G[old]

Lilly Maytree

Sally...
You are my divine appointment!
Blessings)
Lilly Maytree
H

This is a work of fiction. Names, characters, places, and incidents either are the product of the author's imagination or are used fictitiously, and any resemblance to actual persons living or dead, business establishments, events, or locales, is entirely coincidental.

Gold Trap

COPYRIGHT 2011 by Lilly Maytree

All rights reserved. No part of this book may be used or reproduced in any manner whatsoever without written permission of the author or Pelican Ventures, LLC except in the case of brief quotations embodied in critical articles or reviews.

eBook editions are licensed for your personal enjoyment only. eBooks may not be re-sold, copied or given away to other people. If you would like to share an eBook edition, please purchase an additional copy for each person you share it with.

Contact Information: titleadmin@pelicanbookgroup.com

Scripture quotations, unless otherwise indicated are taken from the King James translation, public domain.

Cover Art by Nicola Martinez

Harbourlight Books
a division of Pelican Ventures, LLC
www.harbourlightbooks.com
PO Box 1738 *Aztec, NM * 87410

Harbourlight Books sail and mast logo is a trademark of Pelican Ventures, LLC

Publishing History
First Harbourlight Edition, 2011
Print Edition ISBN 978-1-61116-105-2
Electronic Edition ISBN 978-1-61116-106-9
Published in the United States of America

Dedication

To all who dream of living their dreams, and to my own wonderful family who let me.

1

A Face in the Rain

"Monsieur is brave, bright, and fascinating..."
                                                                    Mary Kingsley

There is a sidewalk cafe in Paris where they say you will meet someone you know, wherever you come from in the world. Not that Megan Jennings was the type to chase after such things. But it seemed fitting that on the eve of her great adventure, she should set out with a bit of fanfare. If such a thing did occur, she would take it as a confirmation that for the first time in her life, she was truly on the right track.

Of course, she had no intention of changing her plans if the little enchantment didn't happen. The die was already cast. She had put on a black vintage traveling suit that one might have seen on the likes of a long line of famous lady adventurers from the Victorian era. She even had an antique broach pinned to the high-neck collar. But most importantly, she had chosen a pair of dark riding boots with laces, which were about as close as she could come to jumping into the shoes of that amazing and intrepid explorer, Mary Kingsley. And Meg was prepared to let them carry her as far back into time as it was humanly possible to go.

Figuratively speaking. The idea was also part of an

experiment to see what effect a person out of the past might have on modern surroundings. Because if there was no effect, if she merely wandered ghostlike through crowds that were so accepting of outlandish styles they were no longer impressionable, then the impact of her entire project would be greatly reduced.

Maybe even worthless.

So, it was on this overcast late afternoon that Meg settled herself at a small corner table in front of the famous cafe, where she had a direct view of the Eiffel Tower in the distance, and could smell the heavenly scent of roses that were being sold from a picturesque flower cart across the street. She ordered coffee in the first words of French she had spoken to anyone other than the voices of the language instructors on her home study course back in the States, and was pleasantly surprised when the young waiter smiled appreciatively and actually understood. So far, so good.

She looked around at the people seated at other tables. No one she knew, yet. And even if, by chance, there was anyone who was scheduled to go out on the same African tour that she was leaving on tonight, she would not recognize them. She had purposely come here first, instead of heading directly for the airport. Visiting this sidewalk cafe was one of the few items on her *"List of Small Things to Accomplish"* that wouldn't take much time.

Meg reached into the side pocket of her carry-all (that had come free with the tour), took out a leather-bound journal that held a finely engraved gold and silver pen in a pocket on the inside cover, and flipped about halfway through until she came to the next blank page. It was at that point her coffee came, and she set things aside long enough to thank the waiter and add cream and sugar from the miniature white bowl and pitcher on the table. She blew softly on the hot mixture and took a sip...delicious.

Then she pulled a pair of delicate gold reading glasses down from the top of her lighter-than-auburn hair (done up into a twist of curls held in place by an antique tortoise shell clasp), picked up her pen again, and wrote: *Question—Is it possible to miss a divine appointment simply because you fail to recognize the moment?*

Hmmm...Meg wondered then if a person could actually go looking for divine appointments, and, if they got good at it, might even qualify for more. Now, that was an interesting thought.

In fact, it put a whole new perspective on that scripture (what was it, again? oh, yes...) that one in Hebrews that talked about strong things belonging to those who practiced enough to be able to tell the difference between good and evil. Definitely something to look into. Because that sort of skill just might prove invaluable considering the places she was headed for. So, she made a note to herself, in parentheses, to research that subject further.

It was at that moment she distinctly felt someone's gaze upon her, and looked up in time to make a direct connection with a man seated near a large front window of the cafe. But other than noticing his eyes were an arresting shade of blue in contrast to his dark, wavy hair and mustache, she could not tell whether or not she might know him.

Peering over the top of her glasses, she could make out a rather distinguished-looking gray suit with a vest. But if there had been a tie, it had long since been removed and stashed somewhere else, and his white shirt was unbuttoned at the collar. He was seated with a fashionably-dressed older woman who was talking over the menu in rapid, fluid French. When he broke off looking at Meg long enough to answer in the same, no further evidence was needed as to whether she knew this person, or not.

Meg didn't know any French people.

Still, there was something about him she couldn't quite put her finger on. Of course, it could be her clothes he was staring at so intently. She had nearly forgotten about them, so she flipped back to an earlier page of her journal titled *"Effects of the Past on Modern-Day Crowds,"* and wrote: *(Mostly ignored, but longer than normal looks from a few particular individuals.)*

Then she took another sip of her coffee. At which point she felt a drop of water against her hand, and then another spattered onto her writing.

"Oh, of all things!" she muttered as she closed the journal and returned it to her carry-all. Now she would either have to cut her visit short or move inside. The few others in the sidewalk dining area that weren't beneath table umbrellas picked up their things and began moving toward the door. No doubt, it would be crowded in there. Since Meg's table was too small for an umbrella, it would probably be best to save this activity for the end of the trip, after all. There were plenty of other things she could do while waiting for her flight.

The waiter returned with a tray and handed her a slip of paper before he began clearing off tables nearby that were already deserted. She turned it over to see what she owed, and was startled to find that it was a personal note instead of a bill. But it was in French.

Which she might have been able to translate if she could take her time and it didn't look as if it was about to rain in earnest at any moment.

"Excuse me…" She forgot all about speaking French and reached out to touch the waiter's sleeve before he moved too far away. "Would you be so kind as to tell me what this says?"

"Yes, certainly. With pleasure, *mademoiselle*." He scrutinized the note with a flair of youthful enthusiasm and pronounced, "This gentleman he will come to you, as soon as"—there was a brief pause before he rattled off the last part in a final burst of confidence—"as soon as the lady she leaves!"

"What?"

"Shall you be waiting inside?" He handed the paper back with a triumphant smile.

"But I'm not waiting for anybody, and I certainly don't…how much do I owe you?"

"Nothing, nothing. Your gentleman, he has already paid."

"I don't have a gentleman, I…" Her gaze turned, almost by reflex, to the man near the window who'd been watching her. It was just in time to see him enter the cafe with a protective arm around the shoulders of the silver-haired lady, and then settle at a table on the other side of the window. But then he looked her way again, and the intensity of that gaze suddenly began to send butterfly sensations all through her.

Along with a very disturbing thought.

What had gotten into her to come traipsing into a restaurant all alone and stare so openly at everyone? In France, of all places! No one but herself knew what she was really doing, and it was no wonder people would naturally assume the most obvious thing. That she was merely a type of…(Oh, dear!). Whatever enchantment she might have been beguiled with suddenly dissolved into a sea of reason. What had gotten into her? Well, whatever it was, it was gone now, and she'd better get herself to the airport and her tour group where she belonged. Before somebody did more than pay for her coffee.

Two taxis had pulled up simultaneously to the curb in front of the crowded cafe in anticipation of the rain, and Meg decided to forego any more sightseeing of enchanted places and take one. She reached for her carry-all and got to her feet.

The waiter smiled approvingly and said, "I will find you a table inside."

"No, thank you," She shook her head for emphasis. "I'm going to catch one of those…"

That was when the man at the window stood up and actually started for the outside door. Why…he was coming in her direction! Meg had a moment of alarm, which was odd, considering she was not the type to scare easily. She dropped her carry-all, then picked it up, again, and finally darted toward the taxi before he could catch up with her.

After a hasty— "Airport, please!"—to the olive-eyed driver, she turned to look out the back window as they drove away. At the same time, there was a resounding clap of thunder and the start of a heavy downpour, but the man made no move to get out of it, only stood there at the curb and watched her disappear into traffic.

"Well, for heaven's sake…" she murmured to herself. "He's just standing there getting drenched!" She felt a slight prick of conscience. "I…I suppose I should have at least thanked him for the coffee. I really don't know what came over me."

"Not to worry, *mademoiselle*." Answered the driver over his shoulder. "He will forgive you, I'm sure, and then love you even more for it!" Then he laughed at the pleasure of his own philosophic comment.

"Goodness…he doesn't even know me!" Meg watched until another car obscured the vision and then turned around to face front. However, the image of him standing there was indelibly imprinted on her mind. When she realized that she was still clutching his note, she turned it over to look more closely at it.

The handwriting was bold and decisive, and there seemed to be quite a few more words than what the waiter had translated for her. "Miss," it began (one was either a Miss or a Mrs. in this country, so that certainly didn't imply anything other than courtesy.) "I cannot let such an extraordinary woman leave without speaking to her. Will you…" Now what was that word? It looked familiar but she couldn't place it.

She leaned over the seat and asked the driver. "Do you know what *nôtres* means?"

"Oh, it can mean many things, *mademoiselle*, depending on how it is used. Ours, our own, one of us, or even…"

"As it is used in the phrase, *voulez-vous etre des nôtres*."

"Ah…it means will you join us. To make one of our group. You see?"

"Nothing that suggests meeting alone?"

"No, not that phrase," he insisted. "Clearly it means more than one."

"Well, of all things." She sighed and sat back against the seat, again. "That waiter didn't speak English any better than I can speak French. I'd have been quite willing to join the two of them, but the way he put it made me think..."

"Not to worry," said the driver. "We French do not mind such things because we like the tourists. Shall I help you practice your French, *mademoiselle*?"

"Thank you, but it's a little late."

"I can drive faster, if you wish. What time is your plane to leave?"

"I meant it was too late to help the restaurant situation. My plane doesn't leave until this evening. But thank you, anyway."

She went back to studying the note, and the next phrase she figured out showed her just where the misunderstanding had been made. It said, "If you are waiting for someone, we would be happy to meet with you later." Now, she really did feel badly, because, looking at it this way, she had been quite rude. Especially, since she hadn't even paid for her coffee. Under normal circumstances Meg had always considered herself to be polite and sociable. With everybody. And she had a great deal of respect for foreigners, too. She really did. In fact, the word prejudice was hardly even part of her vocabulary.

Must have been all those precautionary lectures from family and friends about the dangers of women traveling alone. It had made her start thinking the worst of people. Now, at the very least she had missed out on something that might have turned out to be pleasant. Maybe even enlightening. And wasn't that what she was looking for? Why, it was what this entire trip was about! How in the world could she ever expect to step out into a new and exciting future, if she allowed the restrictions of her past to keep her from even getting through the door? Then the next thought was practically unbearable...

What if she had just missed a divine appointment?

"Stop!" She clutched the driver's shoulder so fast he tromped on the brakes out of reflex. "I mean...could you please turn around? I...I have to get back to that cafe!"

2

A Bad Omen

"I wouldn't go there if I were you."
Mary Kingsley

There was a barrage of French words that had not been included in Meg's language course as the taxi screeched to a halt. The driver turned around in his seat with an exaggerated gesture of throwing up his hands and implored, "You…you stop the heart…*mad'-moiselle!*"

"I'm sure I'm very sorry, but it suddenly occurred to me…"

Now, there was a blast of someone's car horn from behind them, and while Meg turned to look out the back window at who was shouting, her driver stuck his hands and head out of his own window and hollered out an indignant reply. In more French she couldn't understand. After a few moments of verbal sparring, several other cars began to honk, and the two combatants finally drew apart as the taxi eased over to the curb and the irate drivers behind them zoomed around.

During the time it took to turn back and head for the cafe, Meg had the vague sensation they were taking the long way. Under other circumstances she might have complained, but considering the incident she had already caused, she decided it best to be gracious. However, by the time they finally got there, it was only to discover that "her gentleman" and his lady friend had already left.

So, she rode the rest of the way to the airport, silently asking for another chance at divine appointments. Because the knack for recognizing them was clearly going to take more skill than she possessed at present. Still, the small loss left her with a rather melancholy feeling that somewhat dampened her enthusiasm for starting up conversations with her fellow tour participants. That is, until she first looked them all over carefully to see if she felt any "inklings" toward someone in particular.

Not a one.

And hardly a spark of interest in much of anything other than a new compulsion to look for men with mustaches. Of all things! She had definitely not spent nearly six month's salary and flown halfway around the world to suddenly take up some oddly-inspired search for eligible men. For heaven's sake, she had a job to do. Besides, she had fairly well given that idea up years ago, when the avid pursuit of her career seemed to drive most ordinary suitors away. It was a decision she came to reluctantly, after the rather disturbing realization that there was very little about herself that she could describe as ordinary.

So it was that she had made a conscious effort to throw herself into her work in the hopes that her peculiar talents might be more blessing than curse. That she might even be set aside for a certain destiny. But there had been quite the opposition over that philosophy, too. People were forever telling her that her entire focus would change when she finally met the right person.

It was love that was the secret (this from her own mother) because that was the very thing that could suddenly turn an ordinary somebody into the man of her dreams. Well, she had spent a lot of years waiting, and looking, and even praying that just such a thing would happen to her. Only it never had. What's more, she had come away from it all with the growing impression that she had wasted far too much time trying to do what everyone else insisted were the practical ways to go about it.

Now, she had come to this.

Sitting alone in a crowded airport, with every intention of skipping out on most of a tour (for which she'd paid good money). Dressed in her black Victorian outfit (quite the comfortable thing, actually) that had the surprising effect of making her feel prettier than she had for a long time. Must be the feel of the smooth silk and lace of the old-fashioned undergarments beneath. She had gone to great lengths to make sure the mid-length costume was as authentic as it could possibly be. She had even traded modern suitcases for a single canvas duffel of the sort that Mary Kingsley, herself, had taken along on her first trip to West Africa.

Meg sighed heavily and meandered over to an empty seat to settle down for what she had learned would be another hour before boarding time. It was between two separate groups of people who seemed preoccupied enough with their own conversations that they paid little attention to any newcomers they didn't know. Which would give Meg plenty of time to collect her thoughts and finish that bit of writing that had been interrupted by the rain.

Under normal circumstances, Megan wasn't the type of person who made a habit of listening in on other people's conversations. Only this was different. It was impossible not to hear what people were saying in such close quarters. And considering the fact that the human ear did not come equipped with an automatic shut-off when confronted with objectionable material, she must conclude that her only responsibility lay in what she did about it. Well, if it wasn't one thing, it was another.

Meg sighed heavily, again. Then she withdrew her journal from the side pocket of her carry-all and began to thumb through the first few pages. When she came to the list of her own personal rules (the ones she had kept without fail for nearly ten years), she pulled her glasses down from the top of her head and began searching out one in particular.

There it was. Rule number sixteen stated, *"I will not eavesdrop, tell other's secrets, or participate in the spreading of gossip of any kind."* Then she reached for the lovely antique pen, but it wasn't there. Bother! Left at the cafe, no doubt, in her rush to be off. So, she fished through all manner of things to finally come up with one of the common plastic variety. After which she made a note to herself, *"Does not apply to airports."*

Not that she was the type to meddle in things that were none of her business, either. Meg had no criticisms of those who did not think like she did. A distinct effort toward the practice of rule number nine: *"Live and let live."* Of course, she was familiar with the Good Samaritan story, and would have known just what to do if some poor stranger lost their purse, or even if a person suddenly went into cardiac arrest and fell down in front of her. Crowded airport, or otherwise.

This didn't exactly resemble one of those, but in Meg's opinion, it definitely called for some sort of response. Because while Henry (who had occupied the seat next to her) was off in the men's room, his wife Ethel (one seat away) was giving out a piece of disturbing information to Vidalia (two seats down).

"He knows something's up! He was awake half the night trying to figure out where that money went. He even asked me what U.S.M., Inc. was. I had to tell him it was the company that fixed the furnace! Said he wants to see the receipts as soon as we get home."

"Don't worry, honey!" The dark-skinned woman with an even darker dapple of freckles across her large nose gave Ethel a comforting smack on the arm. "Less than a week it'll all be over. You just make sure he takes that little side trip for photographers. Everything's set up."

"Oh, he'll take it all right. It's the only part of this tour he's really excited about." Ethel opened a dark red purse that matched her pantsuit and withdrew a tube of lipstick to refresh. "I only hope I can hold out until then. I feel like he can see right through me. I don't know what's come over me, lately..." She replaced the cap and returned it to her bag. "I used to have nerves of steel."

"That's why we're partners, so's we can help each other out. Just think about having your own money from now on. Here he comes back, now." Vidalia reached into the pocket of her leopard print jacket and handed over a business card. "Better take this, like as if we just met." Then she raised her voice as Henry returned to his chair. "Vidalia Harbin, gen-u-wine psychic. If you want a reading, you'll have to make an appointment."

"Good lord, Ethel!" The heavyset man sat down and brushed a few spots of water from his Hawaiian print shirt, then made sure none had splashed onto the camera that hung from a strap around his neck. "What sort of claptrap are you getting into now?"

"Exactly how much do you usually charge for a reading, Vidalia?" asked Ethel.

"Oh, it varies, honey. Depending on..."

It was at that point Meg shoved her glasses back up on her head, tucked her journal away, picked up her carry-all and moved three rows down. The idea! She hoped she wouldn't have to sit next to any of them when the flight finally boarded. She settled down again and then reached once more into the wide front pocket of her *Bremen Tours* carry-all (the only part of her outfit that wasn't vintage but it was quite the handy, well-made thing) and took out a bundle of brochures. Now, where was that one about the Mole National Park that had such a wonderful map of the reserve? She pulled her reading glasses down into place, again. This might be just the time to take a few practice shots of it with her new camera.

Maybe she should take a still shot, instead. Even though the new video camera could zoom in and pan across each particular point of interest, she had read somewhere that stopping the action with a dramatic photo could present quite an effect. She might even do both and decide which one to use, later. She leaned forward to take both of the cameras out, and then set them momentarily on the empty chair next to her when she felt her slip catch on the laces of her leather riding boots (which she also thought would be perfect for walking through jungles).

As she discretely lifted the hem of her skirt to untangle it, she suddenly felt someone staring at her, again. Not that it mattered so much in this location. Everyone knew the most popular pastime for waiting in airports was people watching. She certainly did a fair share of it, herself. Which was why (with hardly a second thought) she looked up and flashed a friendly smile into another intense blue gaze. This time of an elderly gentleman with wavy white hair and a…a mustache! There she went with the mustache thing, again. But she didn't feel bothered half so much at the moment, because this man was old enough to be her father. He was wearing a light-colored Panama suit and gave her a polite nod before she returned her attention to the cameras.

"What do you say, Gilbert?" She heard him speak quietly to a younger man seated next to him. "I think I've just seen a ghost. This calls for a drink!"

"Yeah? I say I'm not falling for any more of your tricks, Professor, no matter what you see."

Meg glanced over the top of her glasses at the man sitting next to the older gentleman. Black slacks and a white silk shirt that was unbuttoned far enough down to reveal a flashy gold chain at his throat. He had a head full of thick black curls, a dark tan, and was unwrapping a piece of chewing gum as if he had just made a casual comment about the weather instead of insulting the professor.

"Suit yourself, then." The professor rose to his feet. "I'm off to find the nearest watering hole."

Gilbert leapt up to follow. "For sure I'm not letting you outta my sight, again…I'll tell you that much."

"Well, don't crowd me too close, boy, or I'll fire you," said the professor.

By the time the flight finally did begin to board, Meg had a fairly good understanding of most of the personalities seated around the gate area. There was a group of several middle-aged women who seemed to be in some sort of club. They were all dressed in rather similar looking safari outfits, complete with hats, and having a marvelous time together. Next to them was a young married couple, each tanned, blond, and athletic, dressed in khaki shorts, white shirts, and sturdy leather walking shoes. They both carried backpacks, and while they spoke English, there was a distinct Scandinavian accent that tinged their words.

The retired couple Meg stood behind in the line to go down the jet-way had an unusually accommodating relationship. The wife, a redhead sporting enough gold jewelry to draw attention, rattled a non-stop monologue of complaints punctuated by occasional questions directed at a husband who never answered. But he must not have been expected to because the woman didn't seem to have any aversions to carrying on the entire discussion without him.

Once aboard, Meg was feeling rather delighted to have gotten a window seat (even though it was all the way back in row twenty-five and practically in the airplane's tail), when she heard a vaguely familiar voice behind her and realized that the unthinkable had happened. The genuine psychic was stuffing her leopard jacket in the overhead bin and getting ready to settle down right next to her. Of all things! But the feeling must have been mutual, because the first words out of the woman's mouth when their eyes met, were, "Uh-oh. The mystery girl."

"Hello," said Meg.

"Looks like you just stepped outta one of those pictures in the museum we visited yesterday. Been with the tour since New York?"

"No. I only got into Paris this morning."

"What about the orientation and the gala dinner? Don't worry, you didn't miss much. Ice cream sundae turned out to be nothing but a scoop of yogurt with melted jam on top." She squeezed her ample form that was fairly bursting from a black, tight-fitting pantsuit, between the two armrests. "Look at this, here!" She lengthened one end of her seatbelt until it finally closed with a satisfying click. "Thing wouldn't fit round a *Barbie doll!* Well..." —now she turned her full attentions to Meg— "We better call a truce."

"What?"

"On account this is gonna be a long flight."

Meg had thoughts of politely brushing things over, but what was the point? This woman obviously knew exactly where they stood with each other. Besides, she had enough work to do on this trip, herself, without having to put on airs or smooth over any unnecessary misunderstandings. Honesty was the best policy (rule number four). So, she held out her hand and said, "Deal."

It was a mistake, but she didn't realize that until too late.

Because Vidalia latched onto it with both of her own, closed her eyes, and murmured, "I got a feeling..."

"I imagine you do." Meg tried to pull away. "Look, here..." What an absurd situation! "It's been a long day for both of..."

All at once Vidalia gasped and let go as if Meg had

suddenly turned into a viper. "Ooo… la! You got no interest in this tour…you're following a dead woman!"

"Oh, honestly!" Meg tried to make light of the accusation even though a chill rippled through her. "I hope you're not going to be like this for the whole trip, or you'll give someone a nervous breakdown before we even get there!"

"I see danger all around you, girl!"

"Then you'd better keep a safe distance, wouldn't you say?"

"Hmm! Seems a bad omen for me, all right. And I was just trying to be friendly. What's a person like you doing on a tour like this, anyway?" She shoved the armrest between them up to allow a more comfortable space to spread out in.

Then she snapped open the large purse on her lap that sported the same leopard print as the filmy scarf wound round her neck, and Meg couldn't help thinking they made the perfect accent to her personality. Which led her to watch the little ritual that followed with a rather absorbed fascination.

Vidalia peered into a pocket mirror at herself, noticed several wiry curls sprung loose from the large tight knot at the back of her neck and pulled out a black comb that had anchored it there. Like bedsprings suddenly freed from a mattress, a mass of black curls flew out in all directions. Only to be caught up again just as fast, swept back into place, and re-anchored snugly in one smooth motion. A movement so obviously habitual it had become fluid. That done, she reached into the leopard bag and unzipped a pocket inside. But here the routine was interrupted, because what she was after was lost. Which in turn led to an odd assortment of items being flung out onto the seat between them in order to find it.

Meg gasped (she couldn't help it) when some strange-looking thing made of burlap and a tuft of black hair rolled over and bumped up against her thigh. Her hand involuntarily froze in mid-air during an automatic reflex to hand it back. It had a crudely-painted face with pins sticking out all over. Vidalia giggled at her startled expression and then picked it up herself.

"It's my husband." She returned him to his pocket and then gave Meg a confidential thump on the arm. "Don't worry, honey. I been at it for over a year, now, and the worst I ever give him was a headache. I'll tell you what, though. You ain't gonna last long on this trip if the sight of a little something like that is all it takes to scare you. What'd you even sign up for?"

"I'm beginning to…"

"Don't tell me." She paused a few seconds, as if listening, and then pronounced, "Big misunderstanding with that man of yours. I can see it plain as day."

"I don't happen to have any man in my life," said Meg. "Nor do I live in a museum."

"Hmm! I see a man, all right. Dark and mysterious. Tell you something else…" She traced the line of her mouth in a deft red slash before replacing the lid on the finally found tube, pursing her lips together in a satisfying smack and then stuffing all her things back in the purse, again. "I don't have to guess to know what you do for a living. It's as plain as…"

"No thanks," Meg stopped the flow of words with an upraised hand for emphasis. "I'm not the least bit interested in fortune-telling, bad omens, warnings of impending doom, or especially any of the sort of advice you gave Ethel while we were waiting back at the gate."

"I never give warnings lest there's something can be done about it, and I never give bad advice, either. Don't believe in it."

"Well, at the very least it was meddling." Meg reached for the paperback version of *Learning French the Easy Way* she had stashed in the seat pocket ahead of her and flipped it open to where her boarding pass was holding the place.

"It wasn't meddling, it was helping. Woman's gonna need all the help she can get when that monster husband of hers finds out…"

"Would you be good enough…" Meg thumped the book closed in her lap without replacing the marker and leveled one of her sternest no-nonsense stares at the boisterous woman she was being forced to spend the next several hours with. "To keep your opinions and predictions to yourself? We agreed to call a truce."

"That was before I realized we got so much in common."

"In common…what on earth!"

"I avoid your type, usually. But when I seen you comb your hair the same as me…we even got the same freckles!"

Meg's hand self-consciously found its way to the five faint freckles across the bridge of her nose as if they had somehow betrayed her, and Vidalia laughed. It suddenly occurred to Meg that she had made a grave mistake. What on earth had she been thinking? She had been so convinced that traveling with such activities wasn't the same as actually taking part in them. And the amount of money she had spent just to do it!

Even if she could manage to avoid Vidalia for the ten days (which would be tricky since she had booked for double occupancy, and the two of them had already been linked by their seat assignments). The same situation would probably happen all over again. Because the majority of people who signed up for a tour by the name of *Voodoo Relics of the Dark Continent*, would undoubtedly be voodoo enthusiasts.

It had attracted Meg because it was a budget tour. The only one which covered the places she needed to go that would not require a small loan just to be able to afford. The truth was, she was not the least bit interested in voodoo, and never had been. At the time, the reasonable price had seemed like an answer to prayer. She had dismissed that first temptation (she actually called it a temptation) not to go simply because the itinerary followed a trail through the "Dark Continent" in search of dark relics.

After all, everything about Africa seemed dark, if you were to look at it that way. If it wasn't voodoo it was slaves, or the white man's graveyard, or tracking wild animals through dangerous places. She could have stuck with the bird watching tours, but they tended to be along the coasts or lake-shores with overly expensive resorts and boat rides one had to pay extra for. Meg certainly wasn't interested in any of that. Now, here she was with a job to do and a major "thorn in the flesh" before she even got started. Following her destiny wasn't going to be as easy as she thought it would be. That is, if she really had one.

But what if she didn't?

Surely, this whole trip couldn't be a mistake. It couldn't be! But even if it was, and the very thought made her murmur a heartfelt "Oh, dear Lord!" and turn her face toward the window, what in the world could she possibly do about it, now?

3

Footprints

"The only thing to do was to gratefully listen and let things drift..."

Mary Kingsley

Meg felt another insistent thump against her arm and reluctantly returned her attention to her seat companion. "No law against international investments," said Vidalia.

"Did I say there was?"

"You heard what I said to Ethel."

"Anyone within five seats heard what you said to Ethel. But I assure you, I am not interested in what you two will be doing while Henry is off on that photography trip. It just so happens I signed up for that side trip, myself."

"Only thing we're gonna do is attend an investment meeting. You know, like when you get a free night at a hotel when you listen to somebody's presentation about buying into timeshares. That's all it is."

"Well, I don't know why you feel you have to explain it to me."

"On account of you're a..."

She was interrupted by the smooth voice of a

stewardess who leaned across to put a hand on Meg's arm. "Miss Jennings?"

"Private investigator!" Vidalia blurted out.

"Yes?" Meg looked into the lively dark eyes and thought how a person with such smooth chocolate-colored skin and hair done up in many braids gathered into a fashionable knot, would fit in more on the cover of a magazine than waiting on tourists.

"Would you like to move up to 4-D?" Not even a trace of French accent.

"Why...yes, of course..."

"That's first class!" Vidalia accused.

A courtesy upgrade! Meg didn't have to be asked twice and began gathering her things. Whatever the reason, she was grateful for it, and more than a little relieved that she wouldn't have to spend the next few hours listening to Vidalia. Then when she discovered her new seat companion to be none other than the white-haired professor, she breathed a sigh of relief.

At least, this was someone she could relate to.

Except that he was tipping several white pills into a trembling palm at the moment, and she felt obliged to wait while he swallowed them down without water. Then he got unsteadily to his feet so she could slip into the window seat, and a waft of pleasant-smelling aftershave enveloped her. Only it was mingled with alcohol.

"Don't know why they have to board us so early when there's such a beastly long wait at the runway," he muttered. "Hotter than blazes in here." He sat down, twisted around, and looked past the open first class curtain down the long narrow aisle where the coach passengers were still settling in. "Waitress!" he called over the crowd.

The clinking of trays and glasses stopped in the forward galley, the beautiful stewardess poked her head out with a startled expression, and then quickly made her way toward him. The old gentleman hollered the demeaning word out into the main cabin, again, only to be interrupted by a polite, but firm hand placed on his shoulder from behind.

He jumped as if she had pinched him. "Oh, there you are!"

"Is there something wrong, Mr. Anderson?"

He fumbled in an inside breast pocket of his white suit-jacket, shuffled his passport and airline ticket to lay hold of a wallet that seemed practically bursting with money, and came up with an American twenty dollar bill. "Bring me a double gin and tonic, will you dear?"

"Certainly. But you don't need this in first class." She returned the money. "Would you like something, too, Miss Jennings?"

"Not just yet, thanks," Meg replied. Though she was delighted to have been unexpectedly upgraded to first class, the thought of gulping down six ounces of ginger ale before take-off was not appealing.

"Nonsense," said her new seat companion. "A little light wine, at least. Going to be a ghastly long wait before we even get off the ground."

"Well," Meg turned questioning eyes on the stewardess.

"He's right. Busy today on account of all the delays."

"Well, I suppose." If there was time, it would be nice to enjoy a cup of tea. And if they should have green... "Do you—"

"Absolutely not, Professor!" The stewardess

intercepted the man just as he retrieved a pipe from his side pocket. "This is a non-smoking flight."

"All the way to St. Louis?"

"All the way to St. Louis."

"No law against..." He clamped the stem between his teeth and spoke around it with a practiced ease. "Smoking without lighting it, is there?"

She looked at him warily, glanced at her watch, and then relented before turning to get back to her duties. "I suppose not. We'll give it a try."

She returned a few moments later with the double gin and a glass of white wine that she set down on the trays in front of them, and then hustled off, again. Meg took one look at the miniature stemmed glass with the offending liquid and gasped. "Oh, but this isn't what..."

"Would you rather have red?" The professor reached up to jab at the call button. "I'll get her right back here, and..."

"No." Meg stopped his hand more out of reflex than thought. "Thank you very much, Professor, but I think we've taken up quite enough of her time, already. It really doesn't matter."

"When you're on vacation, everything matters. You are on vacation, I take it. What with all that stuff you're carrying around. *Bremen Tours*?"

"The carry-on came with the deal."

He took two long swallows of his drink and agreed. "Good advertising for them and a nice souvenir for you. How long have you been into it?"

"Only since this morning. Even though it started officially yesterday with a brief tour of Paris and an orientation dinner at..."

"Voodoo, I mean."

"Voodoo…why, I'm not into that at all."

"But the bag says, *Voodoo Relics of the Dark Continent*."

Meg glanced toward the continuing tumult in coach for a moment, where even though a great many other bags being stuffed into overhead bins sported the same slogan, the very phrase was beginning to weigh heavy as a curse on her. "It was a budget tour," she explained. Then she lowered her voice in a confidential whisper, "To tell you the truth, I have other plans."

"Well, now"— his blue eyes twinkled with pleasure at the shared secret— "I can see the plot thickens! Not some spy on a clandestine mission, are you?"

"Absolutely not, I'm a schoolteacher."

"Ah, a fellow educator. But not a voodoo enthusiast and not a spy. Let's see. Why else would you be carting around such expensive equipment? I suppose you'd like to meet someone in one of those exotic tourist traps… man of your dreams, and all that."

"Hardly. No, I have long since resigned myself to the fact that I'm too strong-willed and unorthodox to be compatible with anybody in the dream category. A price one seems to have to pay for independence, these days."

"There have always been independent women, my dear. Their mistake was in giving up the femininity they used to hide it behind. There are very few men around who have any aversions to being charmed, you know. But the way you're dressed, I'm sure you're already aware of that." He finished off his drink and set the empty glass down on the tray with a decisive thump.

"Professor Anderson, I do not have this outfit on to charm men. If you must know, it's sort of an experiment I'm working on. Look here"—she reached for the bundle of brochures stuffed into the outside pocket of her bag—"the fact is, I am interested in one of those tourist places. Have you ever heard of Mole National Park?"

"The one where they come knocking on your door at four or five in the morning to announce what animals are drinking at the local waterhole you might want to see?"

"They all do that. But this one"—she pulled her reading glasses down from the top of her head to peer through them long enough to choose the appropriate flyer, and then push the glasses back up, again—"actually allows you to walk right out there. On foot. With a guide, of course. Should be perfect for what I have in mind."

"Ah, so that's it!" He guessed, again. "You're planning to get rid of the husband."

"Oh, honestly!" She gathered the brochures with a disappointed sigh and put them back in the pocket. Did everyone who spent exorbitant amounts of money on a trip to Africa have to be so odd?

"It's cheaper than a divorce."

She looked over at him with a discerning scrutiny. "The term incompatible, Professor, has other meanings besides grounds for divorce. Do you always ask such personal questions when you've only known someone for five minutes?"

"Such questions are more than acceptable on vacations. I don't mind admitting I'm only interested in redheaded characters with arresting green eyes, dressed like something out of the Victorian era.

Carrying around – not one, but two – expensive cameras. Not to mention that copy of *Moviemaking for Beginners*." He indicated the telltale yellow and black binding of one of the books protruding from the bag. Then (without even asking) he traded his empty gin and tonic glass for her untouched white wine and took a tentative swallow. "Not bad. But then, this is France."

"How would you know what kind of cameras I have in my bag?"

He ignored the question and went on with his deductions. "A mere schoolteacher on vacation would have been more than content with her old digital model, or even a couple of those throw away types you can buy at any airport. No, Miss Jennings, I'd say you are clearly up to something."

The engines came to life beneath them, but they didn't go anywhere, as there was still a line of other planes waiting to take off ahead of them. But at least the stuffiness of the cabin began to clear. In a moment, the stewardess returned to meander between the rows in first class offering refills.

"I'd like tea this time, if you don't mind," Meg informed the professor as he finished off her wine. "In case she leaves before I get a chance to order for myself."

"Miss…" He put a hand on the young woman's elbow as she was still serving passengers in the row ahead of them. "Another gin and tonic for the lady, and I'll switch to tea."

Since the two of them were sitting in the last seats before coach, the stewardess simply gave him a nod and turned back to the galley without as much as a glance in Meg's direction. Which seemed rather an odd thing (in Meg's estimation) since she was clearly not traveling with the man.

"Now, what on earth did you do that for?" Meg leveled one of her no-nonsense-in-the-classroom expressions on him. "It just so happens I do not drink. And unless you are trying to cover up the fact that it's barely four o'clock in the afternoon and you've already passed your limits…"

"My dear, there are no limits when one is on vacation. If you must know, I'm gearing up for take-off. They're revving up the engines already, and I've still got the jitters. Hardly any alcohol in these drinks, anyway."

So, he was afraid of flying. Meg's irritation with him melted a little. "Well, has anyone ever told you it's safer to fly than drive?"

"Yes, but has anyone ever told you about the abominable maintenance regulations they have on these African airlines? There aren't any! Statistics are so stacked against us, that there's more chance of a plane crash…"

"This plane is not going to crash," she declared.

"How can you be sure?"

"Because I'm on it. And I have a destiny."

Professor Anderson shifted the stem of his pipe from one side of his mouth to the other beneath the neatly trimmed mustache, and allowed himself a few moments to savor the response. "I believe you," he finally pronounced. "It rings true, yes, indeed. But I don't see how you can be so sure of yourself."

"Well, for one thing, I have a sort of formula I go by that helps me decide if it's safe to go ahead with something, or not."

He glanced back into coach for a moment and then lowered his voice. "I could use that kind of formula," he admitted. "As I'm walking on some pretty thin ground, myself, right now."

The stewardess returned with their drinks, and Meg switched the gin and tonic that had been set down in front of her with the tea, that had been placed in front of him. Black tea.

"Footsteps, Professor. I don't venture out anywhere without a…sort of…trail to follow. Sometimes it's only the signs of someone I trust that has gone on ahead of me. But other times, it's more like unusual little coincidences that pepper the trail with a glow all their own. And if I can't find any of those signs…divine footsteps, I call them"—she stopped dunking her tea bag up and down in the cup for a moment and looked him in the eye, again—"I don't go."

"Hmmm. Just whose footsteps would you be following now?"

"Mary Kingsley."

"Mary Kingsley…" A look of startled surprise came over his face before it was replaced by something that resembled suspicion. "Why her, of all people? She died a hundred years ago. And she certainly never traveled anywhere on a plane. I don't see the point."

"The point, Professor, is that neither time nor death is a part of the equation. The secret is in jumping into her shoes, so to speak, and literally following in her footsteps in order to find out her secrets."

His blue gaze involuntarily dropped down for a closer look at her boots, at which point he gasped and then looked searchingly over her face, again, as if she really might be the ghost he had referred to back in the gate area. Meg made a quick mental note of jotting that down in her list of reactions to dressing like someone out of the past, and then went on with her explanation.

"Of course, I didn't mean Mary Kingsley, personally. She has nothing to do with the actual formula, itself. But then that's not exactly true, either. Because she happens to be the reason I'm even going to Africa in the first place. She's got something to do with my destiny, I'm sure of it. You see, she's the subject of a documentary I want to film. Tentatively titled, *In the Footsteps of Mary Kingsley.*"

This time, the professor startled as if someone had thumped him from behind, snatched the pipe out of his mouth, and threw a look over his shoulder as if someone from coach might be trying to listen in. Obviously, nobody was, so he absently stuck the pipe back into his pocket, and began to chuckle with a nervous sort of relief. "You...you had me going there for a minute...thought I was seeing things! Did Tom put you up to this?"

"I haven't the slightest idea what you're talking about."

"That rascal! I must say, you've done a good job of it, my dear. How much is he paying you?"

"Not a dime. I don't know anyone named Tom."

"Well, I suppose he wouldn't have used his real name. Dark hair and mustache...speaks French like one of the locals. Looks something like me, on account of he's my son. Always up to something!"

"That description could fit any number of people," she replied, although a distinct impression of the man standing in the rain came to her mind. In fact, the professor did seem to bear some resemblance to him if she really...oh, but that was absurd. Absolutely uncanny. Why, a coincidence like that would be nothing short of a..."Professor Anderson, oh, my goodness!" An excitement suddenly came over Meg that she was barely able to contain. "Do you, by any chance, believe in divine appointments?"

4

A Wrong Turn

"However, that is the path you have got to go by if you are not wise enough to stop at home."

Mary Kingsley

"Believe in divine appointments? Not particularly." he admitted. "But if you told me you were an angel and then disappeared out of that seat, I would probably have to consider it."

"There are other kinds of divine appointments." Meg insisted. "I'm talking about the kind where two people are miraculously brought together for a divine purpose."

"Well, then, that settles it. Because I'm about as far as anyone could get from anything divine. In fact, the way I see it, the only reason anyone of that nature should take the slightest interest in me, would be out of pity during a time of trouble."

"Are you in trouble, Professor Anderson?"

"I'm in trouble, or going crazy," he replied. "Either one of which will probably spell disaster."

"Disaster?" Meg was about to ask if he was serious, but it was at that moment the stewardess came by to gather things in preparation for take-off. He breathed a muffled "Shh..." and momentarily froze like a statue. Which left Meg to hand over her barely touched tea (along with his third empty glass) and dutifully fasten both of their trays into locked and upright positions.

By the time the plane rolled forward to the nearby head of the runway, revved up its motors, and spun its tail around smartly to open throttle and hold back all at the same time, he had come to life, again. With a quick— "Hold on, here we go." —the professor gripped the armrests, leaned his head back and closed his eyes.

The plane shot smoothly forward and began to gather speed. Meg left off trying to figure out the professor for a moment, and turned her gaze out the window to watch the ground change to a blur and see all the buildings race by. It was her favorite part of flying, and she reveled in the sensation of speed it gave her.

Only a fleeting sensation, though, because all feeling of movement was lost after the slight dip and elevator feel of having arrived up on the first "step" of the highway in the sky. And once the city below disappeared beneath mile after mile of white billowy clouds, there would be less sense of movement than riding in a car. When the brief experience was over, Meg gave a contented sigh and turned back to the professor, who had his eyes open now and was watching her with a look of… what was that look?

"Are you all right?" she asked.

"Quite. Now that part is over. Taking off is the most dangerous under these circumstances. Once up, you can land a bucket of bolts even if only one engine has half a cough left in it. But I have something of a confession to make, Miss Jennings."

"Call me Meg."

Lilly Maytree

Because life is an adventure.

www.LillyMaytree.com

Inspirational Adventure Novelist

"Meg. There's a reason I wanted to talk to..."

She waited for a moment, but he seemed to have ost the thought. Instead, he cast a hopeful gaze toward e galley. The stewardess was belted into the forward mp-seat and they were still climbing. So, instead, he an to fumble through his pockets, in search of the bottle, again. He gave over his attentions to ning it, tipped several pills out into his hand, then her a wink before popping two of them into his th. Or, was it three?

Meg watched him replace the bottle in his pocket en feel for it, again, as if to make sure it was still "Are you always this nervous on airplanes?" she ed. "Maybe you should try counseling."

y dear, I have enough trouble working out the problems I already know I have, without some young idiot convincing me I've got more."

"I'll bet you don't take yearly physicals, either," she guessed.

"Why would anyone waste perfectly good money just to have someone tell them all their body parts are in working order? It's a conspiracy of idiots."

"Hmmm. And what's your family got to say about all this?"

"My family!" It was more of an expression of exasperation than affection. "Young lady, I get along perfectly with my family. In fact, it just so happens I'm on my way to meet up with that son of mine you claim you don't know. Who hasn't seen fit to come home in nearly a year. Even missed Christmas. Now, whether or not that rascal appreciates what I have to go through even to find him, is another thing."

"Too busy to come home for the holidays, was he?"

"Up to his neck in some new business venture, or other. You know what he's trying to do? He's convinced a fortune can be made by turning an old winery into a health spa."

"At least he's ambitious, Professor. You can be thankful for that. I have a brother who's perfectly content to push buttons all his life as long as he can water ski and race boats on the weekends. Practically drives my father crazy. Health and fitness shows quite a lot of forethought, actually. It's all the rage these days. More rich people wanting to get in shape than buy vintage wine."

"Waste of a lot of good vines, if you ask me. Ah, here comes the lady."

Their conversation broke off then, long enough to choose between chilled salmon and pasta salad or chicken cordon bleu, and whether or not they would like a plate of bread and cheeses before dinner. All this while being handed a warm steamed towel to wash with. The deliciousness that enveloped Meg at the anticipation of enjoying such luxuries (not to mention the adventure that lay ahead of her that was once again beginning to cause a little thrill to ripple through her at the mere thought) all mingled together to distract her.

Then, again, maybe just putting a safe distance between herself and Vidalia Harbin (a psychic, of all things!) was what made her feel better. At any rate, she momentarily lost sight of those "footsteps" she'd been following, and simply ignored the many little things that just didn't add up.

Such as the professor's frequent forays past the barrier curtain into coach, when he had presumably paid extra not to have to stand in line with ordinary people. Or during snatches of conversation when his son's name kept alternating between Tom, and John, or even Robert. Or how, after returning from the lavatory, herself, she distinctly remembered her *Bremen Tours* bag had been sitting upright rather than on its side. Not that it mattered. She hardly expected anyone who could afford an international holiday to be interested in rifling through some fellow-passenger's carry-all.

"Will your son be meeting you in St. Louis?" Meg inquired politely, though secretly, it was beginning to prick her curiosity whether his son and that gentleman in the rain might not be one and the same. Absurdly farfetched. But hadn't she asked for a second chance? Was she a woman of faith, or wasn't she?

"That would be the day," the professor replied. "No, he doesn't even know I'm coming. I figure I'll at least have until that bloodhound of his spills the beans. Might be just enough time to find out what's really going on. You know he's managed to liquidate nearly twenty percent of my assets without asking me? From overseas, yet. Up to no good, if you ask me. Been up to no good for a long time, now." He sighed with a rather poignant despondency and pushed his half-finished dinner aside. "I think he's trying to prove me incompetent."

"Professor Anderson..." Meg swallowed the last bite of her salad as if it were pure ambrosia, dabbed her mouth with the cloth napkin (real linen!), and took a sip of her tonic water. No gin in it, of course, but she had purposely cultivated a taste for the tangy soda over the last few months because it contained quinine. Which was what a person planning a trip through the tropics should do. Back in 1894. "Are you sure he isn't just trying to take care of you?"

He was tipping the brown pill bottle into his palm

again, and gave an involuntary gasp when only one last pill rolled out that seemed at least twice bigger than all the rest. "Blast...blast! Who's been" —he twisted around in his seat and glared back into coach— "tinkering with my blasted pills!"

The stewardess, who was now collecting dinner trays two seats ahead of them, turned around long enough to reveal a hint of impatience that was beginning to replace her former professionalism. She took two steps backward without losing an item off the overloaded tray, and said rather firmly, "Is there something else I can get for you, Mr. Anderson?"

"Another double gin!"

"I'm sure no one's been tampering with your pills, Professor," Meg soothed. "You've been popping them like candy all by yourself."

"I don't know many people who could choke down thirteen pills in less than an hour unless they were nothing but sugar," he argued. "Somebody's definitely been..."

"There, you see? We've been flying for well over two hours, already, and you had no idea. Which is just what mixing wine and spirits in the afternoon will do."

"Listen here," the professor insisted, "If I had taken that many of anything other than antacids, which is all they were, I tell you, I'd be on my ear about now. Wouldn't you say?"

"I'd say it depends entirely on whether they really were antacids. Because if it was something like heart pills, or..."

"My heart's strong as an ox."

"How wonderful for you. Then again, if they were nerve pills..."

"Never taken a nerve pill in my life. Why, I'm in

better shape today than I was at forty! And that's why I resent all the bloodhounds. Especially the ones who treat you like some kind of mental case and tamper with your pill bottles."

"I can see how irritating that would be."

"Irritating! It's degrading! But I'll tell you something, Meg"—he took a long swallow of his fresh drink and then gave her a conspiratorial wink. "There's a certain Mr. Gilbert Minelli who should still be wandering around that Paris airport, right now, wondering where the devil I got to this time." The mere thought gave him a delighted chuckle.

"Hmmm. So that's what became of him." Meg took another sip of her soda. "Whatever is Tom going to say? Or is it John."

"Not a thing, because he isn't going to find out. That nincompoop Gilbert wouldn't have the nerve to tell him. He'd get fired. You can't beat an old fox! Look here..." He withdrew a folded, well-used map from another inside pocket, set his drink on her tray to clear his, and spread it out so she could see. It was a map of France, where someone had marked a neat red circle around a small town in the southern part of that famous peninsula known as Brittany. "Tom's place is just outside of Port Louis, here, and when I pop in on him unexpectedly, he'll have to..."

"Port Louis!" Meg gasped. "You mean St. Louis, don't you? In Senegal?"

"No, I mean Port Louis, in France, where Tom has his blasted broken-down vineyard along the banks of some river in the countryside there."

"But I distinctly heard you ask the stewardess if this was a non-smoking flight all the way to St. Louis." Meg had a brief moment of panic, during which she could only calm herself by a reassuring glance over the back of the professor's seat for a glimpse of her fellow *Bremen Tour* participants. Just in time to catch an accusing glare from Vidalia, who happened to be waiting at the end of a long line to the lavatory.

"Port Louis, St. Louis, what's the difference?" The professor grumbled irritably. "There's a St. Louis in Missouri, too, but I'm not worried we're headed there – I just changed planes in Paris!"

"Oh, Professor, you've made a mistake! This is Air Senegal, it's going to… "

"Of course I know we're on Air Senegal, young lady, I've flown thousands of miles on these blasted African airlines! I often have business in Ghana. I'm going there at the end of the week."

"Yes, but we talked about *Bremen Tours*…and how I was going to…"

"*Bremen Tours* ends up in Ghana. Does it not? I know because I happen to be a shareholder in that company. I like to help out young companies, now and then. I also happen to know they land first in Dakar. I'm headed that way, too. Next week. To get to St. Louis, Senegal, you have to change planes and double back from Dakar."

"This airplane is headed for St. Louis right, now, Professor," Meg argued. "It's landing there first. But whatever made you think an African airline would stop off in some small city in France? It's not a bus service."

"Well it…" Now he glanced back toward coach himself before turning to her with an expression that was beginning to show traces of confusion. "Why it must have been that nincompoop Gilbert! Doesn't even have enough brains to get the tickets straight! He told me we didn't need to change airlines. It was already one of the stops on our tickets and Tom would be..."

Now, his words slowed down and began to slur. Whether from all that alcohol or the pills, she had no idea, but Meg suddenly felt he was not only losing his grip on reality, but about to slip away entirely. "Whatever the problem, we'll get it fixed," she assured. "We'll call Tom as soon as..."

"No-o-oh, we can' tell Tom 'bout this..." He lifted a hand toward his breast pocket, but it was as if he had shifted into slow motion and seemed to have trouble connecting. "We'll tell 'im...tell 'im I had some bi'ness to take care of an'...went on ahead...then I'll – blassst! Blassst-blasss..."

The clutch of items slipped from his hand and tumbled onto the tray. His wallet fell to the floor, and a cell phone skidded onto Meg's lap before he finally came up with a white business card and shoved it toward her. "You call. Jus' tell 'im that...what I said."

"I can't call now, we had to turn these off, remember? But I will as soon as we get there. I promise."

"Tell tha' rascal his ol' dad...has figgurd out what he's up to...and he'll never..." He folded his arms on the tray in front of him and laid his head down, then. "Get away with it... 'cause I...blass-it-all, now I am tired..."

"Oh, honestly!" Meg retrieved the small airline pillow that was wedged between their seats and placed it under his head. She tucked the cell phone back into his pocket and then turned the business card over in her hands.

J. T. Anderson

Professor Emeritus, UCLA Film Institute

Yes, film institute! This must certainly be her second chance at that divine appointment. It had to be. Because what were the odds of being randomly upgraded to first class, only to be seated next to an authority on filmmaking? At the very moment she was taking her first hesitant steps toward her dream of producing educational films! But what did his son have to do with any of it if he didn't even live in the country? Of course, meeting the son might eventually have led to meeting the father. Especially if the conversation had taken that sort of turn. The only question now was...

What exactly was she supposed to do next?

5

Mistaken

*"My deplorable ignorance of French prevented me from
explaining my humble intentions to them."*
Mary Kingsley

The stewardess glanced at the professor, sleeping peacefully now, with his head resting comfortably on the airline pillow. "That was easier than I thought," she whispered to Meg. "I was expecting at least one attempt at lighting the pipe."

"He didn't get off when he should have," Meg whispered back. Nearly everyone in first class was either reading quietly or dozing, now, and they both kept their voices low. "He's on the wrong plane! I think he was supposed to change planes back in Paris!"

"Professor Anderson?" The stewardess shook him gently.

"It won't do any good," Meg informed her. "Between all that alcohol and those pills, he's taken enough to drop an elephant."

"Well, I wouldn't be too concerned. Lots of people overdo things a bit when they're nervous about flying. He'll probably just sleep the rest of the way and be glad when it's all over."

"He isn't nervous about flying, he just doesn't

trust your African airlines with all their..."

Meg caught a slight glimmer of disdain flicker briefly over the beautiful young face. The woman had no accent, but perhaps she had lived abroad somewhere and simply had a knack with languages. Whatever the reason, it didn't hide the fact that she was clearly insulted at the inference. "I mean, well...what do we do if he doesn't wake up? Personally, I don't think he'll wake up for days."

"Then we'll take him off in a wheelchair and call for a doctor. The airport handles these kinds of problems all the time, Miss Jennings, so you really shouldn't let it bother you. Besides, I'm quite sure he intended to go to Africa, tonight. At least he seemed sure enough when he had your seat switched to first class."

"What? You mean it wasn't just a courtesy upgrade?"

The stewardess shook her head with a slow, rather mocking smile. Or was she imagining things? A call button bell went off in the first row, and the young woman turned to see who had rung. Then she looked back at Meg and smiled again. "Maybe he just wanted to talk to a private investigator...I never would have pegged you for one of those!"

"What? Oh, honestly! That was just something Vidalia..."

The stewardess left Meg talking to herself and returned to her duties.

"Well...well, of all things!" Meg looked back at the professor, again. Sleeping like a baby. Imagine someone paying good money to have a perfect stranger upgraded to first class. It all seemed rather desperate in a sad sort of way. But whatever his reasons, he had definitely managed to get himself into a bad situation, now. And Meg was not the kind of person to leave anyone in the lurch at a time like that.

Hadn't he said he was in some kind of trouble?

Which was why she remained in her seat and did not get off the plane when they finally landed in St. Louis. When Vidalia (who was the last person to leave on account of her seat assignment) finally passed by, she was in fine high spirits, and reached over the sleeping professor to give Meg an enthusiastic shake.

"What do you think, girl? The tour guide ended up in your seat, and he personally knows a genu-wine witchdoctor! Gonna introduce me! And wait 'til you see what he give me. It's a…"

"You can show me later, Vidalia," Meg answered, having no desire for a close inspection of some dried toad, or lizard's tail, or any other piece of fetish a witchdoctor might consider valuable. "Right now, I'm going to make sure this gentleman gets settled into the nearest hotel and call his family."

Vidalia leaned over the professor for a closer inspection. "Just drunk if you ask me. The old coot! Serve him right if you just…"

"I'm taking him to a hotel. They've already called for a wheelchair, and…"

"You gonna be way late, I can see that right now. I'll register for us both and make sure we get the same bungalow."

"Oh, you don't have to…"

"I want to!" A peal of delighted laughter bubbled out of her as she hurried her large bulk down the deserted isle. "Kindred spirits gotta stick together!"

Kindred spirits! After that, Meg waited nearly half an hour in the deserted plane. Where was that stewardess? It seemed everyone had forgotten about them. Just when she figured on taking things into her own hands, a wheelchair came in. Propelled by a dark man who looked more like a passenger than a skycap. He was wearing a shiny, multi-colored shirt that reached almost to the knees of his slacks, and a fez-type hat on top of his head to match. He also had a thick gold chain around his neck, at the center of which was some primitive rendition of a crocodile with an enormous red eye. It was her first glimpse of the real Africa.

"Finally!" Meg said. "I thought everyone forgot about us."

"It isn't easy to find a wheelchair at this hour, Megan Jennings." The voice was deep and hypnotic, as if laced with some kind of poison. "It is nearly midnight. Yes."

There was something odd about him. Something that made her uncomfortable. His face looked as if it had been chiseled out of rough black granite, and he had three peculiar lines on his left cheekbone, just under his eye. Those eyes looked very cold and impatient, but it may have been from having to deal with the task at hand.

"The witching hour. Yes." He flipped the armrest up and grasped the sleeping professor under both arms to drag him into the waiting chair. Then he pulled a black bag from an open upper bin, smacked it onto the professor's lap, as if it might keep him securely weighted into the chair. "There." He rolled the large wheels backward a few feet to let her pass. "You are free."

"You don't look like an airline employee." Meg pulled her carry-all over her shoulder, stepped into the isle, and started toward the door. "Where's your badge? And how did you know my name?"

"It is our policy to call everyone in first class by name. I will show you my badge when we get inside. Watch your step. The stairs may be slippery."

Looking back on her arrival, Meg tried to console herself with the fact that any decent person would have done the same thing she did...only no decent person had. Of all the people on flight two ninety-two out of Paris that day, she was the only one who felt compelled to accompany the sleeping professor to his fate. Eventually, even the airline people bowed out.

And that small city in Senegal wasn't what she expected, either. Even though it was nearing midnight, Meg knew the moment she stepped down off the set of metal stairs rolled up against the plane, that the runway was not paved. What's more, there were no other planes around. Not even one.

Instead of the "wind tinged with the ever present smell of burning grass," she had read about in books, she was met with a warm, rather sticky dampness that carried with it the bold announcement that they were practically on the ocean. Having been an ocean-dweller herself for the first half of her life, she could tell. She could also tell in one sniff that the tide was low, and the main occupation for locals must be the fishing trade.

At the bottom of the stairs, she turned around in time to see the professor's head whip back and forth as his wheelchair lurched down the steep steps, with the skycap barely hanging on behind. After that, progress was irritatingly slow over the unpaved ground, and a thought suddenly occurred to Meg. She was going to miss her connecting ride to the traditional village compound in the historic town of Podor, on the Senegal River.

Then (like a prophecy fulfilled) she caught sight of a dilapidated blue bus, with the words Bremen Tours painted in colorful letters across the side and a giant mound of luggage piled on top, lumber away with her fellow Bremen tourists from coach fare. She stood stock-still for a few moments and stared after it. Of all things! Now, she would have to hire one of those "bush taxis" just to catch up with them, again. Another unexpected expense.

But she would think about that later. For now, she judiciously caught up with her film professor and the skycap, and followed them through the small one-story airport building to the customs counter. There, they waited their turn amongst the few remaining passengers who had not been put through speedily with the departing tour.

There seemed to be only one elderly official at this late hour to handle everything. What's more, when her turn finally came up, he was far less concerned with what she had in her bags than what was to be done with "that old man." He didn't open the duffel, or even the carry-all, much less ask her what was inside. If Meg really had been a private investigator, she would have made a note of that.

Private investigator. Of all things! Just where on earth had Vidalia come up with that? And as for being kindred spirits, they would make miserable roommates if they had to put up with each other for the entire tour. She was going to have to have a serious talk with that woman, but she would think about that later, too. At the moment, there was much bantering going back and forth between the skycap and the agent about what was to be done, right now. Most of which was in a quick and unusual sort of French, that Meg found difficult to follow.

But that didn't keep her from putting her foot down when they began to wheel Professor Anderson into a dark adjoining room that seemed to be something of a storage place for unclaimed baggage. The idea! He wouldn't even know the difference, the skycap argued, and the health inspector could look at him first thing in the morning.

"Entirely unacceptable," said Meg, with a definite shake of her head and taking no nonsense from either of them. "You will kindly call for a taxi and point us toward the nearest hotel."

The skycap nailed her with an uncomfortably piercing glare and said, "As you wish, Megan Jennings!" in a way that made her feel as if she had asked to be shot off in the next rocket to the moon instead of just asking for a taxi. He flung a string of words, not even French, to the agent behind the counter that made the older man in uniform jump to his orders as if he had just been poked with a cattle prod.

When the agent disappeared into the baggage room and then hustled out a few minutes later with a golf cart, the bossy skycap quickly loaded it down with their luggage, along with the professor in his wheelchair, and then hopped up behind the wheel. Meg wondered if that was to be the taxi.

"Come, come!" He impatiently motioned her to get into the front seat with him. "I will take you to *L' Hôtel Bonne Nuit*."

She set her carry-all between them on the seat and had barely settled in before he tromped on the pedal that sent them barreling down a wide corridor and out of the deserted passenger waiting area at an uncomfortably fast clip.

"It is only a few blocks away, and I will send a doctor to you there." The golf cart sailed through a set of glass double doors (hurriedly opened by a security guard), and then they were suddenly flying down a deserted main street in a town that bore more resemblance to old New Orleans than her ideas of the real Africa. (And this was the taxi!) The shocks on the little vehicle weren't what they should have been, and Meg found it necessary to keep one hand on the bar in front of her and the other on the wheelchair behind in order to avert catastrophe.

After passing several establishments, they finally came to another relatively small building, three stories high, with a few balconies facing out over the quiet street. The words, *L'Hôtel Bonne Nuit* hung in buzzing pink and lavender neon over a beautifully carved wooden door, proclaiming the remnants of a culture past and that of the modern day. At least, that's what popped into Meg's mind at one o'clock in the morning, universal time, after such a strange and awkward arrival in the land of her great adventure.

At the desk, the skycap continued to make all the arrangements. It was simpler, he explained, since she didn't understand the language well enough. There would also be no misunderstandings about the doctor. All delivered with another of those piercing looks that sent a chill down Meg's spine. Definitely something strange about the man. He was only in his late twenties, no older, yet, he had such a demanding way about him. It made people hop to his every word. Including Meg. But it had been a long day, and she was probably just overtired.

And who wouldn't be at this point?

The room was simple but clean, decorated in a brown and white print that resembled some modern art version of palm fronds. The skycap helped deposit the still sleeping professor into the single bed, fully clothed, and stayed only long enough to pull their luggage inside and roll the empty wheelchair back out, again. After that, Meg handed him two American dollars for his services. A fleeting expression of surprise crossed his face before he finally stuffed them into a pocket and walked away, laughing.

Such audacity!

This was not how she had imagined her first night in Africa would be. At this moment, she should be drifting off to sleep in an authentic thatch bungalow that was situated close enough to the river to hear animal noises. That after having been welcomed into the compound to the sounds of traditional native drums. She might even have taken a few pictures already. But Meg was not one to feel sorry for herself.

Instead, she removed the professor's shoes, jostled him out of his suit jacket, and pulled the brown and white bedspread up over his sleeping form. Then she sat down in a wicker chair, cushioned in the same palm tree print, to look through the jacket pockets in search of that cell phone. It was time to find out if there really was a son named Tom. And if (in some miraculous way) this really was her second chance at that divine appointment she had prayed for. But did God give people second chances like that? If Tom Anderson really was the same man who had stood watching her in the rain...

A glimmer of thrill passed through her.

6

Citizen's Arrest

"At this point in the affair, there entered a highly dramatic figure. He came onto the scene suddenly and with much uproar..."

Mary Kingsley

In the end, the idea didn't hold up to scrutiny. Not that she didn't believe that God (who had created the heavens and the earth) was fully capable of moving people around in any number of ways. Except that He almost always added a logical explanation to go along with it. This situation didn't seem to have one of those. Because if the man in the rain really had been Tom Anderson, what was he doing at the cafe if he was supposed to be somewhere in wine country? It was the professor mentioning he spoke French like one of the locals that had made her jump to conclusions.

That along with the mustache and blue eyes.

But enough of all that. At this point, nothing made any sense, and she was getting far too tired to do anything but finish with her Samaritan duties and then check herself into a hotel room of her own. Catching up with the tour would simply have to wait until tomorrow. Who knew how long it would take for that hotel clerk to find a doctor at this hour?

Meg had a twinge of verging on an invasion of privacy as she turned the professor's cell phone on, but she decided an emergency was an emergency, and chose the phone book option. Then she quickly scrolled down to the first "Tom" listed. She clicked on it and was automatically put through. One...two...three rings...

He wasn't going to pick up.

She sighed and waited for the message, thinking she should go back and look for a John or a Robert, when a pleasantly resonant, but rather impatient voice said, "This is Tom. I'm on a plane so leave a message. Pop...if it's you...wait for me in Accra. Turn your phone on, will you? And quit dumping Gilbert. It isn't safe traveling alone down there anymore, no matter who you are. I should catch up with you sometime in the afternoon. We'll rent a car and drive up together. You and me. Just like old times. Wait for me, Pop."

A few seconds of silence and then a beep, at which point Meg piped in and said, "Hello, Tom? This is Megan Jennings. I sat next to your father on the plane out of Paris. He isn't in Accra, he's in St. Louis. At *L'Hôtel Bonne Nuit*. Room 307. I'm afraid he mixed too many drinks with his medications and won't wake up. Don't worry. A doctor is coming by to look at him. I'll let you know what he says. I think you should come here instead of Accra, though. The professor is...well, he's..."

Just as she was trying to decide how best to phrase her concerns without betraying the professor's confidence, the sleeping man suddenly threw off his cover like a rising bull, and with a tremendous bellow, hollered, "Put 'em up! Put 'em up, you cowards, I can take every one of you!"

Such behavior! It startled Meg so that she dropped the phone and lost the connection. Then she forgot about Tom Anderson entirely as she struggled to keep his delirious father from flinging open the door and running off down the hall. He was still caught up in some disturbing dream about people who were out to get him, and not really awake at all. But finally, her soothing voice and forceful help sent him back to bed, and he was out like a light, again, as if nothing had happened.

Between collecting her nerves and waiting for the doctor, Meg didn't ring back. Not that she forgot. She had mentioned the name of the hotel and room number, and the fact that his father had landed himself on the wrong continent. How much farther was a Good Samaritan expected to go? Besides that, it was obvious that Tom Anderson was not the same man she had seen at the cafe.

He couldn't be. Even if he could speak French "like one of the locals," he was too abrupt and bossy with his father to be the same man who had been so courteous and attentive to the older woman at the cafe. Nor could she imagine anyone who said things like *"Turn your phone on, will you? And quit dumping Gilbert..."* could have the patience to write such a polite and formal invitation as the one she still had tucked away in her purse. The realization of which made her suddenly feel rather disappointed and impatient, herself.

She also had quite enough of experiments with dressing like someone out of the past or seeking out her destiny. It was obviously giving her more trouble than insights, anyway. Besides that, it was stifling in here, and while her outfit might be perfect for walking through jungles, it was much too warm for a stuffy hotel room with an old-fashioned swamp-cooler instead of an air-conditioner.

So, she unzipped her duffel and took out a pair of leather sandals, a mid-length khaki skirt, and a cooler blouse to change in to. One with pale pink orchids over zebra print. Oh, why hadn't she brought even one pair of shorts or comfortable jeans along? The decision not to bring anything other than skirts and one crinkle-cloth dress for the gala dinners, now seemed utterly ridiculous.

This whole situation was ridiculous.

And for heaven's sake, where was that doctor? If he didn't get here within the next fifteen minutes, she would have to muster up enough French to call down to the desk and find out what was going on. Except it had entirely slipped her mind at the moment just how to say she was calling from room three-oh-seven. Three-hundred and seven, probably. Oh...hopefully, the switchboard was modern enough to let them know automatically which room was calling...or maybe the doctor would come...and she wouldn't have to figure it out...such an absurd situation...

****

Falling asleep in the chair was an accident.

When Meg woke up the next morning, she had a crook in her neck and the professor was snoring. What happened to the doctor? None had ever arrived. Now, she would not only miss the first day of her authentic African safari, she had spent the entire night in a strange man's hotel room! What would people think? Not to mention the opportunities she would miss out on to collect a few establishing shots for her documentary. Because somewhere out beyond this bizarre situation, the real Africa was waiting for her.

The thought gave her a sudden sense of urgency.

"Professor Anderson?" She cautiously shook his shoulder, but, as she had predicted, he was still sleeping like the dead. After that, she got down on her hands and knees to retrieve the professor's cell phone from under the chair where it had fallen the night before. "Ten forty-five! Professor!" She leapt to her feet and shook him again. "Professor, wake up. I have to…oh, I'll just leave you a note!"

After which she gathered up her things and hustled off to the hotel lobby. There were people coming and going, tourists mostly, as if some flight had just come in and a wave of more tours was about to launch. Meg moved out of the flow to where another rattan chair (also with palm print padding) was placed next to a large potted plant in an obscure corner. At least it would be a quiet out-of-the-way place where she could sort things out and decide what to do next.

Inquiring at the desk as to the whereabouts of the doctor would be the first thing. Then she would find something to eat. She could smell a wonderful aroma of rich, dark coffee coming from somewhere.

But at that thought, she suddenly felt disheveled and chided herself for not at least freshening up in the hotel room. She hadn't even combed her hair. Behavior which was obviously the result of trying to adhere to rule number twelve: *I will avoid even the appearance of wrongdoing.* Which she made a mental note to readjust the next time she had a moment. She would add (in parentheses) *"except in cases of emergency."* After all, what good were a set of personal rules if they were impossible to follow?

When her gaze fell on a small souvenir stand across the room with a rack of hats, she picked up her things and headed over there. Nothing but tourist stuff. But at this point Meg was not picky, and chose a straw hat in the shape of a narrow-brimmed safari helmet, with a brown and white flowered scarf around it that looked suspiciously like all the upholstery and drapes in this establishment. Nearly ten dollars out of her budget, but she no longer cared.

She also determined to get rid of the *Bremen Tours* carry-all, even if it had been free. Not that it wasn't quite the handy, well-made thing. It's just that the voodoo slogan was beginning to weigh heavily on her, and it suddenly felt more important not to even associate with such practices. She had never given it a thought before she met Vidalia. Meg had always relegated unsavory things like voodoo into the same category as a bad movie she had no interest in watching. But it was important to her now.

So important, in fact, that she ended up with some sort of woven string shoulder bag that looked more like a beach tote (pretty shades of brown, at least) that would barely hold all of her things. But she bought it anyway. It gave a sense of relief to dump everything into the shoulder bag right there at the counter and give the carry-all to the sales lady. Who was happy enough afterwards to point her toward the coffee stand where all the good smells were coming from. Things would look better after coffee.

She ordered an espresso, frothed up with real cream and cane sugar, and the cost was no longer an issue. It was heavenly. She trudged carefully back to her potted fern, seriously regretting not having brought along a suitcase with wheels instead of a canvas duffel that weighed nearly twenty pounds. To make matters worse, the new bag hung much lower from her shoulder than the other one and had a tendency to slip off. But she'd do something to fix that, later. Right now, she was just going to sit and enjoy her coffee for a while.

Whatever had she gotten herself into? At this moment, she should be filled up on a breakfast of fresh bread and chilled fruit that was included in the price of the tour. Why, she should be halfway through a day of floating down a river lined with real African jungle. She really needed those river shots! Now, here she was staring into a crowd of tourists in a lobby that didn't look much different than hundreds of other places around the world. Certainly, she had gone the last mile.

That realization settled things for her. As soon as she was finished, she would take the professor's cell phone and his bulging wallet over to the desk and have them put in the hotel safe (one could hardly leave such valuables in a foreign hotel room, so she had brought them along with her). She would leave a message for Tom Anderson there, too, and then phone for a taxi to…oh, of all things! It had completely slipped her mind where her tour group was scheduled to go after Podor. And she had that entire schedule memorized for weeks!

She set her coffee aside and reached for her new bag to look it up in the brochure. It fell over and a few things spilled out, and it was at the very moment she looked up with an exasperated sigh, that she spotted him. Tom Anderson. He was headed for the front desk with purposeful long strides, blustering through the crowd like a general prepared to kick his troops into line. She would have recognized him anywhere. Because, except for wavy brown hair and a muscular burliness that looked like some advertisement for health and fitness, he was the express image of his father. Just like the professor had said. And he did have a mustache, but that was the end of the mystery. The last thing she could picture this man in was an expensive gray suit, or ordering a late lunch in a sidewalk cafe.

Instead, he was wearing jeans and a light khaki shirt under a vest of many pockets. And he had a backpack slung over one shoulder in such a way that made her think it had been carried many miles in that fashion. Still, there was something of an uncanny resemblance to the man at the cafe (had to be the mustache) but she decided it was definitely not him. Not with an attitude like that. This man, she felt as if she knew already (an Anderson was an Anderson, obviously). And, rather than any sort of mysterious intrigue, he triggered an impulse to give him a piece of her mind about such foolishness going on between him and his father. Evading and chasing after each other like a couple of children!

Without as much as a second thought, she shoved her twenty pound duffel beneath the seat to hide it (one couldn't be too careful in strange places). Then she scooped the scattered items back into her bag, pulled the long strap over her shoulder, and hurried toward the desk. Just in time to hear the girl behind the counter, a young girl, not even twenty, in Meg's estimation, make the startling announcement (in French, and for once Meg understood it perfectly) that there was no J. T. Anderson registered at this hotel.

"What?" Meg's new bag slipped from her shoulder and things spilled out onto the floor. "There most certainly is! I just spent the night with him!"

At which point, Tom Anderson and the desk clerk both turned toward her with the same startled expression. Meg felt the heat of color rise to her face and forgot about French entirely. "Waiting for a doctor who"— the explanation tumbled out in English— "who never even showed up! What if he died in the middle of the night? What, then!"

"Megan Jennings, I presume," said Tom Anderson, casting a critical gaze (yes, critical!) at her safari hat. "I'd recognize that voice anywhere. Do you do that on purpose? Barge in and out of other people's business with some shocking bit of news and then wait to see what happens?"

"Well, I am quite finished with Andersons!" She bent down to pick up the items that had scattered (her new camera, too!). "You will find your father in room 307, just as I said before. Still asleep. I could care less what the two of you do at this point. Personally, I have a tour to catch up with."

"Hold it." He leaned down and stopped her hand as she reached for the professor's wallet. "What are you doing with that?"

"Well, I…"

"Looks like his cell phone over there, too. Now, just what"—his hand tightened around hers— "is going on here, miss."

It wasn't even a question. It was a statement (no, a demand), and it irritated Meg right down to the very core of her being. After everything she had done for these people! She tried to pull her hand away, but she couldn't as much as move it. Why was it that people who took regular workouts so seriously, seemed to have a sort of Mount Olympus air about them? It made her feel small, somehow. Although she was slender, she was not small, yet she felt irritatingly tiny next to Tom Anderson. What an absurd situation! Their eyes locked and held. He had the same distinctive blue eyes as his father, only much more intense at the moment. Almost the same as...

No, that just couldn't be.

He simply wasn't the type. Not the slightest hint of refined manners anywhere. Not only was he staring at her as if she was in pajamas, he wasn't making the least effort to hide the fact. "Would you rather I had left them up in the hotel room?" Meg was beginning to feel rather impatient, herself. "I was going to register them at the desk here, to be placed in the hotel safe. Then the professor could pick them up after he...came to his senses."

"Why didn't you do it, then?"

"I only just got here, Mr. Anderson."

"It's almost twelve o'clock."

"I overslept." Meg could feel heat in her face, again. "Jetlag or something. Do you mind letting go of me, now? I am quite willing to turn everything over into your capable hands and get back to minding my own business."

He let go of her.

Whether it was because he saw the logic, or if he had simply been caught off guard by her quiet submission in the face of an altercation, she couldn't tell. She only knew that, quick as a wink, she heard her father's frequent admonition of *"A soft answer turneth away wrath"* and it worked. She handed him the cell phone and wallet, remembered she had brought the professor's passport along at the last moment, and handed that over, too. Then she scooped the rest of the items into the open bag and got to her feet. Hardly expecting an apology, much less feeling any desire for one, she turned to leave.

"Wait," said Tom Anderson.

She stopped. He was demanding, again. Was it just her imagination, or did the Dark Continent seem to bring out the worst in everyone?

"I'd like you to go up there with me, if you don't mind," he said in a tone that clearly echoed with suspicion. "So we can get things straightened out."

At which point Meg forgot about the benefit of soft answers. "I do mind. I've had quite enough, so you'll just have to straighten things out without me. I'm going to catch up with my tour!"

"I think not." He had hold of her, again. Only this time by the arm and she couldn't move away.

"Well, of all the…" Of all the what, she had no idea. Nor could she think of any more logic to speak quietly. When he began to steer her through a cluster of newly arrived tourists gathering behind them, she said, "Look, you can't just…"

But Meg was interrupted at that moment by the imploring protests (French, again) of the clerk at the counter. "Wait, if you please. Mr. and Mrs. Anderson! You cannot go into room 307!"

"This man is not my wife!" insisted Meg, stumbling over the French words and then realizing her mistake too late. "My husband, I mean!"

"You cannot go!" the girl insisted. "Room 307 is reserved for the Abdu Sadir!"

"I will speak to him on your behalf," Tom replied in a perfect and fluent French that made Meg forget about protesting for a moment and stare more closely at him. "Meanwhile, would you be so kind as to see if there are any messages for, or from a Mr. Gilbert Minelli, and then send a doctor up to the room?"

But the spell was just as quickly broken when he returned his attentions to Meg with an abrupt, "Let's go," (in English) as they started toward the elevator.

She tried once more to disentangle herself from his grip, but it was no use. "Whatever made her think we were married!" she fussed. "What kind of a…"

"Arguing in public, no doubt. Married people are usually the only ones who do that."

"Do you mind? I left my duffel…" This time she at least succeeded in diverting him toward the potted fern. "It's under that chair, and I'd rather not leave it in the lobby!" He let go of her long enough to reach for it, during which she practically lost her shoulder bag, again. All the while, she was contemplating another refusal to go upstairs with him. As she hesitated, trying to decide if it would be worth a public scene, Tom slung the duffel alongside his own backpack, and then continued to steer her toward the elevator. All without a word passing between them.

At the elevator, a large group of people and luggage crowded in, forcing everyone close together. She could feel the strong, hard lines of Tom Anderson's body (he didn't move back an inch!) as she involuntarily leaned against him while some heavy, overly enthusiastic tourist leaned unabashedly against her. Of all things!

"I'm supposed to be with a tour group in Podor." She tried once more to reason quietly with him (it had worked before), but the close quarters made it impossible to turn around or see his face for any sign of effect.

"What made you think you had to stay?" he replied over the top of her hat.

"Well…the professor, of course. Listen, if my own father was afraid of flying and landed himself on a strange continent in that condition, I would only hope some Good Samaritan"—she emphasized the phrase—"would have the decency"—extreme emphasis on that word—"to inform his family and help get him home, again."

The doors opened then and they poured out with the flow of other tourists, toward the long row of dark red doors along the hall. But even after things thinned out he was still holding onto her like some common criminal. As if she might escape at any moment. All appearances aside, Meg was ready to make a scene.

She came to a dead stop in the hallway, yanked her arm from his grasp, and turned to face him. "If you don't mind! I changed my plans, my own plans, to make sure your father didn't wake up in some strange hotel not knowing where he was. And now, you have the…the audacity…to treat me like some petty thief!"

"My father, miss," he looked down on her with equal ardor, "is nothing like you describe him. He is a rascally old man who has dragged my brothers and me into some of the wildest shenanigans this side of Hollywood. He is not on medication, hates pills of any kind, in fact. What's more, he would never get his tickets mixed up. Fear of flying? He happens to have his own pilot's license."

"Which is entirely beside the point," she argued, only a little less forcibly at such shocking news. "Whatever the circumstances, they certainly give you no right to boss people around like this. You're as bad as him!"

"Considering the amount of bossing you must have done to get things this mixed up, I'd say it was..."

"Let's not just stand here in the hallway trading insults, Mr. Anderson. The professor asked me to call you. If you have a problem with the way things have worked out, you'll just have to take it up with him. So, let's get this over with." She pointed him down the hall and stepped aside so he could take the lead instead of shoving her along ahead of him. "Room 307. Last one on the right." Then she lowered her voice in a pretense of warning as he passed. "The Abdu Sadir's room."

His only reply was to take her outstretched hand and pull her firmly along behind.

"Oh, honestly!" Meg complained.

"Pop?" His insistent rap swung the unlatched door open on its hinge.

"Professor Anderson?" Meg glanced around the broad shoulder that was blocking her view, and then gasped at the sight of the empty, ransacked room with tumbled out drawers and the contents of the professor's bag strewn out all over the floor.

The old gentleman was nowhere to be seen.

7

Kidnapped

"I did not want to go across the continent, and I do not hanker after Zanzibar..."
Mary Kingsley

Tom's grip on her tightened in what she felt was first out of reflex and then in frustration. "All right, what's going on?"

"Well, the last time I saw him, he..."

"Where is he?"

"In the restaurant...or lobby...or something." She was unable to quell her feelings of disbelief. This couldn't be happening. It absolutely couldn't be! "Maybe he rifled through all this looking for his wallet. Before he saw my note."

"What note?"

"It's right over..." Meg glanced at the nightstand where she left it, but it was gone. "Well, he...probably took it with him, then. I'll call the desk to have him paged, and you can..."

"I'll have him paged." He pointed to the chair across the room and closed the door behind them as he spoke. "You wait over there."

"You don't think...well...of all things!" She sank into its sturdy depths more out of bewilderment than compliance. "Do you think if I had anything to do with this I would wait around until you got here? The poor man, he'll be absolutely beside himself!"

"My father is never beside himself," Tom dropped their bags on the end of the bed, picked up the phone from the nightstand, and dialed with the same hand while he ran the other through his hair and waited for an answer to the ringing she could hear even from across the room. "But it does look as if he's got himself in over his head this time. Hello, young lady," (it was French, again). Could you page Professor J.T. Anderson please? He's not in the room. And about Gilbert Minelli...Yes? Will you read it to me?"

There was a long moment of silence, during which Tom cast her another accusing glance. He hung up then without saying a word, and continued to stare at her with those piercing blue eyes as if a closer, more determined inspection could somehow explain everything. Which Meg did not appreciate, not for one minute.

"Well?" She interrupted the ill-mannered scrutiny. "What was the message?"

"Anderson is headed for Accra...and the girl..." A look of disappointment flickered over his face before he finished almost reluctantly, "Has the documents."

"He must mean the passport," she offered. Because watching the unmistakable waves of disbelief, and then dread flood into those expressive eyes in such rapid succession suddenly wrenched something in her.

The last piece of advice she'd been given before leaving the United States was, "Whatever you do, Meg, don't get into any trouble with the law. Some people have disappeared down in those places and never been heard from, again." She had lightly laughed it off back then, because she was not the kind of person who needed that sort of advice.

But she had a feeling she may need it now.

"Why did you take his passport?" he finally asked. "Now, he'll be detained at the first…"

"I took it because…well, because of everything you hear about them being so valuable on the black market. Identity theft and all that." She sighed and looked away from him. She had to, because now she was beginning to feel as if she had definitely done something terribly wrong somewhere. But who would have thought?

At that moment, her eye fell on a flamboyant pair of red and black print boxer shorts lying among the tumbled out clothes. Hardly the thing you'd guess a man with a Panama suit might wear. Tom (obviously following her gaze) answered as if she had spoken the question out loud.

"These aren't my father's clothes."

"What?"

"I take it they're not yours, either."

"I should say not! Oh, of all things…now, I've gone and taken someone else's luggage. On top of everything else!" All of a sudden, she was upset. As if that little irritation was the last straw, her emotions rose up and threatened to spill out at any moment. "I suppose I'll have to… I'll have to lug that thing back to the airport and turn it in to…"

"First, we have to find Pop before he lands himself in jail."

"We? Whatever for? I've told you everything I know, what more could I…"

"Because I'm not letting you out of my sight until I find him, that's why."

"You still think I had something to do with this? For heaven's sake, do I look dishonest? Do you think I could…"

"You look like some character out of a low-budget movie. It could be a disguise. You could be in cahoots with the Abdu Sadir, for all I know."

"Oh, honestly! These clothes are really nothing more than…"

He picked up the receiver and redialed the desk. "This is Tom Anderson, again. Would you get someone from the airport to collect the bag in 307? It was brought here by mistake. And do you happen to know when the next flight to Accra is?" He glanced at his watch. "That's the only one so far? We'll try to catch it. If you please. Two seats. Yes. Appreciate the tip."

"I'm not going," Meg pronounced before he even hung up.

"Yes, you are." He picked up her duffel and his backpack and started toward her, as if he fully intended to scoop her up in the same fashion.

"You can't make me."

"Yes, I can."

Meg realized he was strong enough to drag the entire chair out the door if she refused to let go of it, but at this point, she was ready to scream for help or even call the police. Nothing in the world could make her agree to accompany a perfect stranger…

"Unless you'd like to sit in jail on kidnapping charges until I get back. You made the first contact with me. You had all his…"

Meg gasped. "I'm sure once I explain to them and they realize I have no reason…"

"This isn't America. You might not get a chance to

explain."

A sense of absolute dread passed through her at such a thought. Which must have shown on her face because he immediately apologized. "It's the best I can do. And look here, if things do turn out the way you say, I'll pay for your tour to make up for the inconvenience. But we have barely an hour to catch that flight, and there are a lot of places around here he could be snagged in along the way."

"No doubt." Meg didn't mention the sort of establishment she was most certain he was liable to get snagged in, but she obviously didn't have to.

"He does have a ticket booked through to Accra," he reasoned. "We may not be able to check every…possibility here in town…" (Meg knew exactly what he meant by that word) "…before the flight leaves, but it would not be impossible to meet every flight that comes in at the other end after that. Believe me, Miss Jennings, Accra is a much bigger place, and if you are telling the truth, it will save us both a lot of time and grief if we find him before he gets out of that airport."

"Oh, all right. I'll go."

What else could she do? But it wasn't because of his arguments, his threats, or even any of his grandiose promises that she relented. Pay for her tour? What was he thinking? Dropping such large sums of money on the slightest whim must be another Anderson family trait. No, the reason she gave in was because at that moment (and right in the middle of all the confusion) she distinctly recognized another footprint. A very familiar one this time.

It was a wonderful sense of well-being that suddenly washed over her (making an incredible impression following the tumult of emotions that had preceded it). All at once she knew she could trust Tom Anderson. That he was a man of his word. That, as awkward as the situation seemed, this was the right thing to do. She certainly had no such assurances about sitting in some foreign jail all by herself. Tom Anderson might be demanding and arrogant, but at least he was an American. Besides, he could speak perfect French. Which would save a lot of misunderstandings when it came to trying to catch up with her tour.

Those were the reasons that Megan, an ordinary schoolteacher who had spent the last ten years working in a quiet university town, walked off into the Dark Continent with a perfect stranger, without telling so much as a soul. She might have called someone in her family at that point. Except that calling halfway around the world just to hear your father give a lecture you already knew perfectly well…was quite out of the question.

And that's how it was that Meg spent the next hour trailing behind the audacious Tom Anderson as he plowed through the closest restaurant, the nearest bar (they were open even at this hour!), and finally the two similar establishments nearest the airport. In ordinary circumstances, Meg would never have set foot in one of those. Except that he still fully expected her to run off at the first chance she got. He also insisted that two pairs of eyes were better than one.

Meg did peer into the gloomy recesses of those places, but only half-heartedly. For, try as she might to prove her integrity by helping him, she could not bring herself to believe that anyone who could not be roused by shaking less than two hours ago could possibly disappear so fast. The fact that she and Tom couldn't find one person who had brushed up against the boisterous old gentleman, made her begin to suspect that he hadn't even left the hotel. An opinion she tried in vain to express.

Because by that time, they had less than twenty minutes to scramble for the departing flight to Accra, which he stubbornly insisted was still their best bet, no matter where his father happened to be at the moment. So, as Meg stood tapping an impatient foot next to the ticket counter where Tom was hurriedly handing over a traveler's check to pay for it all, her eye caught sight of a ladies' room. Without a word, she slid her passport at him that she was waiting to show for inspection and headed for it.

"Megan..."

"Two minutes! I'll be back before you're finished."

During which time she even managed to take that infernal hat off, run her brush under water, recapture those unruly curls, and anchor them securely back into the clip before rushing out, again. By then, he was pacing impatiently in front of the door that led to the gate. He held it open for her, and then the gate, and they hurried across the grass to where an attendant was waving at them from the top of the metal stairway rolled up next to the plane. They were the last to board.

First class, again! Meg sank gratefully into the comfortable seat with an odd sense of *déjà vu*, and buckled herself in. Tom finished stowing their bags in the overhead bin and sat down beside her with a heavy sigh, as if he had just finished an exhausting race. The plane was only half full. There was the thump of the door being closed, the clatter of the stairs rolled back, and the cabin became stifling hot before the engine was finally turned on and the air conditioning began to work.

It was not a stewardess this time, but a steward who passed quickly through the first class area collecting cups and glasses before disappearing into the forward galley to prepare for take-off as they began to taxi down the runway. Meg looked out the window, anxious to catch a glimpse of things she had only sensed were there in the dark last night. More grass beyond the runway, a faraway line of verdant trees, and a thin line of blue off to one side, confirming her belief that the coast was somewhere nearby. She reached into her bag beneath the forward seat and pulled out her camera...

Only to be stopped short by Tom's hand on it before she could even get it turned on. "Taking pictures of airports and runways is frowned upon in these countries. One of the first things they tell you when you're on a tour. If you really are on a tour."

Now, it was Meg's turn to sigh. "For your information, I happen to have missed my orientation dinner."

"And the reason you were sitting in first class instead of coach with the rest of your tour?"

"Because your father had my..." She stopped because something told her she was quite at the limits of her credibility as it was, without adding the fact that the professor had paid for the upgrade on a whim.

"Did you know him before Paris? One of his students, maybe?"

"I should say not!"

"Pretty expensive camera for a tourist. Know what all those buttons and switches are for?"

"Of course I do." She was glad *Moviemaking for*

Beginners was at the bottom of her bag and not sticking out the top, or he might not have believed that, either. "Why is it so hard for you to accept the fact that there are some people in this world without ulterior motives? I didn't even know your father was a film instructor until I read it on one of his business cards."

"After rifling through his wallet?"

"He gave it to me by mistake. If you must know, he thought it was one of yours. I only noticed it wasn't after he…"

"I don't have any business cards."

8

Suspicions

"He persisted in his opinion that my intentions and ambitions were suicidal..."
Mary Kingsley

This time, Meg found it necessary to use a good offense in her own defense. "I should think you would have several of them. Since I was under the impression you were one of those entrepreneurial business geniuses who can handle his own company and everyone else's besides." Which must have hit home somewhere because she caught a slight glimmer of uncertainty in those expressive eyes.

"Is that what he told you?"

"That and more. In fact, he gave me a message for you. I believe it was, 'Tell that rascal I know what he's up to, and he'll never get away with it.' Which only goes to show, Mr. Anderson, that you are not so far above suspicion, yourself."

A flash of appalling surprise was quickly replaced with irritation. "Now, what's that supposed to mean?"

"It means you could very well have had a hand in orchestrating this whole thing. You and that"—Meg cocked her head as if she were thinking and murmured— "Let me see, what was the word...oh, yes..." She nailed him then, with an intense look of her own. "That nincompoop, Gilbert."

"Why would I even do such a thing? Tell me that."

"To take over the business, no doubt." She said it so matter-of-factly it had a double impact on him.

He looked away for a moment as if struggling to keep his composure, smoothed down his mustache and then muttered something that Meg couldn't quite hear. "Is that what he told you?"

"Now, you're repeating yourself. A bit nervous, perhaps?"

"Not on your life."

"Well, the fact is, he was certainly upset about something, and it concerned you. Talked about you incessantly. Rather as if something terrible had come between the two of you and he couldn't quite believe it."

"Such as?"

"How should I know? I was only the polite listener. But if you want my opinion?" She didn't wait for him to answer. "That was the very reason he felt so compelled to gulp down six or seven drinks in the space of a few hours."

"My father has a great capacity for drinking, miss, whether he is extremely up, extremely down, or anything in between. You can hardly use it as an indication of being upset."

"Nevertheless. He was practically beside himself when he asked me to call you."

"Why didn't he call me himself?"

"Because he was, by the time, we..." Now, Meg's brief confidence began to falter. As much as she wanted to put this arrogant man in his place (how anyone could say "miss" so disdainfully, she had no idea), she couldn't in good conscience betray that heartfelt request of his father not to flaunt any such weakness to Tom. Whether that weakness was the state he was in at the time, or the fact that he had somehow allowed things to get out of control between them, she did not know. She only knew that no matter how "rascally" the old man was known to be, she should not be talking about those things to others. No matter who they were. And not even if they knew about them quite well enough already. Rule number seven: *"I will not only try to believe the best of people, I will express it."*

"Just what I thought," said Tom, as if her very silence was an admission of guilt.

Still, Meg was not one to back down easily, and even though she couldn't bring herself to betray the professor's confidence, it infuriated her that this son of his so obviously accused her of being responsible for everything that had happened. Infuriated and disappointed at the same time. Was there nothing about her that showed any trustworthiness? Didn't she at least look like she had a little integrity? She had never purposely gone against the law in her entire life, and here she was being suspected of aiding a kidnapping. Of all things!

She wouldn't have it.

"Give me"—suddenly it seemed incredibly important that he believe her—"one good reason why I should take the slightest interest in that"—she almost said ill-mannered, but her conscience pricked her again so she left that part out—"that father of yours, much less risk my entire life and future on such a wild scheme as you think happened here."

"How about several million dollars in the Bank of California."

Now it was Meg's turn to give a frustrated sigh and turn toward the window for a few moments to reign in her nerves before answering. "And just how on earth would I get any of it? In front of a plane load of witnesses, yet! Bop him on the head when no one was looking, man-handle him off to a hotel, and threaten him at gunpoint all by myself?"

"You weren't by yourself. I distinctly heard Pop scuffle and threaten to have it out with several others while you were leaving that message on my phone."

Meg gasped at this new accusation and he gave a gentle but insistent tap of his finger against her forehead for emphasis. "Recorded."

"But that wasn't..."

"Hard evidence in any court of law. Why do you think I raced down here so fast?"

"Just how did you race down here so fast, Mr. Anderson? According to your own message, you were on a plane yourself. Headed for Accra. So, why aren't you there, already? Tell me that!"

"I switched planes at the layover in Casablanca, that's how. Because you scared the daylights out of me with that message. If I hadn't heard from Gilbert so soon, we would probably be down at the police station hashing things out there instead of here. But we don't seem to be getting anywhere with all this, so let's quit arguing about it. We'll let Pop settle the whole mess, himself, when we catch up with him."

"As I'm sure he will," insisted Meg.

"Meanwhile, will you quit with the Mr. Anderson thing? The name's Tom."

"That sort of familiarity is reserved for friends," she objected.

He gave another frustrated sigh, leaned back in his

seat, and closed his eyes. "I don't know what to do with you."

"Then what, in heaven's name, did you bring me for?"

"I must have been out of my mind."

"Oh!" Meg snatched up one of the pillows from between their seats, turned toward the window, and tried to find a comfortable position to rest. She was exhausted. Tom Anderson exhausted her.

Even though he had some of the same appealing little courtesies as his father (like opening doors and carrying her bags), he also had the same abrasive way of telling people what to do, and she did *not* like it. Not one bit. Meg usually wasn't one to hold a grudge (what was the point when a person could either talk things out or walk away) only now she seemed to be having trouble in both places. Where exactly could she go at thirty thousand feet? Still, when it finally came time for their meal, the nap seemed to have been at least a little refreshing. That is, until Tom took the liberty of ordering her beefsteak and potatoes when she would have preferred the fresh fruit and crisp salad.

"Should always stick to the cooked food in these places," he reminded her, "unless the fruit is the kind you can peel yourself."

Meg knew that. Hadn't she read all those tourist precautions in the government brochures a dozen times over? She just wasn't thinking about the airlines being considered any part of a "third world." However, he redeemed himself a bit when he asked what she preferred to drink, and then ordered only coffee for himself. At least he didn't resemble his father in that department.

"Where do you come from, Meg?" It seemed the

nap and the meal was having somewhat of a positive effect on him, as well.

"Lately or by origin?" Anything was better than more arguing, so she tried her best to be gracious.

"Let's start with origins."

"I come from three generations of fisher-folk. But don't ask me about fish, I was raised on a tug boat that ran contracts between Seattle and Skagway."

"Born in the gold rush, eh? You sure carry your age well."

"Very funny." Meg took her first bite and had the odd sensation that what she was eating was not really beef. "And what about you? How come you're not one of those self-centered Hollywood types if your father has a life-long professorship at the film institute?"

"What makes you think I'm not?"

"Because you're missing a button off the pocket of that shirt." She shook her head. "Wouldn't do for those types."

"Hmm. Well, he only got that lifelong thing within the last five years. After he developed an ulcer and backed off some on the company workload. Doesn't do as much traveling overseas these days."

Meg noticed that he ate like the Europeans, without switching his fork from one hand to the other. "Is that why you don't go home very often?" she asked. "Because you have to do so much of his traveling for him?"

"Is that what he told you?"

"You're repeating yourself, again."

"Rather uncommon to air all the family skeletons on vacation."

"According to your father, such topics are more than acceptable on vacations." She pulled her reading glasses down, peered through them at her plate for a moment, and then returned them to the top of her head. Then she tentatively tried a bite of the potatoes…delicious. Browned, golden in some sort of sauce that was buttery, sweet, and salty all at the same time.

She looked back at Tom, then, only to catch him watching her with a look of…what was that look?

He turned back to his meal. "Then you won't mind if I continue to catch up."

"I certainly have nothing to hide." But the truth was, he was beginning to make her feel defensive, again.

"Where from lately?"

"Teaching at a private prep school in a small town just outside of Seattle. History and theater, if you insist on knowing the subjects. And…" She took a sip of her tonic water and then wrinkled her nose. "I'm not sure I like this so much without ice in it. Do you think it's really necessary to avoid local ice as well as water?"

"Probably not in airports and the better hotels, but why take the risk? Last thing I need is a sick woman on my hands. I've got enough to carry as it is." He looked over at her and winked then, another blueprint of the family (Meg had seen that wink before).

"Oh, honestly!"

"You were saying?"

"I don't remember what I was saying."

"Something about teaching history and theater. You're not going to get grouchy, again, are you?"

"Grouchy…"

"Let's at least keep up appearances through dinner, shall we? I haven't quite figured you out, yet."

"Nor I you, Mr. Anderson." Meg left off the

potatoes to try the carrots...not carrots, at all...chopped sweet potatoes, of all things. But lovely.

"It's Tom. And would you mind telling me what you're thinking, running around West Africa all by yourself? It's a dangerous place for a woman alone."

"I am not by myself. I'm with thirty other people. At least, I should be, by now. More are supposed to be trickling in today and tomorrow. But I will be by myself on the long way back from here. I'm not looking forward to that. My French is deplorable."

"They speak English in Ghana."

"But my tour is..." She glanced up at him with a mild surprise and caught him staring at her again. Almost as if he knew her, or at least seen her before. But she was not about to let herself get caught up in those thoughts, anymore. "After Podor, we were supposed to take the train from St. Louis to Dakar. I couldn't, for the life of me, remember that this morning. But it just came back to me all of a sudden. Must be finally settling down and eating something substantial."

"Short of money?"

"No. Just on a tight budget. My money has to stretch for three months."

"What are you on, a walking tour? I wondered why you were traveling so light."

"Not exactly. I'm only going to be ten days in Africa. But I've rented a little place on the coast in Scotland where, after that, I'll be able to work without..." She looked over at him, again, wondered what on earth had made her blurt that out, and then gave a pretense of dabbing her mouth with a napkin as she tried to think how best to change the subject.

"Now, I get it."

"What?"

"Why you got yourself mixed up in all this. The fact is, miss, you are…"

At that moment, the steward came up with a bright smile and reached for their trays. "Did you enjoy the biffsteak, sah?"

"Wasn't sure it was beef," Tom replied, "but it was cooked good enough."

"And the wife?" He cast inquisitive brown eyes at Meg.

"He is…not…my husband." She handed hers over, having eaten only the vegetables.

"Ahh…yes, I see!" He smiled indulgently at Tom and left with the trays.

"Oh, honestly! Now, he thinks…"

"Which is just the point I was about to make. You're way too easy to get information out of, Megan. Places you're headed…flaw like that could be suicidal."

9

A Dangerous Journey

"But most newcomers do not get a shock of this order..."
Mary Kingsley

Meg peered at herself in the mirror of the tiny bathroom cubicle, refastened her hair-clip, and had a distinct flash of Vidalia Harbin doing the same thing. She decided to wear it down, instead. It would mean she would have to bother with brushing curls back from her face whenever she needed her glasses, but today it felt preferable to rituals. This was not how she thought reaching for her destiny would be. Where was *"... the Lord going before you to make the crooked places straight and guarding your rear from behind?"*

No, that wasn't exactly the right quote but it was the same idea. The point was, that promise didn't seem to be working for her. Not one bit. Because whatever she had gotten herself into was only getting worse. Yesterday's dread at the thought of having to spend two weeks in the same rooms with Vidalia now seemed like it would be a welcome reprieve compared to this bizarre situation. At least, she knew where she stood with Vidalia.

Which was more than she could say for Tom Anderson.

The fact he had purposely set out to extract personal information from her (and succeeded) made her question whether or not she had deciphered that footstep correctly. And she had been so certain of it! Had she simply been too frightened at the thought of facing foreign authorities with so much strange evidence stacked against her? Or, had she chosen because Tom Anderson had the familiarity of an American? There were, after all, quite a number of dangerous Americans.

Maybe she didn't have enough faith to actually get herself through something as terrible as being taken to jail. Even if she got released when they discovered she was innocent. Just the thought of it! Of course, it was easy to believe faith would get you through any terrible thing while sitting in church on a Sunday morning. But actually coming face-to-face with it gave a person's mind an amazing ability to conjure up vivid imaginations of what awful things might actually happen. That's what made her hesitate. Her own mind.

Which had been playing quite the number of tricks on her, lately.

Such as the fact that her memory of the man standing in the rain was now beginning to turn into the express image of Tom Anderson. Disappointing, to say the least. Because it wasn't often that she compelled the attentions of such handsome men, and she had been enjoying that little memory. Working in a place where one tended to see only the same people day after day, often made her crave such things.

True, the similarities between the two men were rather uncanny. But somewhere along the line, she had elevated the rain man to "dashing prince" status. Tom, on the other hand, bordered very close to being an arrogant brute. What else could you call someone who made a habit of physically forcing people to do things they didn't want to do? For heaven's sake, this wasn't the Stone Age.

What a mess this thing had become!

Suspected of theft, and possibly even kidnapping! It was absolutely the last thing she thought would ever happen to her. Now, or any other time. Not to an ordinary teacher who'd spent the last ten years living a well-ordered life in a quiet university town. Why, she couldn't remember a time in her life when she hadn't been sure of things. She even prided herself on being a good judge of character.

All the way up until she had gone chasing after her destiny.

"Dear Lord"—she murmured into the wet paper towel she was running over her face— "all of a sudden, I can't seem to be able to tell the difference between a good person and a bad one around here. If I can't figure it out on short notice, how in the world am I supposed to tell?"

Then, at that precise moment, she had another flash. It was of a conversation with her brother that had taken place many years ago. When Meg had been quite young. After school, one of the boys in her class had talked her into walking home on the other side of a busy street. They moved across with the flow of other children being shepherded by the crossing guard, and had quite the pleasant walk together. Until the boy stopped at a side street and said, "This is where I turn. You have to go two blocks up to the traffic light and cross back over. After that, go back one or two blocks, maybe three, and turn on your street."

Then he left her there.

Meg trudged on dutifully by herself, but everything looked different from that side. There were no landmarks she recognized coming from that direction, and she couldn't find her street. First one wrong turn, then another…and suddenly she was lost. She burst out crying, wailed her heart out, in fact, while more and more cars continued to race by on busy streets.

Only the sudden appearance of her older brother saved the situation. Sent out to hunt her down before dinner, the carefree youth with hair as red as hers, gave a familiar loud whistle from half a block behind her. Then hollered, "Hey, drop anchor, Meg, have you slipped your cable? Come about, or you'll end up in Port Townsend!" She had never been so glad to see anyone in her life. She flung her arms around him and clung unabashedly, not caring who might see. For once, he didn't seem to mind, either, and was even sympathetic as she told him what happened.

Then, as if it was his duty in the absence of their father, he said, "What in blazes made you walk off with some strange kid who had no manners in the first place?"

"I couldn't tell…I didn't know!" She sniffed. "How do you know, Bennie?"

"By what they do, of course. Any decent kid would have walked on your side of the street and crossed over himself. Keep your eye out for what people do, Meg. It's not always the same as the way they talk."

He put an arm across her shoulders and headed her toward home. But he framed the comforting gesture with the remark, "And quit calling me Bennie, or I'll have to wallop you."

Hmmm. If Megan were to judge things by that long ago standard…The fact that Tom Anderson had made some sort of character judgment, himself, and not had her arrested on the spot was a good thing. The fact that he came rushing down to find his father in the first place, was another good thing. On the other hand, he could have just been playing the part of a concerned son, and his true intentions were merely to set up an alibi. That would not be good, at all.

Still, one couldn't easily falsify the many spontaneous reactions he had in response to her accusations of him during their previous conversations. Which made the score two to one if she counted her own personal discernment that he was, indeed, a good person. But purposely setting out to get as much information about her as he could, without revealing his actual intent…well, now, that made them even again, and…

There was a loud rap on the door that made her jump, and she heard the steward's voice through the thin partition. "You will please exit the lavatory, we are making ready to land!"

Meg hurriedly tossed her things back into her bag and exited just as the plane banked gently in preparation for descent. Which gave her an odd sense of losing her balance that made her reach out to steady herself. Right at the moment Tom reached out and helped her into his aisle seat, at the same time sliding into her empty one by the window. Another courtesy.

"Trying to hide out in the lav so you can get out first and run off somewhere?" he said, just as she was about to mentally mark that down as a good thing.

Always thinking the worst of people definitely belonged in the bad column.

He got another bad point at customs. There were three people working at the counter, so they were standing side by side, and he made no excuses for unabashedly scrutinizing her things as her agent removed each item for a thorough inspection. It distracted her so, that she was late in noticing there was some kind of a problem, and the supervisor had to be called over. She only realized it when Tom's expressive face clouded over, and she turned back to find the two men in uniform conferring in whispers across from her.

Finally, the second man stepped forward and said, "Will you come this way, please?" while the other scooped the rest of her things into the bags and followed.

They took her to a small office behind the counter where another man, also in uniform, sat behind a black wooden desk that seemed to take up the entire room. There were more whisperings as the supervisor informed him about the problem and pointed her toward the nearest of two chairs. The agent carrying her things put her duffle by the door and dropped her string bag on the huge desk with such a thump that several items fell out.

Meg felt a rising sense of irritation at her cameras being tossed around like that and was about to make a remark when her full attention was suddenly riveted to the grotesque form of a human skull. It had a hammered copper ashtray embedded into the top and was holding down a pile of papers. As if it were nothing more than an expensive desk ornament. At whose expense? She wondered if it was real, or just some manufactured replica made to shock tourists. And even though Meg had been fully prepared to personally witness some of these things on her tour (monuments of the slave trade, and all that), it caught her off-guard under the present circumstances.

"Please think carefully before you respond."

"Yes, I'm sorry…what was the question?"

"If you would be so good as to state your full name."

"Oh. Megan Andreanof Jennings."

"Of Russian origin?"

"It refers to a place not a family. I was born off the Andreanof Islands in the middle of a storm. They're in Alaska. I'm as American as I can be. It is a U.S. passport, isn't it?"

"Yes, but false identity papers are not hard to come by." He went back to studying it, as if there might be another clue there. "Why were you listed as Mrs. Anderson on your ticket?"

"A mistake, I assure you. Some hotel clerk who made the reservations back in St. Louis assumed I was married, when I wasn't."

"Oh, I see."

"That isn't what I mean, either. Look, is that what the problem is? The name on the ticket doesn't match my passport?"

"No, but I find it interesting." He looked across at her through his gold-rimmed glasses and smiled. He motioned the others out of the room and got to his feet. "Why did you come to Ghana, Miss Jennings?"

"I'm on a tour."

"There were no tours connecting with this flight." He moved to a brass coffee service that rested on top of a filing cabinet at the back of the room, turned back to her, and asked politely, "Would you like some coffee? Or a sweet, perhaps?"

"Coffee would be nice." Meg didn't want to offend him by refusing (another tip she had learned from the tourist pamphlets). "I'm with *Bremen Tours*. A ten day tour that ends up here in Accra."

"Ah, yes, I am familiar with them. And now, I quite understand." He handed her a very small cup, hardly enough for a few swallows, and Meg dutifully took a sip. It was thick and strong, and nearly took the top of her head off. What in the world was it?

"It is my own recipe," he replied with a smile, as if she had asked the question out loud. "Liqueur, I think you call it in the States. My own brand of espresso liqueur. Now. Miss Jennings. You may not realize, but we have a very delicate situation here. I might have to confiscate some of your things."

"What?"

"It's the new regulations regarding drug runners and terrorists."

She set the little cup down and leaned forward in her chair. "Well, that certainly isn't me, there must be some mistake!"

"Yes, indeed. There has definitely been a mistake. Perhaps you are under the mistaken impression, Miss Jennings, that we are a backward country with a highly inadequate security system? I assure you we are not."

"And I assure you that I am not a security threat."

"You lied on your ticket."

"I told you I didn't make the reservation."

"Yes, and that is what makes this case interesting. Now, if you would have perhaps said you had recently become married and your passport was still unchanged…well, then…I might have thought nothing of it. The name is a small matter, anyway, compared to the nature of your undeclared item."

"But…I declared everything."

"Shall we look through, again?"

"Be my guest." Meg gestured toward the string bag on his desk, and he did not hesitate to dump the rest of the contents out between them.

As if he already knew what he wanted, he shoved aside her two cameras and reached for the batch of tour brochures. He held up the one about the Mole National Park. He opened it, made an expression of mock surprise, and lifted a folded sheet of paper from the hiding place. Meg didn't recognize it.

The man perused it for a few moments. "I've seen many of these illegal documents. They are a menace to all our efforts to make ourselves a respected presence in the world marketplace. Probably no more than a worthless scam, but nevertheless, the government has declared them as contraband."

"I don't even know what that is," Meg objected. "I've never seen it before."

"Yes, everybody says that when they are caught. But, as you can see, it was in your belongings."

"I haven't the faintest idea how it got there!"

"Probably the same way you got here, Mrs. Anderson." He slid the paper across the desk for her to look over. "It is the deed to one of our goldmines…made out in the name of your husband."

10

The Road to Destruction

"No West African path goes straight…"
Mary Kingsley

There was a horrendous pounding against the closed door, and Tom Anderson suddenly burst through with a disgruntled agent still holding onto him from behind. Which made what Meg was thinking to come tumbling out her mouth.

"Tom Anderson…how could you? You snake! You…" She leapt to her feet and flung the paper at him. "You wolf in sheep's clothing!"

He caught it as it fluttered against his chest. "Let's hold off having any squabbles in public, shall we?"

Which in turn caused a delighted chuckle to escape the man behind the desk, and he waved the apologetic agent out the door, again. "Yes, yes…by all means, it is time to bring in the husband."

Meg had quite passed her limits and was ready to go to jail. "Call the American ambassador!" She scooped everything back into her bag and slung it over her shoulder. "Take me to the consulate!"

"One moment," said the man at the desk.

"This instant!" demanded Meg with a stamp of her foot and then a bang of her fist on his desk for emphasis.

"All right." Tom brushed her aside (like a pesky fly) to stand in her place. Then he reached into an inside pocket of his khaki vest to withdraw a wallet that was equally as bulging as the professor's had been. "What's it going to take to get us out of here?" He removed two bills that Meg could not see the value of and set them down on the desk.

The man's eyes widened.

"That's for the trouble she caused." He set down another. "And that's for any trouble you might have explaining all this. And" —he took out one more— "this is for the evidence."

"Evidence…" The man rose to his feet and offered his hand across the table in good will. "The worthless thing. It is worthless, I assure you. But go ahead and take it."

Tom and the man shook hands, (and acted as if she weren't even in the room) after which he stashed the wallet back into his pocket (along with the offending document) and hustled her toward the door. She went along because she was dumbfounded. Speechless, as a matter of fact.

But she came to her senses well enough halfway to the exit.

She stopped and yanked her elbow out of his grasp. "You are nothing but a…"

But he only put an arm (a very heavy arm) across her shoulders and continued to sweep her along. "Not here, Megan. Do you understand? I'll explain everything as…"

The first bar of the French national anthem emanated from one of his pockets, and he steered her out of the flow of traffic and closer to a waiting area before he took out his cell phone. He flipped it open with his thumb. "This is Tom," he answered without letting go of her. There was a long silence, during which Meg could hear a woman's voice on the other end of the line. She tried to pull away, again, but he only held on tighter as he continued to listen.

Meg felt her temper rising in a way she hadn't experienced in years. What right did he have to treat her like this? He was holding her so close she could smell the leather straps of his backpack mingled with a faint trace of *Old Spice* aftershave. She put both of her fists against his chest and pushed. It didn't faze him. The harder she pushed, the tighter he squeezed, and the sound of his voice when he finally answered didn't betray even a hint of effort.

"Mother, take a breath. Now, listen. I have his passport. Yes. And all of his money, too. All of it. Yes. Isn't that what I just said? No, he wasn't. I'm going to meet him in Akosombo."

At that moment Meg came to the ultimate end of her limits. She had exerted every ounce of her strength for nearly a minute, until, like a contest of arm wrestling, it gave out suddenly and failed her, when in spirit she would never have given up at all. Not for one minute. But instead, she went limp all at once (she couldn't help it) with her forehead leaning against his chest, and such a great wave of frustration swept over her that she burst into tears. The iron hold went immediately gentle in response, then the slightest of tightening, again, in a gesture of apology.

Which so infuriated her that (without even thinking) she drew back one of her still-clenched fists and hit him in the stomach with every last bit of force she could muster. It caught him off-guard. He staggered half a step backward, let the phone down from his ear, and Meg distinctly heard— "has ruined my plans, again, Tommy, that reprobate! You know every time he gets with Eddie, it's like"—but it still wasn't enough for him to let go. He gasped (as if he only just could because the wind had been knocked out of him) and sank back into one of the empty chairs of the waiting area, with Meg simultaneously having to follow suit in the one next to him.

"Mother…" The voice on the other end was only an incessant drone now, because he had put the phone up to his ear, again. "I'll handle things with Eddie. Take the wives and kids on holiday like you planned, and the rest of us will…just have to meet back up at the end of it instead of the beginning. That's the only thing that's changed…I know you can…it will, I promise." He slowly returned the phone to his pocket and looked over as she sat there, still trembling from the entire experience, and an unchecked flow of tears streaming down her face. "Megan…"

She sniffed and began to rummage through her bag for a package of tissue. "Don't talk to me! And don't think because I'm crying that you got the better of me, Tom Anderson! I'm…" She found the tissue and snatched one out so fast that it tore in half. "I'm just worn out, that's all. Do you hear me? I'm worn out!"

"Thank God, or you'd have killed me." He rubbed an unconscious hand over his stomach, took one slow, deep breath, and then another. "Swing like that ought to be registered as a weapon."

"Pushing people around who are smaller than you…" She blew her nose. "Well, maybe you'll think twice next time."

"I will."

"Serves you right. But you made me lose my temper, and I hate that!"

"I'm sorry."

You've got me bawling, like a baby, and I can't stop!"

"I said, I'm sorry."

"Well, just..." She sniffed, again. And then hiccupped (for heaven's sake!). "Just save your apologies for your wife and kids and let me go back to my tour! Or, home even! I'm that upset."

"I can't let you go, yet, Meg."

"Why, because you need me to smuggle more illegal documents for you? Take me to the consulate. I want to talk to the ambassador!"

"Listen." He took another deep breath, let it out slowly, and got gingerly to his feet. "I didn't put that thing in your bag, Pop did."

"I don't believe it! And there's not a thing you can say to..."

"It wasn't my signature on the bottom of that deed." He reached for her arm and helped her up. "It was his."

"I'm not going!"

"Yes, you are."

"I'd rather go to jail!"

"No, you wouldn't." He resituated her duffel and his backpack on his other shoulder. "Will you please not make me force you? I'm a little worn out myself after all this."

Megan took a deep breath of her own, held her chin up (like a good martyr) and rose slowly to her feet. She put the tissue into her pocket, but had to take it out again when she realized she was still wearing the same clothes since yesterday, and succumbed to another jag of tears. Tom held onto her arm as they started walking, but it was more to steer her clear of obstacles than drag her along this time.

When they came to the glass doors that led outside, he held the nearest one open for her. "And I don't have any wife, or kids," he informed her as she went through ahead of him, still sniffing. "Don't think I'll even be tempted after this experience."

They took the first taxi he could flag down.

It was old and run down and smelled like grease. The windows were either open all the way or missing, and an uncomfortably warm humidity that seemed practically stifling hung heavily around them. And it was rush hour. The streets were crowded with people coming and going everywhere. Horns honking, loud music spilling out of dingy little bars and nightclubs they passed. This was not the Africa Meg had come to see.

The taxi driver was a heavyset older man with a bald head and a face that reminded her of a raisin. When he smiled, one of his teeth was gold. Tom rattled off an address as if he had done it a dozen times and knew right where he wanted to go. Which seemed very suspicious, under the circumstances, and made her uncomfortable all over, again.

"I thought you said we were going to sit at the airport and check every flight in from St. Louis," she accused. "Now, where are we going?"

"Somewhere I can pick up a car. We've got to drive to Akosombo. Pop talked a friend into taking him there in a private plane so he could avoid being detained at customs. We have better connections there."

"So, if you already heard from him, why do I have

to go? He told you I was innocent, right? Did you even ask him? Hopefully you mentioned I've been accused of smuggling, now! "

"I haven't heard from him, personally. Only Mother has, and she has a tendency to get overly excited about things." He reached for his wallet and removed several bills. "He told her he was robbed. And since you had everything he said was stolen…"

He paused to lean forward as the cab pulled in toward the curb and handed the money to the driver. They were stopped in front of a rundown car lot that also had several goats and chickens meandering around the yard (right in the middle of the city). How long was this nightmare going to continue?

Meg slid across the seat to get out on the curb side, and refused Tom's outstretched hand to assist her. But she didn't let herself lag very far behind when he turned and entered the building: there were several strange-looking characters milling around the sidewalk in front of the entrance. A little bell on the door rang as they came in, and after a few moments, a dark man in a red t-shirt that said *Uhuru* on it, entered from a door behind the counter. Meg had seen that word before, but she couldn't remember what it meant.

"Tom Anderson!" A white, brilliant smile in a handsome face.

"Hello, Mick." They shook hands.

"Welcome, welcome! I didn't expect you until next week."

"Something came up, and I'm in need of a quick ride to Akosombo." He set their bags on the counter. "Can you do it?"

"I can. But man, that road! Hard rains the last few days and it's not so good over the mountain."

"What's it doing raining so hard this time of year?"

"You tell me. The whole planet is going crazy. My cousin says the road crews are out, but I don't know how far they are. Might make it if you take it slow, though."

"Well, I have to get there, so I'll take my chances." He reached for his wallet. "Give me something that can handle it."

"I always do, my man. I always do." He turned away to retrieve a set of keys from a row of others on a cork wallboard before stepping up to an outdated computer to begin typing in information with a quick agility. He hit the execute button, and as a printer under the counter began to tap out the paperwork in a steady hum, he looked up and flashed Meg a smile.

"First trip?"

She nodded, waiting for some off-color remark about her relationship with Tom. Well, she wasn't going to say a word…not one word. Let him do the explaining this time, she was tired of it all.

"Freedom," Mick explained to her as he reached back under the counter for the paperwork and then slid it across with a pen so that Tom could sign. "It means freedom. But it is also the name of a music group. And so the drums."

There were two large drums under the black lettering on his shirt, and she had been staring at them. "I see," she murmured, trying at least to be polite. After all, it wasn't his fault that she was in this predicament.

"You shall have to hear them sometime when you get back this way."

He led them out a side door then, and pointed

towards an ancient jeep that not only looked like
something left over from the world war, but also
seemed as if it had been pieced together from several
different vehicles. Tom tossed their things into the back
and opened the passenger door for Meg. Then he went
over to where Mick was taking five-gallon cans of
gasoline out of a shed and began to help carry them.
They set three in the area behind the back seat that
opened from the outside.

"Good luck, my friend," said Mick as they shook
hands, again.

"Thanks." Tom opened the door and climbed in. "I
have a feeling we'll need it."

"Goodbye, lady friend." He smiled at Meg
through the open window as he closed the door after
Tom. "Stay out of the jungle at night."

"I'll try." His ready friendliness made the situation
seem a little less sinister, somehow.

****

That melancholy time between light and dark
didn't last long in the tropics. By the time Tom had
made a second stop on the outskirts of the city for
some fresh fruit and bottled water, along with a box of
crackers and canned American cheese to take along,
night had fallen. Meg refused the offerings. She wasn't
hungry (how could she be under circumstances like
this?). Things were growing worse by the minute.

She knew it was going to be a long drive, and she
was not looking forward to it. The engine was noisy,
and a distinct smell of gasoline seemed to waft in
through the windows after every acceleration. It was
still uncomfortably hot and humid, and the longing for

a cool shower was almost overpowering at this point. She hadn't slept in a decent bed for days, and suddenly she was close to tears, again. Of all things…why…she hadn't been this emotional in years!

She reached into her bag sitting on the seat between them, and rummaged around in the dark for her package of tissue. Tom took a long swallow from a bottle of water he had been drinking and then set it back into a plastic cup holder that looked as if it had been added as an improvement sometime back in the eighties.

"Why don't you crawl into the back seat and try to get some sleep, Meg. Should be a better breeze back there with all the windows down. It'll cool off more once we get higher up the mountain, too."

"Why do I think you've done this before?"

"I've done it quite a few times. Our company has some business going with one of the towns up here, and we make the trip every couple years. Don't worry about what Mick said about the road, I know where I'm going."

He didn't have to offer twice. At least she could stretch out back there, and she wouldn't have to keep up appearances. She really didn't care what he thought about her anymore. Looks weren't everything. Which just goes to show how low a person can go when they let themselves slip into a decline. Her own behavior over the last forty-eight hours had shocked even herself. Why she had broken nearly half of all those personal rules she had kept under control for years!

By all rights, she should probably at least help him stay awake. Especially since the faster they found that errant professor (who had some definite explaining to do, in her estimation), the faster she could get back to being her own normal self. The trouble was, she wasn't exactly sure who that was anymore. But there was one thing she did know. Any person who could be accused of a felony, practically kidnapped and hauled across two countries by an intimidating stranger without losing her mind entirely, had to at least be halfway stable. Maybe even commendable. And who was to say she wouldn't come out of these trying experiences a stronger and better person because of them?

That's what they always said in church, anyway. That trials and tribulations made you stronger. Well, if they did, Meg decided, (as she plumped up her duffel to use as a pillow) she ought to be feeling like one of those Amazon women by now. Considering the fact that there was little left that could be worse, she gratefully surrendered herself to the welcome escape of total exhaustion, with a comforting assurance that if the car broke down, or even ran itself into a ditch…it could wait until tomorrow to be dealt with.

No, let Tom Anderson deal with it.

11

End of the Road

"Clearly that road was not yet really healthy…"
Mary Kingsley

Meg fell asleep to an unending series of bumps and jolts, twists and turns, and an endless changing of ancient gears that ushered her into welcome oblivion. But, in what seemed like only moments later, she woke to a fragrant, humid warmth that had replaced the stifling heat of the night. A slight almost cool breeze moved across her face. Was she dreaming? When she opened her eyes, it was only to be met with a ragged tear hanging from the cracked and aging canvas-topped jeep, which reminded her exactly where she was.

But it was much too quiet.

The first thing she saw when she pulled herself up to look over the front seat was that Tom Anderson was not there. The second thing she saw made her gasp and lean as far over as she could to gaze up through the windshield with an astonished, "Uh-oh…oh…oh, dear!"

An enormous tree had fallen across the road and now towered nearly ten feet in front of them without any possible way around. On the driver's side, a steep, heavily wooded hillside barred their way, and on the other, an equally steep embankment that tumbled off toward…she stuck her head out the open window on the passenger side. It was a wide lazy river that looked like a molten strand of silver in the early morning sun. It lay some several hundred feet below. And there in the crook of the closest bend an entire herd of hippos were lounging in the cool depths. She could faintly hear the explosive blasts of air as they surfaced. Why, they sounded like whales when they came up! Yet, they also honked at each other like giant, deep-throated geese. The incredible scene nearly took her breath away.

"That's a lot more worth filming than an airport runway," Tom spoke quietly beside her, and she only just then noticed that he had been leaning against the side of the car, eating an orange, and watching the antics of the faraway herd, himself.

Meg ducked her head back inside, and her fingers fairly trembled trying to get her camera out. Then she opened the door to step outside. Now, this was what she had come for, this was the Africa she wanted to take back with her! But who knew how long she would have to capture the moment? And what was it she'd read in the book about filming at such distances? No time to look things up, now, because if the herd didn't move out of sight around the bend, Tom Anderson could very well take a notion to…

"You have a tripod?" he asked.

"Yes, but…"

"It's the only way you can keep it stable this far away. Then you can use the zoom to close in." He set his half-eaten orange on the roof of the car and wiped any remaining moisture on his pant leg before taking the camera. "Want to be in the picture?"

"Heavens no, not looking like this." She leaned back into the car long enough to pull her duffel across the seat and unzip it to search out the tripod.

"You look fine. Besides, you can cut out anything you don't like later on."

"Well, I'd have to cut out everything but my lower half, because I don't want anyone to recognize me." She brought out the black and silver stand that was telescoped into itself several times and held tightly together with a compact clip.

"Nothing to do with gold, I hope."

"Oh, honestly! Is my name J.T. Anderson? You're the one who ought to be worried. Manhandling me across the country like some..." She had never assembled the two items before, and reached for her glasses to give the bottom of the camera a closer inspection. They weren't on her head. With hardly a second thought, she handed the things to Tom and climbed into the back seat, again, to see where they might have fallen off during the night.

"Well, it'll be a relief if all I have to do is apologize. Nothing could make me happier."

"What?" She backed out with the glasses in hand, but by that time he had already set everything up a few feet away on the edge of the road. "Don't tell me you're finally starting to believe me!"

"To tell you the truth,"—he leaned down to peer through the lens for a moment— "I believed you the first time you called Gilbert a nincompoop. Only someone who had Pop's complete confidence would have been let in on that opinion."

Meg was shocked. "Then, why, in heaven's name, did you drag me all the way up here?"

He straightened and looked over at her. "You mean, in spite of every piece of evidence pointing to you? Probably because I had the worst feeling the minute I let you out of my sight, something terrible would happen."

"Tom Anderson!" She stamped her foot. "The only terrible thing that's happened to me in the last twenty-four hours has been you!"

"Don't let's start arguing, again, Meg. It's too nice a morning. Now, do you want to be in the picture, or not."

"I do, but I have to put something different on," she finally replied.

"Well, hurry up before the light changes."

What else could she do? She wanted that footage, and she might never get such an opportunity again. Especially if she missed every sanctuary and mini-safari in the tour, only to catch up with them when they ended up in Accra. Now, here she was with Tom Anderson not only waiting for her to take pictures, but actually helping.

And that's how it happened that Meg's opinion of him suddenly changed as quickly as a coin flipping over onto the other side. What's more, that momentary flash of temper melted into a mixture of gratitude and the most tolerant sort of faith in his blustery, but enthusiastic approach to situations. He certainly knew how to get things done. Which left her without feeling the slightest need to explain any of her actions to him. Something that, after the stress of the last two days, was actually quite a relief.

She took her duffel around to the other side of the jeep and removed her Victorian outfit. She put on the black cotton blouse with long sleeves and high collar, and the matching mid-length skirt. She exchanged her sandals for the riding boots and fastened a wide leather belt around her waist. Tom was involved filming the herd by the time she came around, again, and stopped only long enough to give a quick inspection. As if he wasn't the least bit surprised to see her looking like that.

On the contrary, he reached out and took the glasses from the top of her head, and then, on impulse, it seemed, brushed the curls away from her face. "Where's your hat?" he asked.

"She wouldn't wear that kind of hat."

"But she wore her hair up most of the time. So you better put it back like it was, yesterday."

Meg stopped fumbling with the antique broach she was trying to pin at her collar, and cast him a questioning glance. Taking it as an appeal for assistance, he put her glasses into his shirt pocket, and then slipped two fingers between her neck and the thin cotton collar before pinning and fastening the clasp. Her pulse quickened at the brush of his fingers, and he answered the response as if she had accused him aloud.

"It was only to keep from pinning it to your throat, miss priss." Then he turned back to the camera. "For someone who wants to jump into the shoes of Mary Kingsley, you've got the inhibitions of a..."

"Tom Anderson, you've been reading my journal!"

"Under the circumstances, it would have been foolish not to when I saw the opportunity."

"You said you believed me since yesterday! In which case you had no right..."

"Believed you were the lady at the cafe."

Meg gasped.

"Doesn't mean I was convinced you aren't involved in all this." He straightened up and this time his eyes softened when he looked down at her, again. "Now, I'm convinced."

She felt her irritation begin to melt under that look, before a terrible thought occurred to her. He might only have said that because he read it in the journal. Could be a ruse, using the scenario of the cafe, and just another crafty way to get more information out of her. "Well, it was a" —she turned away on pretense of searching for the tortoise-shell clasp but mostly to reign in the tumult of her feelings—"an invasion of privacy!"

"For a girl who didn't hesitate to rifle through someone's wallet and take all their valuables in the first place, I admit, privacy was the least of my worries."

"And to think I was beginning to trust you!" She swept her curls up in a brisk, smooth motion and clipped them in place.

"You can trust me, priss. I promise." He waved her toward the embankment as he started filming, again. "No more debates, now. We're losing the light. This early sun is just right to give you a sort of silhouette effect against the river. So, just walk back and forth a few times at different angles until it feels comfortable."

"Then you...you don't think all this is crazy?" The realization that he had sifted through her innermost dreams and deepest thoughts (the only one in the world who ever had!) just as easily as she had rifled his father's wallet, made it suddenly important that she know.

"Crazy? It's brilliant. Film biographies are a dime a dozen. But you've got a unique edge with this idea of…how did you put it…jumping into the shoes of the woman, grabbing hold of the current of adventure-seeking curiosity that drove her, so you can plug it into the bored young minds of today. Well said. And well done."

"But I haven't done it, yet." She began to pick her way gingerly down the slope and was glad she had the knee-high boots in case she should run into any snakes.

"You're here, aren't you? Everybody talks about their dreams, Meg. Not many are brave enough to actually go after them. In fact wait 'til we're finished here, and…hey…watch out…"

She stumbled over a fallen branch and nearly lost her balance. Tom lifted his head and looked at her over the top of the camera. "Can you do it without your glasses? I was trying to keep away from the glare."

"I can if I concentrate," she replied, without looking back. "But it feels like walking on a giant sponge. Could ruin the whole scene if it doesn't work out."

"It'll work out."

"You seem awfully sure."

"Well, it's what I do for a living."

"But I was under the distinct impression" —her voice grew fainter as she moved farther into the brush— "that you were in the health and fitness business."

"That's Mother's latest project. I'm only handling the business end of it until she gets on her feet. A little off to the right. That way I can catch you just in front of the herd. Beautiful… that's beautiful."

After which, ensued about ten minutes of

clambering over the hillside, and then, a rather tumultuous return toward the top. Where, at some point, her left foot sank into a rotten log that immediately came alive with termites and centipedes when it burst open. She squealed and jumped aside, only to lose her footing and topple backward into the thick underbrush. By the time she stood up, again, one side of her hair had escaped its confines, and she scrambled back up the incline, having had quite enough of "being in the picture" for the effect of an illusion.

Tom reached out a hand with a satisfied smile and helped her over the last steep spot in front of the still running camera. "You're a regular trooper, Meg...no wonder you've been so hard to handle all this time."

"What did you expect? It's what I came here for, wasn't it? I should hope I would at least be able to...Oh...Oh!" She felt the skitter of an enormous beetle in her tumbled down hair and flung it off.

"Now, where's the prop boy when we need one? Mary Kingsley would have never let such a fine specimen escape. If we had a jar to scoop him up in, we could..."

"I do have one. Don't let him get away!" Meg scrambled for her duffel with renewed vigor and found it. At the same time Tom scrambled in the other direction to capture the giant bug before it escaped back into the brush. A few moments later, she scooped it into the jar with a stick, and Tom swung the camera around to catch the event. It wasn't until after she tightened down the cap that he finally pronounced, "Perfect," and clicked off the camera.

"Are you sure you got it?" Meg asked. "The whole thing?"

"Absolutely."

"I'll let him go, then."

"Might as well." He removed the camera from its perch and began to fold up the tripod. "Since the doctor she was collecting them for is long since gone."

"Well, I never mentioned that in my journal. How do you know so much about Mary Kingsley, anyway? You're the first person I've met...other than the professor...who even knew who she was." She watched the beetle skitter back into the grass and then straightened up with a sigh. "Which I have every intention of trying to change."

"Did Pop know you wanted to do a film about her?"

"He was totally shocked when I mentioned it. Insisted you were paying me to dress up like this. Whatever gave him that idea, I'll never know. "

"Now things are starting to make more sense."

"Two educators having a subject in common is no reason for one of them to slip an illegal deed to a goldmine off on the other one. I could be sitting in jail right now if you hadn't paid all that money. I don't understand it. Not one bit!" She looked back longingly toward the river. Even at this early hour, the sun was already beginning to feel hot. "Could we take just a little more time? To wash up?"

"In the river?" His blue eyes registered astonishment as he handed over the camera and tripod. "Not on your life...that river's full of bilharzia. So is almost every other body of water around here that isn't connected to the ocean."

"Do you really believe that? I mean, Mary Kingsley was in and out of every river in this region, up to her neck in slime time and again, and nothing ever happened to her."

"Megan, I'm surprised at you." He gathered the remnants of breakfast off the roof of the jeep and began packing up as he talked. "Hardly anything is the same as when she was here. Bilharzia didn't really take over until we got the bright idea of damming up the rivers and breaking the natural cycle of cleansing and fertility all these people used to depend on. The fish they made their living with are gone, and that giant, man-made lake pushed thousands of people back onto soil so infertile they can hardly grow anything anymore. Can barely sustain their families. It's a real mess."

He handed her a bottle of water before stashing the rest of them into his backpack. "But I'll tell you what. As soon as we get to Akosombo, I'll put you up in the hotel overlooking the lake, and you can use up all the water you want while I go get Pop."

"You mean you're finally going to let me get back to my tour?" She took the half of a peeled orange he held out to her and separated one of the succulent sections.

"I didn't say that, exactly. But if you promise to stay put until I round up Pop so we can straighten things out, I won't insist on hauling you all the way to the Little De Ambe with me. It's a pretty rugged trek to get back into there."

"De Ambe...but I thought you said he was in Akosombo."

"He would have been if we could have intercepted him at the harbor when they came in to refuel last night. By now, they'll be at the Little De Ambe because that's where we usually stay. So, I'll have to track him down from there."

"And just how long is that going to take?"

"Up and back, could be a couple days. If the roads are as bad as this one."

"Tom, my tour will be half over by then! I might even miss the Mole National Park, and that's the most important part of the whole thing!" She sat down on the edge of the backseat in the open doorway and began to unlace her boots. It was starting to get oppressively hot, now, and she would just as soon wear the sandals.

"Better leave those on."

"What?"

"We're still about eight miles from town, so we'll have to walk it. Might meet the road crew somewhere along the way, but who knows how close they..."

"Eight miles!"

"Would you rather stay here by yourself and wait for them? Might take a long time depending on how much they have to clear before they even get this far."

"If you can trust me to wait for you in Akosombo, why can't you trust me to drive the jeep back and—"

"Not on your life. It'd be too hard to find you again if you skipped out on me. One missing person is enough to worry about without having to add another." He reached over the seat for her duffel.

"But what about the Jeep? What if somebody steals it? And if you already know where he is, what's the point in dragging..."

"Mick's vehicles are well-known around here. He's got family on both ends. Things like this happen all the time. He gives commissions to anyone who returns one, which makes doing business with him more profitable than stealing from him. As for Pop..."

He tossed his backpack up onto the fallen tree. "I won't know where he is until I'm looking at him. This gold thing has me baffled. Isn't like him to fall for something like that...he knows the ropes around here. And slipping the deed into your bag? Isn't like him to sneak around like that with anybody. Much less, a perfect stranger. Something is definitely wrong. Way wrong."

"He thought someone was trying to prove him incompetent. To be honest"—Meg snagged her glasses from his pocket as he leaned back in to put the keys into the ignition. She put them on long enough to read which of the two plastic bottles she had taken out of her string bag was sunscreen, and then pushed them back on top of her head— "He thought it was you."

"Are you serious? Sure, I hired Gilbert Minelli to tag along with him, but..." Now, it was Tom's turn to be convincing. As if she were a judge seated behind the bench, he began to explain in a *'whole truth and nothing but the truth'* sort of tone.

"He seemed very insulted by that."

"I only did it because he still insists on walking the streets at odd hours. Anytime he feels like it! Thinks nothing's changed since the fifties. But, believe me, Meg, incompetent is the last word I would use to describe my father. Much less think of him that way. He's one of the craftiest people I've ever known. Better wear your hat."

"I don't like it. If it gets too hot, I'll use my umbrella."

"Well, you better get it out, then. Even the sun's more intense since Mary Kingsley's day."

"Will you please stop ordering me around? I'm quite capable of taking care of myself."

"But you're out of your element." He waited for her to get the umbrella out of the duffel, and then zippered it closed for her before tossing it up onto the tree with his backpack. "And for being in the country less than a week, you haven't exactly set any records for staying out of trouble."

"That, Tom Anderson, is a matter of opinion. And where might I ask is your hat?"

"Right here." He pulled an Australian bush hat from one of the pockets of his vest and looked over the jeep a final time as he put it on. "Ready?"

"As I'll ever be, I suppose. But just out of curiosity"—she ducked her head and one arm through the strap of her string bag so it wouldn't constantly be slipping from her shoulder, and then handed him the old-fashioned black umbrella with a curved handle to set on top of the tree— "Why did you..." Now, just how on earth was she going to get up there? "Why did you waste so much time helping me with my camera this morning if you were in such a hurry to get to Akosombo?"

"Had to wait 'til the sun came up. This is not the kind of place to be wandering around in the dark. As for wasting time, I never call capturing the perfect shot a waste of time." He pulled himself up on the fallen log and then paused for a moment to look down on the other side. "You almost never run into the same opportunity, again. And just for your information..."

He turned and reached down to lift her up after him (with one hand, yet!). "It just so happens I've been trying to talk the company into doing a documentary on Mary Kingsley, myself, for about three years, now."

Such a coincidence was almost too staggering to register. "My Mary Kingsley?"

"*Travels in West Africa*, published in 1897...I read it a few years ago. Yep, she's the only one I know of. So, what do you say, priss, after we get this thing with Pop straightened out, maybe we can do a deal?"

"Don't tell me you teach at the film institute, too!"

"Nope. I'm a producer."

12

Turning Point

"'You don't seem to feel these things, Miss Kingsley.' Not feel them, indeed! Why, I could cry over them..."
Mary Kingsley

Meg felt lightheaded at the sheer shock of such a coincidence. She hardly believed it (after all, he had read her journal)...was he trying to manipulate her, again? She was about to mention her skepticism (what were the odds?) except that, at that very moment, he jumped down on the other side of the tree and then reached up to take her by the waist and lift her down after him. The way he slowed down halfway to setting her on the ground, looking at her with that softening in his eyes, again, as if she were someone to be cherished, made her feel all fluttery inside. In a rather unnerving sort of way.

"Tom Anderson,"—she dropped her hands from his shoulders as soon as her feet touched the ground—"you're looking at me as if you'd seen a ghost."

"I almost feel like I have. To find you, again, and like this, seems too incredible to be real. But there can't be two of you, you're so outlandish, Meg, you drive me crazy. Like some slippery thing I can't keep hold of."

"I wouldn't say that." Meg objected, even though

inwardly her heart pounded. "You've managed to drag me halfway across the continent, kicking and screaming. How much more hold do you need on a person?" This close she smelled the leather straps and that hint of *Old Spice,* again, and to make matters worse, the addition of the hat suddenly reminded her of someone she had seen in movies (of all things! What was happening to her?).

"I need to hear you say it, Meg. That you're her. That extraordinary lady who ran away from me at the cafe when it started to rain. I suspected it might be when you finally took that crazy hat off and put your hair up, yesterday. But, I'll be honest with you, the first thing I thought was that you really were part of this mess."

Meg gasped at the inference.

"That you must have been tailing me that day for some reason. Some kind of a decoy while they roped Pop into…"

"But, Tom, I would never…"

"Then when I saw the clothes and the journal while they were going through your things at customs…I knew it was true, and it almost floored me. I had to read the journal. It was the only way to get to the bottom of this thing. Stayed up most of the night, reading it with a flashlight."

Meg suddenly realized she was holding on to his vest and self-consciously let go of it. "You don't…" She took a step back to put more of a decent distance between them. "You don't still think I could have done something like that, do you?"

"Not any more. The things you wrote in that journal, Meg,"—he moved close to her, again—"made that encounter seem a lot more amazing to me than this mix-up with Pop. Then to meet, again, like this, do you know what that means? Doesn't it amaze you, too?"

"Not if it isn't true. And if it is, why did you wait until now to tell me? You never gave the slightest hint of anything like that back at the airport."

"You were in hysterics. You wouldn't have believed anything I said, then."

"Or, maybe the only reason you know about the cafe is because you read my journal. You could just be trying to get more information about your father...and I wouldn't blame you. But I'll tell you right now you don't act the least bit like that man at the cafe, because he was..."

She turned away from him more to collect her emotional bearings than the physical ones, but was suddenly awestruck by the beauty of the scene in front of them. They were in a place where the forest made a canopy above them, and away and ahead there were still traces of an early morning fog that snaked along in wisps on the ground. It rose in front of the tall trees in a ghost-like shroud, almost like steam. Meg could see why they were called "smokes" in this region and felt as if she were standing in some enchanted place that might disappear into a dream at any moment. The rocks along the edge of the road were covered with ferns and mosses in various shades of green, and although she could no longer see the river, she could hear the sweet, long, mellow whistle of some exotic water bird calling into the morning.

"That man in the cafe had no idea his father had just disappeared." Their eyes locked and held, again, when she turned around. "Thing like that would shock anybody. I'm only human."

She broke the spell by starting off over a swampy piece of roadway (she had to do something…anything!), but he took her arm and fell in step beside her, as if it had become something of a second nature to him. Then he helped her up and over a slide of rock and debris that had come down from the hillside when the tree fell across. "You have to admit you've been something of a trial, yourself, priss. That swing of yours, yesterday, practically laid me out."

"I was at my wits end!"

"Obviously."

Meg was beginning to get upset, again. Not so much that her man in the rain might actually be Tom Anderson, but because if he was (and if this really was her second chance at that divine appointment) well, she had never acted so horribly in her entire life as she had in these last two days. He had seen her at her very worst. Her lowest point. And what "dashing prince" (much less any ordinary man) would want anything to do with someone who behaved like that? Not that she was trying so hard to impress Tom Anderson. Dashing prince, or not, now that she knew more about him, he was, without doubt, the most audacious, outspoken, demanding man she had ever met.

"I don't normally go around hitting people," she began to explain. But then there was a break in the canopy of trees above them, and the sudden intensity of sunlight made her pause long enough to open the umbrella. It gave her an immediate and rather cooling sense of shade. "To tell you the truth, I don't know what's come over me, lately. I've broken half the standards I've based my entire life on, just since I got here."

"Pretty ingenious way of dealing with it, though,"

he teased. "Just cross out the part that isn't working for you and write something else."

"They're my own rules, not traffic regulations. I only write them down as a form of commitment to myself." She tipped the edge of the umbrella to look him in the eye for emphasis. "Myself, Tom Anderson. Aren't you the least bit ashamed for invading a person's private thoughts?"

"Not your thoughts."

"Oh, yes, the criminal treatment. But now that you know I'm an ordinary person with decent intentions, you could at least apologize."

"I don't apologize for things unless I mean it. And you, Megan Jennings, are the farthest thing from ordinary I've ever run up against. As for your private thoughts...it was a pleasant journey, and I'm glad I took it."

"Well, just because you barged into my soul, doesn't give you the right to stay. You weren't invited."

"Doesn't change the fact that I'm in, though, does it."

Meg retreated back into her personal shade, having had quite enough of looking him in the eye. Only to have him tilt the edge back up. "The channel runs both ways, you know. Seeing you dressed like that in the cafe was something of a shock. Sort of like stepping off into the deep end of the ocean. Feels like I've been treading water ever since."

"But you said I looked like something out of a low-budget movie."

"That was the second time. When you were wearing that crazy hat and wild print shirt. Tourists are always dressing up in their own version of safari outfits. I didn't realize it was you. Besides, you had me all riled with that phone call. I couldn't figure you out. Then when Pop wasn't even there..."

"And I did have all his things." She sighed, feeling a weight of disappointment in the decision to take them, now that she was looking back on it. Hindsight might always be perfect, as the saying went, but why hadn't the Lord tapped her on the shoulder about that? She didn't even feel a prick of conscience to warn her it might be wrong. Yet, that one false step seemed to be the beginning of this whole ordeal.

"Then, again..." He shifted her duffel to the other shoulder and moved to her opposite side. "Now that I've come across some explanation about the way you think..."

"In a very unmannerly way," she reminded him.

"Don't be so stubborn, priss."

"I wish you wouldn't call me that."

"What's it going to take for you to forgive me? For the journal thing, I mean. I can't quit calling you priss, it suits you too well."

"Oh, for heaven's sake!"

"In a pleasant sort of way." He lifted the edge of the umbrella to look under it, again. "Would it help if I answered your big question?"

Oh, dear. She had forgotten about that long tirade she had written down a few weeks ago describing her continuing determination to avoid relationships with anyone who wasn't a believer. Not only that, but how that very decision was often the source of her lonely days. The thing had come dangerously close to self-pity (or, at least, crying in her soup). And while it had been something of a relief to express it back then, it now felt as embarrassing as having someone walk in on you in the shower. And Tom Anderson…of all people!

"The answer is, yes. I've been a Christian for a little over a year, now." Then he let go of the umbrella and continued. "I wish I could say it's been longer, but we weren't raised that way. The search seems harder when you have everything you want growing up. Pop's always been a spoiler, and the rest of us didn't mind taking advantage of that. That is, until Mother ran into this group of people who were different than anyone we ever met. Did a complete turnaround. Before that, her only goal in life was to retire quietly into the secure and predictable life of the rich and famous."

"And you?"

"I watched her for a long time, thinking it was just a phase. She's always throwing everything she's got into something, or other. The type that's easily led. But it's been nearly two years now, and she just keeps getting more and more stable. Pretty wonderful, really. A little over a year ago, I followed suit. We all did. That is, everybody but Pop. It's been harder for him, because he's always considered himself wonderful enough, already. Does that answer it?""

Meg felt herself in the glare of his spotlight, again, and tried to return the subject to him. "So, did you just accept a different set of standards to live by, or did you truly sense a change? If you did change, that is."

"For me, it was more of a relief than a change. I'd grown pretty cynical wondering what the point was all those years. Like, why should we try so hard to right the world's wrongs if it was going to make so little difference in the over-all scheme of things? By the time I'd been all the way around the world, I was fairly disgusted with most of it."

"Maybe you just didn't see the right things," she offered.

"Which adds to your list of proofs that there's somebody out there trying to keep us from those things, doesn't it?"

It was a lightning leap directly into a subject Meg tried mostly to avoid, simply because it leaned toward fanaticism in the more conservative circles she normally traveled in. A distinct effort at following rule number ten: *I will not try to talk others into believing the way I do, but accept wherever they happen to be on life's road at the moment.* And number eleven: *I will only give opinions when asked.* "Well, I'm not one of those people who sees demons around every corner, if that's what you're thinking. Believe me. I consistently manage to miss out on most of life's good things by causing enough trouble all by myself."

"Like checking into a hotel with a perfect stranger, and then…"

"You…of all people"—she interrupted him—"should know that sitting next to your father for any longer than twenty minutes relegates you to personal levels. I was trying to do the decent, Christian thing. Besides, just because a person isn't perfect doesn't mean they can't try to be. Or at least believe in the hope that it really is possible to change from…"

She stopped talking because, once, again, Tom Anderson had enticed her into revealing the most personal things about herself. Things she had never dared mention to anybody. They sounded so wildly audacious when she said them out loud! No one else in her world had ever seemed to be the slightest bit interested in striving for the sort of things she did.

They were all too content with the "nobody's perfect" philosophy, and inclined to leave any changing *"from glory to glory"* entirely up to God. Yes. Come to think of it (and oh, dear!), she had written a good long tirade about that subject, too.

"From *'glory to glory,'* Meg?"

She gasped. Had he just read her mind? She peeked at him from under the umbrella, again, as if looking him in the eye would help her to explain." Just because I have the habit of making lists and thinking on paper doesn't mean I'm entirely convinced of the outcome myself, you know."

"But it does go a long way toward clarifying things, doesn't it. Writing down thoughts, even your own questions, can bring things into a better focus, somehow."

"Maybe you should try it sometime."

"I have. I've been keeping a journal for years. Mostly for compiling a book of my travels one of these days. But yours is different. It's almost as if...it isn't just your journal."

"Of course, it's mine. Whose else would it be?"

"Where do the answers come from, Meg? Some of those discussions come close to being a two-sided conversation. Do you hear voices, is that it?"

"No, but I wish I did," she admitted. "It would certainly make things easier. The questions I write down...well, they always get answered sooner or later. I'll remember something or hear some bit of wisdom from somebody...but most of the time they come through my own thought process, and I...somehow...just know. Like figuring it out, I guess."

"You must do an incredible amount of Bible study to find that many scriptures to fit so perfectly into each subject."

"Not really. They just sort of pop into my head...like remembering a song I heard somewhere. When I go to look one up, I'm often amazed to find it's even in there. It would probably be a great improvement on the process if I did do more Bible study, though. Then, again, there's always something, or someone, getting in the way of that."

"Which brings us to your *'enemy of your soul'* theory."

"You certainly didn't skip any parts, did you?"

"I'm only bringing it up because I believe the same thing," said Tom. "And do you want to know why? Because when you add that one factor to life's equations, all the rest seem to make sense. All the struggles over everything, the constant clashes between good and evil. It's the reason for everything. The whole point. It's also the reason all hell breaks loose whenever you bring up the subject. Literally. It's like blowing an enemy's cover. You're going to get a fight one way or the other."

"Doesn't seem to be any way around it. None I've found, anyway."" She began walking, again, and he moved back to her other side, as if there might be a better view under the umbrella from there.

"I think there is. It's by people working together. And considering you and I are not on opposite sides, Meg, we can at least agree to stop fighting with each other and put our heads together on this thing. Our meeting might possibly be a divine appointment, do you realize that? Seems we're a perfect match for something, you and me. Not just in the kind of work we'd like to do, but even in the way we think. We could be called to the same purpose, what do you say about that?"

"What do I say? I'm still praying you're not the devil, that's what I say. A perfect match, how should I know? You might have everything about me figured out, but all I have to go on about you is a list of good points and bad points that have turned out just about even over the last two days."

"What about always trying to believe the best of people?"

"For heaven's sake! Is that how it's going to be from now on? You holding me accountable for my own ideals?"

A smile came first to his eyes, then the corners of his mouth, before he made a concerted effort not to give in. "From now on, Meg? I'll take that as your vote for me being part of your destiny. And I believe in divine appointments, too...very much so."

"You could be a wolf in sheep's clothing," she accused. "Talking like this just because you read my journal."

"Didn't I say I was a Christian?"

"So did Judas."

"And he regretted his mistake, didn't he? Besides, if I am a wolf, it will show. You have to agree with that."

"And why should I?"

"Because it's what you do that proves who you are. A person can say anything. But what they do...that comes straight out of who they really are."

"I don't have enough time to test out that theory. Under the circumstances."

"What if I could prove it to you in the next few minutes?"

13

Dangerous Ground

*"What you have to do with him is to be very thankful you
have had the honour of knowing him."*
                                                        Mary Kingsley

"I can't imagine anything you could say or do that
would change my mind that quick." But inwardly, she
wasn't so sure, because she suddenly found herself
wanting very much to believe him. Oh, why did things
have to be so many shades of gray instead of simple
black and white? If only there was some sort of sign
(did God still do that these days?) not lightning, or
anything, just the smallest little hint of…

His only reply was to unzip one of his smaller vest
pockets and take something out that flashed a
reflection of the sun when he held it out to her. "You
left it on the table at the cafe. The waiter gave it to me
because he thought we knew each other."

Meg slowly took the antique pen she had so
carefully selected for her journey into the past, and felt
her emotions begin to churn. The Lord had just
answered that thought as quickly and easily as if He
had been walking, here, between them. *"For I know the
thoughts...saith the Lord..."* (what was the rest of that

scripture?) And if this was her man in the rain, the dashing prince, then Tom Anderson must truly be her divine appointment. A divine appointment! But to what extent and for what purpose?

"I...went back there, you know." She began rather hesitantly because she found herself having to reign in the sudden desire to tell him everything she was thinking and feeling at the moment. She couldn't just throw herself at him. What had gotten into her? "But you had left already, too."

"I was drenched and my grandmother insisted."

"That was your grandmother?"

"Mm-hm. She likes to eat there when I'm in town. But if I'd known you were coming back..." He lifted the edge of the umbrella to look under, again. She was struggling with her emotions and clutching the pen close up against her as if it were a lifeline. "What's wrong, priss? Disappointed that it was me?"

"It's just that this whole situation is so complicated and confusing! You thinking I'm a criminal, and I..."

"I said I didn't, anymore."

"And I don't know anything about you! Who you are, or where you come from...and why you would have the slightest interest in someone like me!"

"Maybe I can clear that up for you, too. I'll start by telling you what I'm the producer of." He let go of the edge of the umbrella when she put the pen away and began looking for that package of tissue. "Ever hear of the *Adventure Company*?"

"The one hosted by Bertram Hunter? Of course. I love that program."

"Bertram Hunter is my oldest brother, Bobby."

"Well...my goodness... no wonder you looked familiar when you put that hat on." Now it was Meg's turn to tip the umbrella up and look at him as if she were just seeing him for the first time. "But you don't have the same name."

"Bertram Hunter is just a stage name. His real name is Robert Anderson.

"So, there really is another Anderson son named Robert. Is there a John, too?"

"Johnny's the youngest of us. Anyway, it's more or less a family business that we've been at for quite a few years. Moving back and forth across the continents, trying to inform the public about the state of things in the natural world. We're actually due in Akosombo next week to do a follow-up on the dam."

"But what's the dam got to do with the state of the natural world?"

"It's the largest manmade lake on earth. You can see it from space. Besides breaking up the cycle of life along the riverbanks I was telling you about, the sheer weight of the thing is the problem. It's actually causing earthquakes."

"Earthquakes! I should…" Meg returned the tissue to her bag, grateful for the switch to a lighter topic and more than a little relieved she hadn't burst into hysterics, again. What an effect all this was having on her! "I should think something like that would be all over the news."

"The tragedies of third-world countries have never been first choice topics for the nightly news." He helped her over another rockslide. "Which is exactly why my father started the *Adventure Company* in the first place. To familiarize people with people instead of problems."

"The human connection. I quite agree. I'm…" She realized he didn't let go of her hand after she stepped down. "I'm trying to make something of a human connection myself with this film project."

"Probably why you caught his attention. Pop's always been a soft touch for anyone trying to reach for something."

"And you?"

"I'm usually the one who has to follow up behind him and make things work."

She self-consciously pulled her hand free and offered him her umbrella. "Would you mind?" She searched through her bag for the digital camera. "I'd really like to get some pictures of this steamy fog before it all drifts away."

His only answer was to close the umbrella and hang it from one of the straps on his backpack as he walked along.

"Tell me"—she stopped to look through the lens—"What was your reason for wanting Mary Kingsley as a film subject?"

"Love of the human spirit, I guess," he replied. "What it's capable of. I've got an insatiable interest in heroes of any kind. Seems to be a shortage of them these days."

She filled a frame with Tom's hat and the back of his head as he continued walking, and then snapped a picture when he turned around to see what she was doing.

"Pretty handy with that thing."

"This camera has been one of my best friends for a long time." She took a few pictures of the steaming trees and then caught up to him. "What made you settle on Mary Kingsley?" She took the umbrella, again.

"Well, a little over two years ago, I happened to be

killing some time during a layover in London, waiting to connect up with my film crew. We were headed down here to shoot a documentary about the gorillas of the Cameroons." He glanced down through a brief opening in the nearby brush below them and then pointed. "Look, the hippos seem to be traveling along with us, but it's the same bend, actually. We've just come around to the other side of it."

Meg stopped to watch for a moment. "Am I seeing things...or is that really a pink one down there?"

"You can see that far away without your glasses?"

"Far away I can see perfectly. It's close up I have problems."

"Ah, so, that's it. Well, the younger ones can be that shade, sometimes. They grow out of it though."

"It's...oh, it's just the most amazing place I've ever been!"

He laughed at the exclamation, and it suddenly seemed to be the most pleasant sound Meg had heard in a long time. "You're awfully easy to please, Meg," he said. "A good sport, too, considering everything I've dragged you through."

"If you still think that at the end of all this," she replied as they continued on. "I'll believe you. Now, go on with your story, please. You were killing some time in London."

"So I thought I'd take in the Royal Geographical Society's Africa collection. Anyway, I saw this hat. A strange-looking, battered, fur thing that didn't even have a brim. Of no use under any African sun, in my estimation, and there it sat in a place of honor all by itself. Well—"

He steered her clear of another swampy spot that she would have stumbled right into because she had been staring up at him instead of the road. Of course she knew about that hat. Mary Kingsley's hat. Knew about it and wanted to see it with all of her heart.

"Knowing how great a value the Africans place on respect"—he went on—"I suddenly wanted to know everything there was to know about a woman whose very hat was enough to inspire awe. Turned into something of an obsession for me. Been driving the rest of the crew crazy with it ever since."

"How so?"

"For wanting to veer off the present and dip into the past, I guess. Like I said, historical biographies are a dime a dozen in this business. Especially, if you don't have something new to tack on."

****

The wisps of fog finally began to disappear, and by ten o'clock, they had been walking in the direct sunlight for quite some time. And even though they came under another leafy canopy, again, the heat was stifling. Meg's boots (practically new because she bought them expressly for filming) were starting to give her blisters. Just when she felt the most incredible urge to sit down on the riverbank, even if she couldn't stick her feet in the water, Tom motioned her over to the side of the road.

"Better sit on this and rest for a while." He set the duffel down for her. "As beautiful as they are, lounging on riverbanks around here isn't too enjoyable. Most of them are infested with ants."

He was reading her mind, again.

He handed her one of the remaining water bottles from his backpack, and brought out the last orange, along with the cheese and crackers. They had been talking nearly non-stop, and it wasn't until the silence of taking a long drink of water that Meg suddenly heard the unmistakable sound of something large moving through the trees a short distance away. A tremor of fear rippled through her. She glanced up at Tom. But he ignored it, intent only on drinking the entire bottle of water down at one time.

He seemed very much at home in this environment. Almost as if being out in such places suited him more than suits or crowded cities. Still, no matter how strong and fit he looked, she wasn't at all certain he could overcome an enraged lion or elephant, should they happen to run into one. Whether or not this was lion and elephant country, she had no idea. But her imagination was working overtime.

"Tom, do you" — Meg handed him half the orange she had just nervously peeled — "Do you have a gun in that backpack?"

"Of course not. You can't carry guns on commercial planes these days."

"But how are we going to protect ourselves if some wild animal charges us?"

"They're more afraid of us than we are of them. You know they actually try to avoid people? Besides," — he sat on the ground next to her — " of all the times I've been here, I've never needed one. And I'm too much of a conservationist to enjoy hunting."

After that brief rest, they continued on for what seemed like hours. They talked about any and every subject that entered their minds and were continually surprised at how many things they had in common. They both had aggressive fathers and adoring mothers. Except Tom's mother was French (no wonder he spoke the language so perfectly). His grandmother still lived just outside Paris, but his mother had spent years in the States, even before she married the professor.

When the road began to pitch into a steep decline, Meg found it easier to close the umbrella and use it as a walking-stick rather than shade. She felt oddly unsteady all of a sudden. What was the problem? She loved hiking. Could walk for miles without getting tired. But there was Tom Anderson walking along beside her as if it were a couple of cool blocks in a park, while she suddenly felt eighty years old. Well, she wasn't going to say a word. Not one word. Better to ignore it and keep talking.

"The professor must know a lot of influential people around here if he can just call up somebody to take him wherever he wants to go in a private plane."

"Pop has a lot of friends everywhere. He's like a magnet that way. Besides, it was about the only thing he could do without money or a passport. I just can't figure out why he ditched Gilbert. Seemed for a while they had ironed out their differences. But where the devil does that put Gilbert? He should have called in by now. Or at least left another message. We're out of range with all these trees and hills, though, so we'll have to wait until town to find out."

"Strange being in the back regions of Africa and seeing so many people with cell phones. You would think they would need more consistent electricity."

"They're pretty ingenious about that," he replied. "You'll see when we have to film in some of the more remote places. There are street vendors set up to charge them off car batteries."

Meg might have been more properly impressed if he hadn't sent something of a thrill through her at the mention of filming in remote places. Maybe he really had meant what he said about working on her Mary Kingsley film...with a real film crew, yet! As if she wouldn't gladly trade a voodoo tour (she had plans of skipping out of the voodoo parts, anyway) for an experience like that. Maybe that's what had attracted the professor to her, too. Hadn't he been unusually interested in her cameras? And if Tom had been talking to him all along about Mary Kingsley...well, it was no wonder he...

"Do you want to rest, again, Meg?" He broke into her thoughts. "You should be careful in this heat until you get used to it."

"I do feel a bit lightheaded. But let's just get this over with. Besides, maybe we won't have to do the whole eight miles. I think I smell smoke somewhere...do you?"

"Hopefully, it's the road crew."

"Tom, you...well, you don't suppose we'll run into any unsavory characters, do you? The kind who like to rob stranded people like us, on the road?"

14

Bush Pagans and Cannibals

*"I must warn you also that your own mind requires
protection when you send it stalking the savage idea through
the tangled forests"*

Mary Kingsley

"Shhh...do you hear that? Voices." Meg stopped
walking and listened. "Oh, and look...just above the
tops of those trees, I'm sure that's smoke."

"I think we've found the road crew," said Tom.

Within another few minutes, they came upon the
slow-moving crew, burning the giant trunk of another
tree that had fallen across the road. There were six or
seven workers, along with an old flatbed truck that
was loaded with saws, axes, shovels, and other road
clearing equipment. The task was nearly finished, and
even though most of the men were just visiting around
the fire, no one noticed Tom and Meg until they were
less than a hundred feet away.

"What the devil happen to you?" A dark man in a
blue, sweat-stained work shirt looked up with a
startled expression.

While Tom began to explain, Meg suddenly found
it impossible to concentrate. Everything seemed to be
happening around her in a movie-like slow motion as

the wafting fire engulfed her in its sickening heat. A man standing nearby offered her a battered, metal canteen, and she gratefully reached out for it before Tom noticed and waved it away.

"Thanks, anyway," he said. "But we tourists have to stick to bottled drinks."

"Tom," Meg objected, "I hardly think…"

"Do you have anything bottled?" he asked their hosts.

"Got beer." Another man replied with a broad smile.

"Beer!" The man in charge gave the offender an incriminating glare. "I told you once already, next person bring beer on this government job gonna get beheaded!"

"What?" Meg was appalled.

"Have his pay chopped, he means," Tom explained. "How far is it to Akosombo from here? Think you could give us a lift in your truck?"

The town was only a little more than a mile away. After some debate over who would drive the American and his lady (as Meg was referred to) they started for the truck. For some reason the men seemed to think the task required two men, so Meg was squeezed into the cab next to the driver, and while Tom was busy tossing their bags up on the back, another man squeezed up against her from the other side.

"Oh, but where's Tom going to…"

"You sit on top, missy." The man scooped her onto his lap to the overpowering accompaniment of the smell of beer and sweat. "Plenty room for all."

Meg had heard it was typical to crowd as many people as possible into vehicles in these regions, but, between the heat and her exhaustion, she felt she actually might be ill if she had to breathe such fumes for any length of time. Much less bounce along a sodden, pot-holed road on a strange man's lap. Just as she was contemplating if it would be more polite to insult someone by refusing the courtesy, or throw up on them, Tom climbed up into the cab and collected her (like a piece of luggage someone else had been holding for him) to sit on his lap, instead.

"Better get as close to the window as you can, Meg." He rolled the window down before closing the door after him. "At least you'll get the feeling of a little fresh air when we're moving."

Meg gratefully turned away from the offending workers and leaned her head toward the window, instead. At least Tom smelled like leather and *Old Spice*. It was a bumpy, noisy ride, and they had to ease their way gingerly around another fire that was little more than smoldering ash where yet another tree had fallen in the storm and been cleared away earlier. Still, they came into the town in less than twenty minutes, and the men dropped them off in front of a bustling outdoor cafe overlooking the Akosombo Dam and Lake Volta.

Tom found an empty table, and Meg sank into one of the wicker chairs beneath the shaded patio while he stashed their bags underneath and sat down across from her. Moments later, a young waiter in a white linen jacket that had been donned over T-shirt and blue jeans, appeared to take their order.

"Minerals for both of us, and something to eat." Tom reached for the cell phone in his vest pocket. "Go ahead and order, Meg, just make sure it's cooked. I'm going to try and get hold of some people."

"All right, but I'm not the least bit interested in

minerals."

"It's just a common term for bottled soft drinks." After that he was engrossed in looking up numbers and left the lunch choices to her.

She glanced at the smiling, eager young face and asked, "What sort of cooked food do you have?"

"Tin soap, and..."

"What?"

"And chicken in castor oil."

"Well, of all things, I don't think I could possibly..."

The look of alarm on her face made him shake his head and point a dark, graceful finger to a printed card on the table. It read "Tinned Soup" and "Chicken in Casserole."

Meg smiled with relief and he grinned.

"Chicken?" he asked. "It is quite good."

"Yes, please," she replied, "for two."

After he had gone, Meg sighed and sat back comfortably. She was exhausted. Again. And her feet hurt where her boots had rubbed. The lake beyond the shady veranda was large and lovely, with a shimmering wave of heat that turned the forest along the opposite shore into dancing shadows of green and blue. In a few moments, the waiter returned with two open bottles and set them down on the table. It was ginger ale.

"I'd like some bottled water, too, please. I'm very thirsty. I've practically walked all the way from Accra."

"Accra.." he gasped. "Sakes alive, missy...on the Akosombo road? At night?"

"Well, we've only been walking since this morning. We came the rest of the way by jeep. But I feel like I've walked the whole way. This heat..." She pushed her hair back from her face and realized how disheveled she must look. "The heat here is incredible."

"Always hot before the rain comes. This is a cool place to cheer up."

"Do I look like I need cheering up?"

"Akosombo road at night and nobody ate you? That's a good reason to cheer up. Too many leopards and bush pagans on that road at night. Gawd must have blessed you."

"What's a bush pagan?" she asked.

"Meat hunters. *Niama*. *Niama* is meat. Snake, crocodile..." He reached across the table and pressed one of his fingers to her forearm. "Meat."

"You're only trying to frighten me," Meg chided, as she would have done with one of her students. "I am quite aware that the animals of this region are more afraid of us than we are of them."

He laughed. "Enjoy your minerals, then. I will bring the chicken."

She looked over at Tom. He had taken off his hat, tossed it on the empty chair next to him, and then ran a hand through wavy hair to try to bring some order to it while he talked quietly to someone. However, when Meg stood to her feet his attention was instantly riveted back on her.

"I'm just going to freshen up," she assured. "I'll be back in a moment."

He relaxed and went on with the conversation, and Meg meandered through the crowded tables and headed for the nearest restroom. Tourists mostly. But some of the women looked local; dressed in colorful light scarves and cool dresses, and many of them wore ornate jewelry. Most of the men she could see wore western clothes, except some of them also had colorful sarongs tossed over a shoulder. One even had a brightly-colored head covering to match. Rather like the fez-type hat she had seen on the skycap the night she arrived.

She felt a little better after she had washed her face and rearranged her hair. But she was more than looking forward to a cool shower and a real bed after they ate. She hoped Tom would manage to work things out with the professor in time for her to visit the Mole National Park, it was the only part of the tour she would be disappointed to miss. Getting to know each other as they had on the road today, she was almost certain he would agree to her connecting back up with her group instead of waiting the two or three days until he got back. Especially if she gave him the itinerary and agreed to meet up with them after it was over. Of course, she had no intention of bringing up the subject until he had rested a bit and eaten a good meal.

Making her way back to the table seemed to take a lot longer than when she had left. What was the problem? And she suddenly had a splitting headache. It wasn't that large of a place, yet she couldn't seem to locate her seat. Where was Tom? Why, he wasn't at any of the tables. She scanned the area for the familiar figure, only to finally catch sight of him at the bar off in one corner, sitting on one of the bamboo stools, engaged in an intense conversation with…

Meg suddenly felt a chill go through her. Was her mind playing tricks on her? He was talking to the stewardess from her flight out of Paris (yes, that was the same girl, she would have recognized that exceptional beauty anywhere!), and...of all people...that most unnerving skycap who (in Meg's estimation) was responsible for this entire mix-up. Only today he was dressed in a black, western-style suit with a white shirt opened nearly to his navel beneath it. But that was the same gold chain with the red-eyed crocodile resting against his chest. Such audacity! Hadn't he been the one to book the room that night? Hadn't he been the very person to send for the doctor who never even came?

Now, things began to come terrifyingly clear.

Who better than a stewardess would have the opportunity to spike someone's drinks? And all that waiting before anyone came with a wheelchair...it was to make sure the other passengers had plenty of time to disembark the plane. That man was no skycap! Meg had been uneasy about him from the very beginning. Suppose there really had been some sort of conspiracy between them and Tom to kidnap the professor, and she had gone and stumbled right into the middle of it? Had these two people flown to Akosombo ahead of them?

What could they have done with the Professor?

Whatever it was, they were up to no good now. Meg could feel it in every fiber of her being. And it was at that precise moment that the skycap looked up from his drink and made immediate eye contact with her in spite of all the people around them. The effect of this strange man's eyes, as if those eyes somehow saw exactly what she had been thinking, made her suddenly afraid. It was a feeling she had no control over.

She was in terrible danger and not a soul on earth knew where she was! Why, if someone were to go looking for her, she wasn't even in the same country anymore! Now, she was almost sure Professor Anderson's disappearance had to involve some sinister plot that Tom was somehow at the center of. Hadn't the Professor admitted his son was "a rascal" and up to no good? Who was to say these people hadn't already done something terrible to him, for those millions of dollars in the Bank of California, and then cleverly managed to lure her so far away that no one would ever be able to find her, again?

But how could that be? She had felt so sure of Tom in spite of all his blustery pushiness. In spite of everything. Not only had he convinced her that he was the man in the cafe, he had even managed to make her feel they were on the same side. To the point that she was actually starting to depend on him. Then another thought occurred to her, a desperate hope that could explain everything and keep things right between them. Because she suddenly wanted very much to have everything right between them.

Maybe he didn't know those people.

They could have been following both of them, and he was walking into a trap this very minute. Tom could simply be talking like any other tourist conversing with local people. He might even be asking if they had seen the Professor when his plane stopped here to refuel. Without the slightest idea who those people were. All she needed was the assurance (another sign!) so that she could believe that. Meg suddenly wanted desperately to believe that.

Then, almost at the very moment she had inwardly sent up that desperate little prayer, Tom reached into his vest pocket, took out a folded paper, and handed it to the girl. Meg felt her heart sink. As if she might even faint right there on the spot. Because she knew exactly what that paper was. She had no doubt about it.

It was the deed to the goldmine.

15

The Last Straw

"There are so many ways of accounting for death about here—leopard, canoe capsize, elephants, etc.—that even if I were traced—well, nothing could be done then, anyhow..."
Mary Kingsley

Some people could live out their entire lives without ever knowing their limits. But Megan knew she was at the absolute end of hers. Not only were her senses of right and wrong, and good and evil not functioning properly, but she had the most insatiable desire simply to turn and run.

It was at that moment that the waiter walked by with their meal. Only it wasn't chicken at all. It seemed to be two plates of chopped vegetables on top of rice, and a banana. Two minutes ago, she would have complained. But instead, she motioned the young man closer and whispered, "Excuse me, but...could you tell me where the police station is? I need to know how to get there from here."

"Don't tell, missy. There will be questions, I will get the sack, and I have two wives to support. I swear on my life, there are no bush pagans in Ghana, anymore."

"Oh, I'm not going to tell about your bush pagans." Her head was pounding now, and she could hardly hear anything. Someone had put some coins into an ancient jukebox, and it was blaring. "I've simply had some trouble and I need help."

"Where is your husband?"

"He is not my husband!"

One of his eyebrows shot up in mild surprise, and the meal nearly slipped from his tray. "I thought all Americans were Christians!"

"Oh, never mind. I'll just ask someone else!" Meg turned and left the place as quickly as she could because she couldn't stand a minute more of any of it. She shot a quick look over her shoulder at the bar, but, to her horror, the skycap was no longer there. A feeling of panic set in. Who cared where she was headed anymore? She just needed to get away.

After that, it felt as if she were a child who was lost, again. She began to run down the crowded street in such a state of fear that it took two blocks before she suddenly felt as if she were going to drop dead. Literally. Then, as happens at such times of stress, she automatically fell back on the most rudimentary principles of her upbringing. She must do the right thing. At all cost. Immediately.

"Excuse me," she spoke to the nearest passerby on the street. "Could you tell me where the police station is?"

It was a pleasantly plump older woman dressed in a bright canary-colored toga with a matching bandanna wound round her head. "The police? Why you standing right in front..." She was interrupted by the most enormous clap of thunder Meg had ever heard in her life, and they both ducked out of reflex.

"Oooo – lawd! Here, it come!"

There was another and another, and then a deluge of warm rain poured down with the force of a giant shower having suddenly been turned on. People huddled beneath canopies and into buildings, and within minutes the road was turned into a running, muddy torrent.

The old woman laughed delightedly and then pulled Meg into the overhang of the building they were standing in front of, as if she were in too much of a daze to look after herself. "This is it – right here where we are." She gently pushed Meg through the crowded doorway and inside. "Go in there, now, and tell the man your troubles."

Meg was thinking how she never in her life had seen such a crowd at a police station before she realized most of the people gathered there were seeking shelter and not all on official business. She finally found her way to an old wooden counter with two uniformed men behind it, and behind them a door over which the word "Commissioner" had been painted in black letters on the bare wall. There was a line (or rather a cluster) of people in front of the officer nearest her, so Meg made her way past them to the other man, who seemed busy with paperwork.

"Excuse me," she interrupted him, "I'm afraid I've gotten myself into some trouble and…"

The man was tall, extremely dark skinned, and slender. "All these people," he said, without looking up at her. "Have troubles. The commissioner is a busy man. If you want him to hear you…you must wait."

"But somebody is—"

"Wait." He still didn't look up at her. "If you want you can sit."

The bench along the wall was already occupied to capacity, so, Meg meandered over to wait at the end of the line. There were several women and a few men arguing with the other officer, and just as she neared them, he held up both hands and spoke above the din.

"One at a time, please. You,"—he pointed to a middle aged woman who seemed to be the senior member of the group—"say what happened so I may write it down for the commissioner."

"We were only going to a party," the woman explained.

"A drum party?" the officer interrogated.

"No, sah. It is my brother's birthday, and my father has called all of us home. We were waiting on the train and that monkey-beard porter…"

"Do not call names, please."

"That porter tipped over our food box, and he should pay something for it."

"He said you had illegal goods in your food box, mama. We will have to inspect it."

"Then we will miss the train!" she protested.

"The food box, please."

One of the men moved away from the crowd to retrieve a large wooden crate against the wall. There were three small girls seated on top of it, all with spotlessly clean togas and slicked back hair. The man shuffled them and their bundles off and pulled the crate by one end to the front desk.

Meg realized it would take at least half an hour to go through the contents, and turned to see if any spaces had been vacated along the bench. Still packed. She decided to move where she could at least lean against the cool brick wall, and went to stand next to the girls. That's when she noticed the smallest girl was carrying a coffee can along with her things.

Meg's head was still pounding, she felt shaky, and she realized she hadn't had anything but a few sips of the ginger ale before she left the cafe. She wondered if Tom would come looking for her, and then chided herself for the thought after what she had seen. Even though she had begun to feel more comfortable with him than without him, she realized it could not be right. One simply couldn't continue to keep company with someone who was so deceitful that you had no idea they were being deceitful. But, in spite of everything, it gave her a melancholy feeling to think of that. Oh, the depths to which she'd sunk!

She sighed, looked down at the three shiny black heads beside her, and caught a direct view into the coffee can. There, half wrapped in a piece of cloth, was the unmistakable form of a human hand. Everything blurred. The last thing Meg was aware of was the sound of rain still pounding against the metal roof like gravel, and the cool sensation of the cement floor as she slid down onto it.

****

Someone called for the commissioner, and she was only half-aware of being carried off somewhere, and the voices around her blended into a pleasant hum before she drifted off completely. Whether it was a few minutes, or a few hours before she came to herself, she had no idea. A cool wet cloth was moving soothingly over her face and forehead, and she recognized the distinctive smell of leather and *Old Spice*.

"Tom, I…" She opened her eyes in time to catch a perfect vision of her man in the rain, his hair all wet and glistening, and he was watching her with the most tender look of concern. She raised herself up on one elbow, then, only to have a shooting pain behind her eyes force her down, again. But not before she got a good glimpse at where she was. "Oh, Tom...how could you?" she moaned.

They were in jail.

"Take it easy, priss, you're not in trouble. This was the only handy place to lay you down in. It's raining torrents outside. What did you run off like that for? Just when I was beginning to trust you."

"How did you...find me?"

"You asked the waiter where the police station was." He reached over to rinse the cloth in a bowl of cool water that was on the floor. Meg noticed then that his hair really was wet (it had been no vision), and he was nearly as drenched as she was. "But I would have ended up here eventually even without his help. There's no consulate in Akosombo, so the police station is the next logical place." He pressed the renewed cloth against her forehead, again, and then moved it around to the back of her neck.

Meg should have refused anything from him but she couldn't help it. She had never had such a pounding headache in her life. "You...you knew those people!" She managed to accuse.

"I know a lot of people around here. It's where I pick up the boat to Yeji."

"But I saw you...give them the deed!" For heaven's sake, was she going to start crying, again? What a disturbing influence this man had over her!

"I didn't give anyone the deed. All I did was show it to Miriam, here, since she knows this country like the back of her hand. There's no exact location on the thing. It's just listed as one of a series of mines belonging to..."

Megan was up on her elbow, again, but she paid for it with another shooting pain and had to drop back down. She hadn't noticed they weren't the only ones in the cell.

"Lay still, now Meg." Tom insisted. "Before you..."

"She's the stewardess! The one on my plane out of Paris!"

"It's no crime to work part-time for the airlines, Miss Jennings," said the familiar voice. "Especially if it provides access to the many places a person might need to go."

"Well that...that part-time skycap of yours is a kidnapper!" said Meg. "Where's the commissioner? I want to file a complaint!"

"No, you don't," said Tom.

"Yes, I do!" insisted Meg. "I want to see the commissioner!"

"And who is hollering for the commissioner?" Boomed a low, authoritative voice from the open iron doorway.

Meg put a hand against the cloth that was now back on her forehead, as she eased up on her elbow, again. "I am." She insisted to the middle-aged man in uniform, with a bright silver badge on his chest to prove his identity. "I want to file kidnapping charges against a Mr...." She looked over at the stewardess. The lovely young woman was wearing jeans and a multi-colored blouse instead of an airline uniform and her long braided tresses were pulled back into a ponytail that fell nearly to her waist. "I don't even know his name!"

"What is she talking about?" The commissioner asked.

"She means Sol Horn," said Miriam.

"Sol Horn!" The expression he cast Meg was incredulous. "His father is one of the most respected spiritual leaders in this vicinity."

"By spiritual leader he means the local witchdoctor." Miriam informed her. "He's no skycap, either. Matter of fact, I was just talking with him about how he happened to be in Akosombo when he was scheduled to work the tour all the way from St. Louis."

"Disrespecting the old customs is not a sign of maturity and independence, Miriam," said the commissioner.

"I'm sorry, Father."

"Father!" gasped Meg.

"I thought she might have heard something about this gold scam," said Tom. "Or, at least help us sort out how Pop got himself involved."

"It's part of a smuggling operation to get gold out of the country and bypass all the expensive government regulations. Solomon's at the center of it, all right, but, so far, I haven't been able to catch him doing anything illegal. There's a stakeout set up for tomorrow, though, because we got a tip they're going to try to move a big shipment out during a drum party." Miriam hopped down from the stool where she'd been sitting and headed for the door. "We'll know more when we actually talk to the professor. But in the meantime, I'll see what else I can find out."

As she passed by the commissioner, she slipped the gun from his holster in one smooth motion and tucked it into the waistband at the back of her pants. But rather than being alarmed, the imposing man simply reached out and snatched it back before planting a resounding smack on her backside. She squealed, but kept on going.

"Why won't she just settle down and raise children?" he implored Tom and returned the weapon to his holster. "And now I have to get back to that mob out there."

"We'll be out of here in a bit," said Tom.

"Take your time. Nobody is waiting to get in here."

"What about my charges?" asked Meg.

"You want my advice?" He spoke to Tom rather than Meg. "Put her in a taxi and take her to the nearest…"

"I demand justice!"

"Megan." Tom warned.

"Come back in three days, and I'll give it to you," said the commissioner.

"Three days! Somebody could be dead in three days. What do you say to that?"

"I have no intentions of listening to the hysterical rantings of some wild young woman with a touch of heatstroke. I have enough wild women in my life."

"Heatstroke…" Meg snatched the cloth from her forehead and threw it at Tom.

"Shall you be needing a backup for this situation?" the commissioner teased.

"I think I can handle it." Tom got to his feet. He had been sitting on the edge of Meg's cot.

The commissioner walked away laughing.

"I'm not going," said Meg.

"Yes, you are."

"You can't make me."

"Yes, I can."

"Where's my bag? I'm going to call my father!" Meg struggled to stand and gave him a shove with every ounce of strength she had left...and promptly fell in a heap onto the floor.

16

Fever

"I was fearfully tired, and my legs shivered under me after the falls and emotions of the previous part of the day..."
Mary Kingsley

Meg dreamed she was back home. Not the charming little cottage she had rented on the coast of Scotland that was waiting for her return. Or even her own lovely apartment on the edge of the park across from the school where she'd taught for so many years. It was home much farther back than that. She was on the old *Glory B.*, her father's tugboat, and its calm, steady engine was thumping beneath her comfortable bunk with the familiar peace and security of her early youth.

Mom must be baking an apple pie in the galley, her special recipe with just the right balance of cinnamon and nutmeg, and the slightest hint of lemon. Meg was hungry, and she struggled her way through dreamy sleep and opened her eyes. Why, this wasn't the *Glory B.*, at all. But she was definitely on some kind of a boat...and it was underway! There was a curtain of mosquito netting tied above her, and the little she could glimpse through a nearby porthole showed the flat smooth waters of the lake with a bit of its tropic fringe in the far distance.

A sense of apprehension invaded her. This was not where she should be. This was not the Volta Hotel. Nor was it the local medical clinic, if anyone had been truly concerned about her health. She stirred uncomfortably, still fighting a dull throb in her head, though not half so intense as before, and tried to sit up. Only to feel a reassuring hand on her shoulder to lend assistance.

"It's all right, priss," Tom said quietly. "Everything's all right."

"But this isn't the Volta Hotel, and you promised!"

"Now, don't look at me like that, Meg. It was my only choice." Tom sat in a chair pulled next to the bed. He'd changed clothes and was wearing a light denim shirt that made the blue of his eyes most striking in contrast to his dark hair and tanned skin. On a small nightstand between them rested a half-eaten piece of apple pie and a cup of coffee. Next to that lay an old edition of *Safari* by Martin Johnson he had obviously been reading. "I couldn't leave you alone in Akosombo in this condition. I'd go crazy."

"Well, I'm not far from crazy, myself!" She noticed she now wore her own teal-colored pajamas, and gasped. "What..." She pulled the cotton sheet (the only cover on the bed) up to her chin and threw him an accusing glare.

"You were soaking wet when I brought you in here," he replied. "But don't look so worried. The nurse did all that."

"What nurse?"

"The ship's nurse. A highly capable woman who takes care of any emergencies that might come up on the circuit from Akosombo to Yapei. Name's Judith Banuko. Used to work for the Peace Corps."

"Where is she now?"

"In the dining salon eating dinner, no doubt. You've been sleeping for almost four hours."

"And where have you been this whole time?"

"Right in this chair, miss priss." He was clearly beginning to lose patience. "What kind of person do you think I am?"

"That's just the trouble, Tom Anderson, I have no idea what kind of a person you are. Keeping company with people like Sol Horn." She reached for his unfinished pie and took a bite…it tasted heavenly.

"He was talking with Miriam before I even got there. He's never been one of my favorite people, and he knows it. Probably why he didn't stay long."

"And what's Miriam?" Meg reached for his coffee and caught a barely detectable expression of satisfaction that came into his eyes. Even the cold coffee was delicious.

"One of the best private investigators I know. Definitely the best around here."

"Then what made you side with the commissioner instead of me when I said Sol Horn was guilty of something about all this? We should have pressed charges right then and there. He would have at least been forced to explain himself."

"Megan, you can't just press kidnapping charges against someone when there's no proof. Especially, when it didn't amount to anything more than an inconvenience."

"That man is responsible for everything that happened. I'll bet you anything he even knows where the professor is right now."

"We already know where he is. He and Gilbert drove down to Dakar to meet Eddie Campbell, and the three of them flew to Little De Ambe, this morning."

"You heard from Gilbert?"

"Not directly, but I talked to Eddie just before they were due in. Haven't heard from him since, but he and Pop tend to veer off the path a bit when they get together."

"Then, for heaven's sake, Tom, why didn't you tell me that instead of letting me rant and rave, and make a fool of myself back at the jail?"

"You were ranting and raving about everything at that point. You were out of your head, Meg. You were even babbling about cannibals."

Her eyes grew wide at the sudden remembrance. "But there really are cannibals! Right here in Ghana! I saw a severed hand, with my own eyes, wrapped up in some kind of…"

"It wasn't human. Miriam told me about that."

"How would she know?"

"After the waiter told us you went to the police station, she got ahead of me while I grabbed up our things. Anyway, it was a gorilla hand. Almost as bad, in my opinion."

He sighed at her look of skepticism and tried to explain. "They smuggled it down from the highlands for some special occasion or other. It's a delicacy. But the gorillas are protected now and it's against the law to kill them. Still, there's a lot of poaching and illegal traffic going on. But what a shock for you, Meg! At first, they thought that's why you fainted. Had no idea you'd been trudging through the heat all morning."

"It was the last straw! I've had quite enough of all of this! Do you hear?"

Tom got to his feet. "I'll go get you some dinner. You'll feel better after you eat something."

"I'd rather get dressed and get it myself."

"Not on your life. You're supposed to stay in bed for at least a day. Standard procedure for a mild case of heatstroke in this part of the world."

"Will you hand me my bag then, please? I would at least like to call home."

"Nope." He started for the door.

"Give me one good reason why not!" Her head began to pound, again. "I have more than proven myself, Tom Anderson! And you can hardly expect…"

"Oh, you've proven yourself, all right. But I think one member of the Jennings family"—he opened the door— "is about all I can handle at a time."

Meg threw her pillow at him, but it only went halfway across the room and had no effect on his exit. Enough of this, she decided. She was going to call, anyway. Then she would get dressed, and take her complaints to the captain of this vessel. After that she would rent her own stateroom (no matter how much it cost) and get off at the very next port of call. She would rejoin her tour. And if Tom Anderson wanted to get in touch with her again, for any reason, he better have his father along. Alive and well.

Only she would have to do all that before he got back. Because any physical confrontation between them was decidedly stacked in his favor. Maybe it would be better to find that Nurse Judith person. Every man she had encountered since her arrival had automatically sided with Tom. Meg threw off the sheet and swung her feet onto the floor.

The room had white walls and wooden floors that looked dark and ancient. A small closet occupied one corner, and in another, a folding bamboo screen that partitioned off the space behind it. Probably a sink and commode. She found her duffel in the closet along with her string bag. But her cell phone was gone. The audacity! Now, who was acting like a common thief?

It was better than she thought behind the screen. Instead of having to wash in a small basin, there was a short hose and shower nozzle that could be connected to the faucet. One simply stood over a wooden grate and let the water run down into a drain in the floor underneath. There was also a fresh towel hanging nearby. Meg hadn't had a real shower in nearly four days, and even though the water only had one temperature, lukewarm, it felt wonderful.

After that, she donned a fresh khaki skirt and green print blouse (that practically matched the shade of her eyes), along with a wide leather belt. She certainly couldn't go looking for the captain in her pajamas. She still had the towel wrapped around her freshly washed hair, and was just beginning to rub moisturizer over her face when she heard the click of the door. Didn't even have the decency to knock!

She kept on with her ablutions and didn't say a word. Maybe Tom would simply leave a tray and go away. Now that she was on her feet, and quite capable of taking care of herself. By the time she had finished brushing out her hair and using her reading glasses to keep it back from her face, the smell of some delectable stew was more than she could take, and she stepped around the screen. Tom was reading, again, but he looked up as soon as she made an appearance.

"Feel better, priss?" he asked.

"Will you please stop calling me that? And you had no right to take my phone."

"Let's talk about it later. Come and eat, first. While it's still warm."

"You don't have to stay and watch over me, you know. I'm quite…"

"I like watching over you, Megan. It's turned into something of a habit."

"Well, if you cared anything at all for me…" She sat down on the edge of the bed and picked up the bowl of…what in the world was that? She reached for her glasses to give it a closer inspection.

"It's their specialty here," Tom answered the inquisitive look. "Sort of a peppery peanut butter stew. In fact, no matter what you order, roast beef and potatoes, chicken, whatever, you end up with that. I ordered you a bowl of clam chowder, if you're interested."

"Clam chowder?"

"I thought that's what a descendent of fisher folk might like best."

How was it he could be so exasperating one minute and so appealing the next? "I happen to love clam chowder," she confessed before giving the stew a tentative taste.

"You were saying?"

"I say this isn't half bad, and I'm starved."

"Before that. You said if I cared anything at all for you. Of course I care for you, Meg. We wouldn't have come this far if I didn't."

She stopped eating and cast him a long, thoughtful look. He was going to talk her into something, again. She knew it. He would make it sound so logical she wouldn't be able to resist. She hadn't been able to resist anything he had said or done, yet. So, she decided to tell him all of her suspicions, right now. Everything. While he was still in a frame of mind to listen. Because even though he had out-matched her at every turn, she knew, without doubt, that he was also vulnerable to her. Hadn't he admitted the channels between them ran both ways? There must be some way to tap into them, again. She would try something unexpected. Catch him off-guard. Wasn't the best defense a good offense?

Yes, she had sunk even to that, now.

"See, that's the point, Tom, you never ask me," she began. "You just say, this is what we're going to do, Megan, and then make me do it. You don't listen to me about anything."

"I'm listening, now."

"Only because you feel guilty for giving me heatstroke."

"Megan, I did not give you heatstroke." Then he raised his hands in response to her look of accusation. "Although I'll concede that I am responsible for putting you in the position to get it. For which I not only apologize, but also feel very bad about. I wouldn't hurt you for the world."

"But you still don't trust me enough to even let me call home."

"Do you trust me?"

"You haven't exactly given me a chance to trust you, Tom. You just plow on through and insist on having things your way."

"Only because you refuse to do almost everything I tell you."

"Most people who disagree on things discuss their differences." She pointed out. "Or even argue about them, instead of going straight to blows."

"Wasn't me throwing the punches, priss."

"Oh, it's…it's just that you exasperate me so!" She sighed at the futility of arguing with him and decided to try a more emotional approach. "Besides, you don't have to. You're quite capable of overpowering me without resorting to blows. No matter what I think. I'm only on this boat because you literally hauled me aboard like so much baggage. You don't care what I think!"

"Of course, I do."

But, rather than giving her the upper hand, the sudden look of disappointment the remark had cast over his face sent an arrow straight into her own heart.

"Meg, why did you run off from me, again?" he implored as if the true root of the thing could no longer be withheld.

"I told you. When I saw you with…"

"No, you would have said something about it right then, if that's all it was. Instead, you ran away from me. Because you couldn't trust what we talked about all day more than what you saw. Do you actually think I could betray my own father?"

"Oh, I don't know what to think, anymore." Then, like a boomerang, her own emotions began to churn (now, how had that happened?). She suddenly felt miserable she'd let him down in some way. She set her unfinished dinner aside and tried to explain. "The truth is, I feel like you deliberately swept me off my feet today."

"Since when is taking pictures on some thorn-infested, insect-ridden hillside, and then marching someone six and a half miles in a tropic heat, an attempt to sweep them off their feet? No woman in her right mind would…"

Disappointment welled up inside her like a storm about to break. He didn't even think she was in her right mind! And how had it come to matter so very much what he thought about her, anyway? But it did. Very much so. She sniffed (oh, dear!) and reached into her pocket for a tissue. It was empty.

"Don't start that, again, Meg. It tears at my heart when you cry."

But she couldn't help it. How could anybody? "You're right. I haven't been in my right mind since I met you! All that talk about Christianity and being a perfect match, called to the same purpose, you said, *divinely appointed*!" She stood to hunt for a tissue. "Maybe my divine appointment was nothing more than getting in the way of whatever underhanded trick you were trying to pull over on your father!"

"You know that's not true." Tom reached into his pocket then and handed her a folded handkerchief. "But it can go either way from here, Meg. It's up to you. Look, we've been given a wonderful vision, you and I, of what each of us has the possibility to become. But the only way to get there is to have some faith in it. We have to believe the best of each other, no matter what we see. I can't be your...dashing prince..."

Meg gasped. Had she actually written that down? She covered her eyes with the handkerchief out of sheer embarrassment.

"Unless you call me back to that. Over and over, Meg. However long it takes. And you can't be my perfect, or shall I say...pristine...lady out of the past unless…"

"Pristine?" She cast a doubtful glance over the top of the handkerchief. "I hardly think you could consider me 'pure as the driven snow' after the last few days, no matter what you saw back at that cafe. You read my journal, for heaven's sake. You know I haven't remained pure to much more than a single ideal I started out with!"

"That's not all it implies. In fact, that phrase is actually a distortion of the true definition of the word. What it really means is, uncorrupted by civilization. Typical of the earliest time or condition. Absolutely... utterly... perfectly...original... Meg. More importantly, it's what it means to me when I call you that. Except when you're being so stubborn I can't even ..."

"Priss, as in prissy, is what you mean most of the time."

"That's why we've got to keep calling each other back to our original visions of each other. Don't you see? Maybe it's possible to become the perfect someone we each thought we saw. In fact, maybe consciously making an effort to believe in it – against all odds, Meg – is the only way dreams like that can survive."

"Tom, you can't possibly believe I could actually turn into someone like that."

"I do. I think maybe everybody could. What if it's something you have to choose to do? A believe-it-or-not type thing."

"What an incredible idea that would be. I've never heard anything like it. And wouldn't it put quite the different twist on things if it really was all up to us."

"If it is, I choose you, priss." Then he announced more emphatically, "I choose to believe that's the real you."

It was the nicest thing anyone had ever said to her. It touched Meg right down to the very depths of her being. And to think he could say something like that after the way she had treated him over the last two days, or even the last few minutes, seemed nothing short of amazing. No one had ever seen anything beyond ordinary in her, not in her entire life.

"But suppose it's impossible, Tom? Think how disappointing to reach for the moon when you can't even touch the trees most of the time. It would…"

"So much better than where we are now, though," he finished the sentence for her. "No matter how far we got with it. The very act of trying would have an effect. It would be like stepping stones across a river, Meg. Glory to glory all the way."

Her eyes welled up and spilled over, again, at such a beautiful thought (she couldn't help it; she cried as much at beauty as she did at sadness), but she inwardly chided herself that every emotion she possessed seemed so intensified beneath his gaze. As if she had no control over sharing her deepest feelings with him.

"So, come back to me, priss." He entreated. "Just like you were in the cafe. If you don't, we might never reach the places and things we were truly made for. Neither one of us. Look…"

He put a hand on her arm and coaxed her toward him. "Just finding each other in this crazy world was a gift, an incredible gift! It shows God must have a little bit of faith in us, too. Don't you think? Enough to give us a divine vision of each other. And a divine appointment just to catch it. We don't dare waste it, dearest, otherwise…"

He pulled her onto his lap and took the handkerchief she was crying into. "Otherwise we'll just turn into a couple of"—he gently wiped the tears away—"eccentric, old, lonely nincompoops!"

Meg could no more resist those soothing words than she could deny her own name. Instead, she put appreciative arms around his neck and declared with the most heartfelt sincerity, "I'll never doubt it, again!"

In turn, he circled her in that strong embrace that had once felt so confining, and simply held her for a few moments. Which, this time, surprisingly, gave her a most wonderful sense of security and well-being. Then he ran a hand through her still damp hair and kissed the side of her face so softly it sent a ripple of sensations all through her. "Promise you won't run away from me anymore, Meg." It was barely more than a whisper into her ear. "No matter what happens."

"I..."

A sudden loud rap against the metal door interrupted her reply. "Message for you, sah!" A man's voice called out from the other side, and the noisy banging sounded, again.

"Oh..." Meg tried to pull away from him to answer it.

Tom held her tighter instead of letting go, and insisted, "Promise."

17

Dark Prince

*"That gentleman is exceedingly amiable and
charming...handsome, exuberant, and energetic. He shows
me...with a gracious enthusiasm...all manner of things."*
Mary Kingsley

"I promise I won't run away," said Meg.

As if satisfied, he rose, lifting her with him, and
then reluctantly set her down to head for the door and
answer it, himself.

"The captain shall see you on the bridge, sah!"
echoed a voice from the companionway but Meg could
not see past Tom to connect it with a face.

"I'll be right there." He reached into the pocket of
his jeans and drew out a bill of foreign currency that he
handed over, and then shut the door again. He turned
back to Meg.

"Probably just a message from my crew saying
they've landed in Accra," he explained. "But I'll have
to go up there and make some arrangements for a
reply. Shouldn't take too long. Go back to bed, though,
will you, Meg? Nurse's orders. She said she'd look in
on you later. Meantime, just bang on the wall if you
need anything. I'm only in the next cabin over."

"But, Tom, I feel much better. Why can't I just

come with..."

"Nurse's orders," he repeated. "Besides, I've already had to listen to her about bringing you here like that in the first place. Judith and I go way back. Now, listen, priss, I have a plan. So, I'll pick you up first thing in the morning for breakfast and we can discuss it."

"What sort of plan?"

"First thing in the morning."

"I won't sleep a wink wondering what it is." She began arguing, again. "So you might as well..."

He put a hand under her chin to tilt her face up and stopped the flow of words with a kiss. Not a demanding kiss: it was a very tender and affectionate one. But its effect on Meg was immediate. All manner of emotions welled up from the very depths of her being that she could barely keep from bubbling to the surface. As it was, she reached up to put her arms around his neck, again, in search of that place where, only moments before, she had felt so wonderfully cherished and secure. Except this time, he caught her against him, and lifted her right off the floor.

He laughed, as if the pure pleasure of having her reach out to him instead of push him away was something of a triumph in itself. It was that same delighted laughter she had heard for the first time, in the forest. "There," he pronounced as he set her down. "I've wanted to do that all day. Only I didn't dare risk another one of your swings. But I'll tell you something. I'd risk two of them to get that kind of response, again."

"I really don't know what's come over me." She could feel the heat of color creeping into her face. "Hardly an hour ago, I was going to complain to the captain about you, and now... well, now, you've completely changed my mind. Swept me off my feet, again. How did you do that? And that cabin next door...well, after the last two days...it suddenly seems like a long way away."

The smile that came first to his eyes and then the corners of his mouth made her suddenly gasp at the inference of her own words. "Oh...that's not what I meant!"

"Might not be far enough, priss. Especially if you ask me to stay."

"But I wasn't talking about...well, of all things...now, you probably think..."

"I think it's pretty amazing how much I could love you in such a short time," he confessed. "And I adore it that you have those kinds of feelings for me, Meg. Which is why I'm not even going to ask. Until you're mine, anyway." Then he flashed her the most appealing smile and winked at her. "Wouldn't want to offend the Giver of such a perfect gift."

Meg hardly knew what to say. She was too overcome with the sudden feeling that he was the absolute, most wonderful person in the world. But before she could collect her roller-coaster feelings enough to answer, he brushed the side of her face with a final kiss and headed out the door. Leaving her wondering how she had ever gotten along without Tom Anderson. Which was quite the turnaround from an hour ago. But she couldn't help it. Not even a bit.

It was strange how, ever since she had met him, Meg hadn't been able to keep from telling him exactly what was on her mind. The words seemed to tumble out all by themselves. It was an odd sort of familiarity she'd never shared with anyone else. Not even her family. There really did seem to be an open channel between them that either could tap into at will. It was something she'd never experienced before. But she hadn't been prepared for the intensity of feelings that could come rushing back through that very same channel.

Meg's life suddenly fell into place like the last piece of a puzzle she had been working on for years. The picture that became clear at that moment was so much more beautiful than she had ever imagined, that it took a series of constant reminders that what had just taken place had really happened. She had come on this trip in a hesitant effort to make something of her own natural talents that she could offer back to God. Resigned, almost to the point of hardness, that there was no one in the world who would ever be able to put up with (much less, understand) all those strange idiosyncrasies that made her who she was. To which the Lord's loving response was to hand her...

A perfect match.

Was that possible? But Tom Anderson was a lifetime in the making, even as she had been, and they had traveled halfway around the world from opposite ends to accidently run into each other. Twice. Even if it was possible, did the Father of Heaven really take such a personal hand in the earthly interests of His children? It was mind-boggling! But even figuring it out suddenly didn't seem to matter.

Because, no matter how she tried to explain it, the pure thankfulness that bubbled from her heart at that moment was proof enough that God had honored her efforts to reach out for more by giving her the deepest, most secret desire of her heart. The one that had been there so long it seemed impossible. The one she had set aside like a childhood fairytale and almost didn't even believe in anymore. A perfect match. Then, again, maybe she was just dreaming. Maybe they both were.

Would they still feel this way tomorrow?

It was a question she need not have worried over. Because something equally as amazing seemed to have taken place while they were apart. By the time Tom returned the following morning, all doubts had dissipated into such a comfortable acceptance on both sides. It seemed they had been together forever, instead of a mere few days. What's more, the warm glow left over from the things they had said to each other the night before, seemed to cast a shine over everything they did. Even simple things became special.

It started with breakfast on an outside deck. The boat was one of the oldest vessels left on the lake, but the *Volta Queen* made up in charm what it lacked in amenities. Just how many *Volta Queens* there had been over the years was contestable. Tom said he liked it for the peaceful Old World atmosphere, rather than most of the modern ones that were more like floating bars and dance clubs. It was there that Meg finally got to meet the nurse, a middle-aged English lady who was married to a West African marine engineer.

She was short, with generous proportions. Her blonde hair was beginning to gray and tied with a colorful scarf at the nape of her neck. She joined them at their table, without being asked, and clapped Tom on the shoulder like a teacher who had just caught him cheating on an exam. "Is this your idea of letting her sleep in, Thomas? It's barely half past seven." And then to Meg, "Feeling better, luv? You were asleep when I peeked in, last night."

"Much better," Meg replied, liking her instantly. "Thanks for everything you've done."

"I can't keep her down. She was awake at six-thirty," said Tom.

"That's not what I heard from the boys in the kitchen. You telling them to have tea sent in to her at six."

"Judith, you're as much of a snoop as the last time I was here. Maybe even worse."

"How else can I keep boredom away when all I do is pass out aspirin for headaches and fever?" She gave Meg a playful wink and turned over the cup that was upside down in a saucer in front of her. "Seriously, though, don't go dragging her through more forest, today, or down any rapids. Quiet bit of lunch in Yeji, and then a good long nap afterward. Wouldn't want a relapse, now, would we."

A young man in a white steward's jacket came up to the table with a steaming pitcher. "Tea with lemon for you, Mama Jude?" he asked as he poured coffee for Tom and Meg.

"That would be grand, Kori," the nurse replied. "And a bit of toasted biscuit, this morning, too."

"Word of warning, Meg," Tom handed her the little pitcher of cream for her coffee. "Judith's a knuckle-rapper if you don't do what she tells you."

"Only for scamps like you," said Judith. "You know,"—she turned back to Meg—"he once took three doses of malaria pills all at once and went off on a hunt, after I expressly forbade him even to think of getting out of bed."

"She hit me with a clipboard when I got back."

"It was the only thing I had in my hand at the moment."

"Good thing it wasn't a…" The French national anthem interrupted the banter, and Tom took his phone from a vest pocket and looked at it. "About time," he muttered as he flipped it open with his thumb. "Gilbert, where the devil are you?" He got to his feet and whispered aside to Meg, "It's a bad connection. I'm going to the upper deck for more reception." And then he wandered off.

"Well, I'll be honest with you, luv," Judith said after he was gone. "Whatever it is you see in that man is beyond me."

"You don't think he's wonderful?"

"That one? You must be kidding, he's anything but. Throws regular tantrums if he doesn't get his way, but I take it you haven't seen one of those, yet."

Meg was about to mention it probably came from being spoiled as a child, when an amazing thought suddenly popped into her head. "I think he's…quite a prince, actually," she replied, instead.

Judith laughed outright at the idea. "A dark one, if you ask me. But if you don't mind that wild look in his eye, you must be made for each other. Watch out for the werewolf, though. Especially when things go wrong."

A remark that Meg might have taken more seriously if she had heard it twenty-four hours earlier. Instead, she found herself wondering how such a wonderful man could be so mistaken by everyone else. What's more, it was equally amazing that a person like him could actually be enamored with someone, like herself, who was so set in her own quirky ways. That's when she realized (with a sense of utter amazement) how falling in love had happened to her just the way her mother predicted. Two people who seemed ordinary to everyone around them, became nothing short of extraordinary to each other.

Meg was much too caught up in the enchantment of that discovery to consider warnings. She even found herself wishing that Judith might not stay too long, so she and Tom could get on with discussing his plan. Whatever it was. Probably something about the Mary Kingsley film, but she was inwardly hoping for something more.

However, just before their arrival in Yeji, when they finally were alone, she still couldn't get him to reveal anything about it. Not even after they pulled up to the dock of the tiny lake port. It was a small town, crowded against the waterfront, with forest pressing in from all sides. After they disembarked down the gangway several minutes later, they made their way over to a bush taxi. Just as Meg noticed it was carrying a large mysterious basket on the backseat, the driver climbed out and handed the keys over to Tom.

"Three o'clock, you be back then," said the wiry old man who held three fingers up and jabbed them into the air for emphasis.

"Back by two-thirty," promised Tom. "I've hired a boat to go upriver at three."

"A pirate boat."

"Not this one. It belongs to the Ashanti."

"Worse! They say he is on a rampage! There will be a drum party tonight to appease him."

"Appreciate the tip," Tom replied as he opened the door on the passenger side for Meg to get in.

But just as she was thinking how thoughtful it was of him to hire a taxi instead of walking the few blocks to a restaurant, he turned off on a side road, instead. It seemed they were headed out of town. As he began barreling down the narrow dirt road through the trees, it suddenly occurred to her that he was not taking her out for the "bit of quiet lunch" that Judith Banuko had suggested. Judging by the large size of the basket on the seat behind them, it was not a picnic, either.

"Is this the plan?" she asked.

"Not, yet. It's just something I wanted to show you first."

"Tom Anderson, just how long is this teasing going to go on?"

He reached across the seat and took her hand in his. "Trust me, priss. You'll love it."

However, when he made another turn into what seemed like nothing more than a pig track that twisted and turned its way into deep forest, the nurse's warnings suddenly began to reverberate through Meg's mind. *"Throws regular tantrums if he doesn't get his own way... that wild look... watch out for the werewolf..."*

"Tom, do you know Judith thinks you're a..." Better not come right out and say it without testing the waters, first. "Well, practically a monster?"

"Telling you stories about me, was she? Well..." He shifted down to a lower gear and plowed through a mud-hole with a practiced ease. "She comes by it honestly. My brothers and I used to tease the daylights out of her."

"Like taking too many malaria pills and going on wild hunting trips?"

He laughed at the recollection (Meg was beginning to love the sound of that laugh), and she tried to press the matter before giving in to the charm. "I thought you said you were too much of a conservationist to hunt."

"In our family, shooting means with cameras. But

Judith's always been such a busybody, it was more fun to let her think we were poaching on the reserve or taking a canoe down some wild river in the middle of the night, instead of telling her the truth."

"You never did any of those things, then?"

"I didn't say that." He turned into a sea of tall grass and pulled to a sudden stop under a high jungle canopy in the middle of nowhere, and turned off the ignition. The silence that descended after the roar of the engine seemed to carry weight. "But don't look so worried, Meg. Most of those shenanigans were a long time ago. It's been over two years, now, since I've even been back here. I've changed since then. Especially, when it comes to lifestyles."

He reached back over the seat and opened the basket. It was filled with several different kinds of fruit that looked to be enough to feed an army. Nestled into the middle of the mound was a chilled jar of some icy drink, along with a few pieces of bread and cheese. He opened the jar and handed it to her. "Take a taste," he suggested. "It's the best mixture of fresh fruit and ice you'll find anywhere."

"It is delicious," she agreed after she had tried a sip. But she couldn't help feeling he was trying to distract her, and prompted him to confide more. "Just out of curiosity, how has your lifestyle changed, exactly?"

"I guess it would be more appropriate to call it a change in perspective. See, I suddenly discovered there was more than just one road in life. There are two of them. One insists you have to take whatever comes along and learn to deal with it. But then I found out you can get off that road, anytime you choose, and take the other one, instead. Which, personally, I like much better. Because that one leads from..." He gave her a disarming smile. "*Glory to glory.* Not to mention I found you there. Now..." He opened the door on his side. "Ready for lunch?"

"I'm ready to hear your plan."

"After lunch."

"That's what you said at breakfast. You can at least tell me what it's about."

"I've been trying to think of the best way to tell you, but nothing's coming to me." He leaned forward to look through the windshield at the top of the canopy for a moment, as if searching for something, then turned back to her with a resigned sigh. "The truth is...you're not going to like it, priss."

18

Dangerous Business

*"But as for those traders! Well, I put them down under the
dangers of West Africa at once..."*
Mary Kingsley

Tom's words caused a feeling of apprehension to invade her, and she slowly set the jar on the ledge of dashboard. What was this leading up to? "Maybe you should let me decide. That is, if you haven't already." Their eyes locked and held. "Well. I see you already have."

"I'm sending you on to Yapei, Meg. To catch up with your tour."

It was the last thing she expected to hear, especially after all the talk about finding the professor together and showing her how the company worked in the remote regions. And about being a perfect match. What had changed his mind? Didn't he realize she no longer wanted to...

"They should be at the Mole National Park by tomorrow, so you can just continue on up there with Judith. That way you can get another day's rest, and I won't have to worry about..."

"But I'd much rather go with you, Tom."

"And I'd like to take you. Only the trek is too

rugged for you right, now. Heatstroke is no joke, even a touch of it."

"I feel fine. Really."

"Here's the deal. While you're visiting the park, I'll pick up Pop and Gilbert from the Little De Ambe, and then meet you in Kumasi. Works out all the way around, that way. Your group will head there next to visit the markets, and…"

"How is it you know so much about my tour? I can't imagine you passed the time thumbing through all my brochures, yesterday, waiting for me to wake up."

"I know a lot about *Bremen Tours*, I own stock in that company. I'm also good friends with the man who runs it. We've known each other since we were in college. Anyway, he leases us one of his planes whenever we need it. He's got two of them that run sightseeing trips over the De Ambe goldfields."

His gaze was suddenly riveted on something moving in the tall grass ahead of them, and he lowered his voice. "Which is where I think Pop is headed."

"What is that?" Meg whispered back, following his gaze.

"A chimp. There's a whole family of them out here I've been trying to make friends with for years. They're pretty elusive, though, because they've been poached and sold off on the black market nearly to extinction in these parts. This is the last band left."

He reached slowly over the seat for a piece of fruit and tossed it out the open door to where the movement had last been. There was a rustling and rippling of grass, and then a dark, somber face rose up slowly and stared directly at them. Meg caught her breath.

"Why, he looks so intelligent," she marveled. "Like he might say something any moment!"

"Would you like to hear him say something?"

"What,are you going to introduce us?"

"Roll your window up, first."

He smiled at her skepticism and waited while she complied. Then he handed the bread and cheese off to her before slowly getting out to set the open basket of remaining fruit on the roof. The chimp didn't move, but he didn't back down, either. He simply watched and waited.

"Will he come this close?" Meg asked when Tom slipped back in, again. Then on second thought. "Oh, but won't we just be helping to make him a good target for poachers? If he gets to trust us, I mean."

"This is Adongo Pondi, and he doesn't trust anyone. He's more than just some smarter-than-average chimp. He's a throw-back from the monkey wars. When so many of them roamed this country they would battle it out for their territories. Men included. There're all kinds of legends about bands of them coming down out of the trees to attack native hunting parties that intruded."

"Now they're all gone?"

"All but Adongo Pondi and his band. He's staked off this circle, here, and declared himself king. Not only will they fight anyone who comes into it, they actually go on raiding parties to the outskirts of town when they feel threatened. The people are afraid of him, now. He's like the boogie-man."

"Then what are we doing here?"

"Just saying hello."

"But aren't we in his circle?"

"It's all right, he always remembers me. I just have

to let him know who it is." He leaned his head out the door, cupped his hands over his mouth, and gave a long low whistle that sounded like, "Woooo—up!" Then raised and held a clenched fist up in the air.

The chimp lifted both arms in spontaneous reply and screamed out a much louder version of the same sound before giving over to jumping and beating his chest with wild excitement. All at once, there were a hundred answering cries from the treetops as innumerable dark shapes began dropping from the trees and running toward them. Tom closed his door only moments before the little van was completely overrun with monkeys. They clamored over the top and sides of the vehicle until it began to rock with their thunderous pushing and shoving, and determined efforts to squeeze past each other to get at the fruit and look through windows.

"Now's the time, if you want a picture," Tom had to raise his voice over the din. "They'll take off as soon as the fruit's gone."

Meg startled, as if coming suddenly awake, and her hands shook just taking the cameras out of her bag. Then a strange thing happened. As if they had prearranged every move and done it a thousand times before, the two of them began to work in tandem. For the next fifteen minutes Meg snapped frames while Tom shot footage of wild antics and close-up joyous expressions through the glass of what could only be called an out-and-out celebration over the surprise.

When it was over, Meg dropped her hands to her lap, still clutching the camera, closed her eyes, and took a deep breath as if only just remembering she needed air. "Oh, Tom! That was just the most...exhilarating experience I've ever had!"

Tom ran a hand through her curls to push them back from her face and then kissed her. "I've got lots of experiences like that for you, Megan. So much I want to share with you."

"Please take me with you!" She circled his neck with her arms and leaned her forehead against his. "I feel like I've been waiting my whole life for things like this. I can't bear to miss a minute!"

"Don't make it any harder, priss, I can't give in. But I'll get back as soon as I can. I'll pick you up in Kumasi in two days, and the three of us will fly back to Akosombo for the shoot."

"Only three of us?"

A ripple of anger flickered over his face. He looked out the window for a moment, as if trying to keep it under control, and then answered. "That rat, Gilbert, is up to something. He hung up on me this morning without even telling me where they were. When I get hold of him, he's fired. I'm going to throw him on a train in Kumasi and ship him home."

By the time they returned to Yeji, Meg found the prospect of rejoining her tour actually depressing. The dread of having to go separate ways seemed to grow with each passing minute, and nothing they said or did could dispel the ominous mood that was growing darker as the moment of his departure arrived. When they stood, at last, on a cluster of docks in front of a small boat harbor where Tom had rented a launch to carry him upriver, he reached into a vest pocket and handed her cell phone back to her.

"To call home?" She realized the thought was hardly an inclination, anymore.

"If you want. But don't be too hard on me, Meg. I'd rather wait until better circumstances to have to make a first impression. Mostly it's for you and me to stay in touch whenever we can. I put my number on there for you, but I'll be out of range until Little De Ambe. It's nothing but river, swamp, and rocky hillsides between here and there."

He gave a wave to a man who was starting an engine on a small boat some distance away, and reached into another pocket for his bush hat. "I'll have to trek a mile and a half where they drop me off, and then I know someone who has a jeep I can drive the rest of the way. About five hours in all. Just about the same time you'll be pulling into Yapei, so I'll give you a call."

"Tom, I have the most awful feeling," Meg confessed.

"I'm not very happy leaving you, either. But the quicker we get this thing over with, the better. Keep out of the sun, Meg, will you? Have to be careful about that for the next few days."

"I will."

"And remember the mosquito netting around beds in this forest country is not for decoration. Don't fall asleep without...."

"Tom, I'll be fine. Those aren't the kind of things I meant. Something just doesn't seem quite right about all this. Nothing seems right. I almost hate to leave, it's so…"

"Don't miss that boat, Meg."

"But what if something happens to you?"

"Whatever happens I can handle it. So, don't worry. It'll be over before you know it."

"I don't see why we can't just wait for them, if they already have a plane to use…isn't that how they got there?"

"For some reason, Eddie still isn't answering his phone. Not last night, or all day today. It's probably just a matter of waking up somewhere with a hangover. Whatever it is, though, I have a feeling I should have been there, yesterday."

"Well, I..." Meg looked over at the tin building that housed the office, and then turned back to look at the town that was only a block away. Beyond that, she could even see the top stacks of the *Volta Queen* that was moored up at the wharf beyond. "It's almost as if I had run into some kind of strange magnetic field and my compass is out of sorts."

"Stay close to me, then, priss." He put a hand under her chin and leaned down to kiss her goodbye. "Because mine's working just fine." Then he kissed her, again, and headed off toward the boat that was waiting for him at the far end of the dock,

She waved one last time when he turned around, and then watched until the boat finally disappeared around a bend in the river. After that, she started back toward town and the melancholy mood still felt so heavy, she decided the only way to break it was to buy something at a little souvenir shop she'd had seen near the wharf. This region was famous for beautiful cloth, and she'd planned to purchase some, anyway. There was a nice selection on a table outside the shop and, in the half-hour that remained before the boat left, she would have just enough time.

Once there, she found a light colorful shawl and was tying it over her blouse the way she had seen so many of the African women do, when she heard someone scream a few feet away from her. It was a noisy, crowded place, and a burst of laughter from a group of women in the same area made her think they were just having a good time. Only, just as she turned around to go inside and pay for her shawl, she heard an emphatic— "Pssst! Mystery girl!"—from behind a large rack of dresses.

Meg stopped short and stared, just as a purple headscarf with an enormous knot tied on one side rose up over the top like an emerging periscope, only to reveal a familiar face beneath it. "Why, Vidalia Harbin, of all things! Shouldn't you be at the…"

But instead of the friendly greeting she expected, the dark eyes grew wide with fright, and the woman reached out and pinched her, instead.

"Ouch! For, heaven's sake, what did you do that for?"

"Had to make sure you weren't another ghost! Been seeing ghosts all over the place." She stepped from behind the rack and gave a furtive look in all directions as if to make sure it was safe. She wore a long flowing sarong in the same purple shade as her headscarf. "Meg, where have you been all this time, girl? I thought you were dead!"

"Dead…"

"When the old coot came back without you, I…"

"Vidalia, what are you saying? The professor wasn't booked on our…"

"He showed up all right. In the same shape he was on the plane. Like that through most of the trip. But then when I seen Henry last night looking the same way…mmm-mmm! I knew I was in a fix worse than…" She tugged at a maroon-colored neck scarf as if she couldn't bear the heat a moment longer, and Meg caught sight of a huge gold chain with a red-eyed crocodile underneath.

"Where did you get that thing?" It was a dead

ringer for the one she had seen on Sol Horn.

"It's what the witchdoctor's friend gave to me. Remember? Only, now, it won't come off! Been trying to get somebody around here to help me, but soon as anybody catches a look, they get all kinds of scared and run away from me! Have to keep it covered up, or they treat me like one of the walking dead. Must mean something awful!"

"It means something, all right. Now, listen, Vidalia, we've got to get this straight. When exactly did you see the professor? Because I was told he flew into a place called Little De Ambe, yesterday."

"Maybe he did and maybe he didn't. All I know is, last night, him and Henry got dumped in the back of the van on its way to that investment meeting I told you about."

"Was he with a younger man? With curly hair?"

"Just Ethel's husband, Henry. Remember? That's who it was. Unloaded 'em both in the middle of the night after the boat brought us all over. The ferry from Mole National Park. Only a couple of us were going to the meeting. Ethyl chickened out on me at the last minute, her and her nerves of steel. Next thing I know, there was Henry. And him supposed to be off on that photography expedition! Only just when I caught a glimpse over the back-seat and was trying to figure out what was wrong with him...well, that's when the curly-haired guy come out of nowhere and started a scuffle."

"That had to be Gilbert Minelli! Where are they now? Do you know?"

"Bottom of that goldmine, if you ask me. Right where I'd be if I hadn't run off and hid under the wharf when that Minelli guy, same one was asking all those questions about you back in Podor..."

"About me? Was the professor with him, then?"

"Nope. Just him. Didn't see him anymore after that. But the old man rode with us on that awful road trip through the back country in Mali, didn't even stop there! All the way to Ouagadougou, in this here Volta region. That ain't how this tour was supposed to go. The other guy didn't show up until last night, when he threw a swing at the witchdoctor. Knocked him flat, too."

"Then what happened?"

"Saw a rat as big as a cat down there under that wharf!"

"With Gilbert and the professor, I mean!"

"Oh. Somebody important drove up and they all ganged up on him. Heard them say they'd take those four up there first, then come back and find me, later. Oooo-la! Scared the…"

"Four?"

"Another lady from the tour was with us."

"Vidalia, where's the mine? Do you know?"

"Not sure exactly. On account of I never been there, myself. But you could ask Belle Daube. She might know."

"Who's that?"

"Woman that runs the store, here. If it hadn't been for her, I'd be…"

"Can we trust her?"

"Every time you say that witchdoctor's name, she spits. I think we can trust her." She shifted a large, woven grass carryall to her other shoulder. "She helped me out with this outfit, too."

"Come on, we've got to talk to her!" Meg grabbed Vidalia's arm and started inside. "I've just got to find the professor, and that goldmine might be close by!"

The inside of the store was like walking into a witch's den. After the glare of outside it felt dark and damp. There was a strong smell of incense and…something else Meg couldn't quite make out. The first thing that caught her attention was the head of a panther protruding from a portion of the wall, with fangs bared and a single claw stretching out beneath, as if it were just tearing through and about to spring on some unsuspecting prey.

The ceiling was hung with all manner of baskets and nets (for capturing human souls; Meg had read about that in one of the brochures), and there were bins and tables stuffed and stacked to overflowing with sticks and shells, pieces of leather, and…bones. It was a shop of bones. Big ones, little ones, and numerous wall hangings made out of bones. She felt a chill just being inside, even though it was nearing ninety degrees out in the street.

"That be twenty dollar." The old woman behind a bamboo counter pointed to the shawl Meg was still wearing and moved over to an ancient cash register.

"Oh…" Meg slipped her bag from her shoulder and fished for her wallet. "Yes, of course. Do you happen to know…" She pulled out a combination of local currency Tom had forced on her before he left. "I'm a friend of Vidalia, here, and…"

"American twenty dollar," the woman corrected her. Two of her teeth were missing, and she had something brown in her mouth. Which seemed rather out of balance with the lovely full length green toga and matching scarf she was wearing, tied attractively in the African style.

"Oh." Meg looked in the zippered section where she kept the change from the last traveler's check she had cashed, and withdrew a twenty-dollar bill. "Here you are. It's a lovely shawl. Everything out there is beautifully made."

"All made in my village, missie." She took the twenty, snapped it to make sure it was genuine, and then leaned close to squint at the buttons on the machine. She punched one. There was a loud ring, of the sort one used to hear on children's bikes, and the drawer sprang open against the woman's stomach. She lifted the tray of local currency and slipped the twenty underneath. "De Ambe." She slammed the drawer closed, again. "Just down the river. All these goods are made by my people in De Ambe."

"De Ambe?" Meg could hardly believe what she was hearing. "You mean, De Ambe is somewhere near here?"

"Near to some, far to others," the woman replied. "My grandson and I go home every night, if that is what you want to know. I invited Vidalia to come home and stay with me until the boat comes back, but she would rather sleep with rats!" Then she laughed as if the thought delighted her, and leaned down to spit a stream of brown juice into an old brass spittoon near her feet. Why, she was chewing tobacco!

"But I was told De Ambe was some dangerous primitive place at least five hours from here." Meg still couldn't quite believe what she was hearing, and had to make sure.

The woman smiled a tolerant smile and shifted her mouthful from one side to the other. "De Ambe is a beautiful place. Like Paradise. And very modern. Aram Fada, who is the headman there, is the only man, maybe in all this Volta region, to have a dish."

"A dish?"

"To bring in the television. He has a dish. And there are drum parties and music every night. Wonderful music. The witchdoctor"—she spat, again, and this time it was more like she was trying to get rid of some terrible taste in her mouth—"plays in a reggae band twice a month in Kumasi, Accra, Dakar, all over. A good friend of my husband."

"Would you happen to know if a Professor Anderson arrived there yesterday?"

"Professor Anderson? He is a great name. If he came, we would all know it. His sons are coming next week, and there is to be a big celebration."

"Well, then, is there a…" Meg came right to the point. "Some kind of a goldmine in De Ambe?"

"There is, but it is broken down. Cost too much to get anything out right now, so Aram Fada doesn't allow it. But some devils are getting something out by selling pieces of it to any child of an ostrich who believes them."

Vidalia gasped and grimaced as if someone had smacked her, and the old woman laughed at her discomfort.

"Have you heard of anyone named Gilbert Minelli?" Meg ventured.

"Mmm…" The woman's eyes twinkled at Meg as if she were a cat playing with a mouse. "I heard of somebody with a name like that who tried to hit Sol Horn on the chin last night." She spit again, at the mention of the name, and then laughed with outright delight when Meg's expression turned as equally shocked as Vidalia's had been.

"What happened to him? Do you know where he is now?"

"Well…" The woman moved down the counter a

few steps and picked up a small bundle of some noxious smelling herbs. "Same thing happens to anyone who is so foolish. He got himself turned into monkey brains."

19

Hunter's Blind

"Every hole in the side walls had a human eye in it."
Mary Kingsley

There was a deep loud groan of the whistle on the *Volta Queen* as it called passengers back to get under way. Meg gave a start and grabbed Vidalia by the arm. "Come on, I've got fifteen minutes to get my luggage off that boat before it sails! Don't go away, Belle Daube. We'll be right back."

"I'll be here."

It wasn't until they were standing on the wharf, again (and Meg had made serious efforts to avoid Judith), watching the boat pull away that she had a momentary twinge of guilt. She was doing exactly what Tom told her not to, and he had barely been gone an hour. She was also breaking one of the last remaining rules she had not changed in her journal. But there was simply no way around it. Rule number two: *"I will always keep my word,"* would have to be revised to include: *"except in matters of life and death."* But she would think about that later. Right now, she had to tell Tom everything she'd heard.

So, while Vidalia sank down onto a nearby bench to catch her breath, Meg took out her cell phone and tried to call him. Three rings and it shifted over to, "This is Tom. Can't talk right now, so leave a message, and I'll get back to you."

Out of range, already.

Meg flipped it closed and put it back in her purse. Choosing the right words to explain would take some thought. He was just getting over the last time she left him a message. But if De Ambe was a shorter distance by some other river that only certain locals knew about, and if the professor really had been taken to the abandoned goldmine that was near there, then time was of the essence. Who knew what kind of condition he might be in by the time anyone got to him? Or, worse, yet, what they were planning to do to him before that.

Whatever the plan, Sol Horn certainly couldn't do away with everybody involved in the scheme: there would be no way to cover up such a large crime in such a small place. Not and get away with it. At that point, Meg realized exactly what she must do. She had to somehow talk Belle Daube into revealing that shortcut to De Ambe. Of course, she had no intentions of trying to handle everything, herself, because this was definitely turning into dangerous business.

They were going to need help.

She took the phone out again, and pressed zero. "Could you connect me to the police station in Akosombo, please?"

Vidalia, who was now fanning herself with a tour brochure, cast her an accusing glare. "Not gonna turn me in, are you? I had no idea that thing was illegal."

"I'd like the commissioner's office. Yes, thank you, I'll wait." She covered the phone with her hand and whispered. "Don't look so worried. I'm just getting in touch with someone who might be able to help us. If we run into any trouble, we're going to need…Oh, hello, sir, this is Megan Jennings. The lady who fainted on your floor, yesterday?"

Another startled look from Vidalia.

"Yes, I know it hasn't been three days, yet. But I was wondering if you could give me Miriam's number. Especially if I promise not to bother you, again, even when my three days are up." Meg set her bag down on the bench and felt around for a pen. "I do, honestly. I will…" She scribbled the number on one of her own tour brochures. "On my honor. Yes, sir. Thank you."

Miriam didn't answer, either, but Meg left a brief message saying that Gilbert and the professor were trapped at the bottom of a goldmine, but she had no idea where Eddie Campbell was. Could she please bring help? There, now. That was all she could do in that regard.

"Well…" She sat down next to Vidalia and fanned her own face for a moment. All this activity was making her feel light-headed, again. "Let's get something cool to drink, and then go back and try to talk Belle Daube into telling us how to get to De Ambe. The short way."

"Ain't gonna catch me in De Ambe. It's where that witchdoctor lives. Not an eye in his head, but he sees without them. Scared the bejabbers outta me."

"That's impossible. It must have been some kind of a trick."

"You can believe what you want, but I seen what I seen."

"We'll feel better after we drink something."

"I can't buy anything. I'm busted flat. Called my husband to wire me money to get home on, and I'm just hoping he'll do it before he finds out." She sighed and dropped the drooping brochure back into her carryall, again. "Figure he'll divorce me when he does."

"Divorce you?" Meg felt a sudden wave of compassion. "I'm sure once you explain...I mean, you can't be held entirely responsible for falling in with bad people."

"Oh, he won't mind about that. It's the other thing I'm worried about."

"What other thing?"

"Spending two thousand dollars on shares in a bogus goldmine. Ooo-la!" She shook her head miserably. "If I get stuck someplace like this for the rest of my life, I'll kill myself!"

"Oh, Vidalia! Nothing's that bad. You should've taken my stateroom like I suggested and gone back to the tour. That way you could have got home on your original ticket out of Paris."

"I told you, I wouldn't go back to that tour if you gagged and tied me. Even threw the voodoo doll of my husband away. Don't want nothing to do with that stuff anymore. I'm a changed woman."

"You're kidding. You mean, you've renounced voodoo? Why, Vidalia, I think you have had a change of heart."

"Heart attack is more like it. Almost had one those when I found out that witchdoctor runs the tour company."

An uncomfortable twinge pricked at Meg. Hadn't Tom said he was good friends with the man who ran the tour company? That they were practically in business together? And how was it that he had been coming here for years with no idea of the shortcut to

De Ambe, when a perfect stranger like herself had found out about it within the first hour of asking around? But, she pushed the disturbing thoughts aside; that wasn't believing the best of him, no matter what things looked like. And she was absolutely determined to do that from now on.

But why did things always have to look so bad?

She returned her attentions to Vidalia. "Well, you've made a start in the right direction, anyway. Come on, that's all the time for rest we can spare." She got to her feet and picked up her things. My, she had forgotten how heavy her duffel was! "I know a little place just down the street where they mix up the best tropical fruit drinks I've ever tasted. And don't worry, I'm buying."

"You're a real friend, Meg. Not many people like you in this world."

"Oh, you'd be surprised how many of us there are. Let's get Belle Daube a drink, too, and take it back to the shop. I heard someone say once that a gift can make a way for you."

"Better watch out, girl. That woman's talked me out of every last cent I had left."

The refreshing drink did loosen the old woman's tongue. Not because there was anything more than fruit in it, but because no one had ever given her something for nothing. She even agreed to let Vidalia sleep in the shop, at no charge, until her money came in.

"Now, about this goldmine in De Ambe..." Meg began in earnest.

"There are goldmines everywhere around De Ambe," said Belle Daube. "Enough for everybody."

"But I'm specifically interested in the one they are

selling pieces of. How far away, exactly, is it from the village?"

Now, the old woman looked at her as if she were a bit disappointed.

"Oh, not to buy a piece," Meg assured, "I only want to…"

But their window of common ground had shut, and a look of sheer craftiness flowed back into Belle Daube's eyes, as if she had only just come to herself. "De Ambe is not a village. It is a town."

"It's quite large, then?"

"No, it is quite small. Yes, quite. Villages are larger than towns. Towns are small things. We do not make trouble for tourists in De Ambe, missie. In case you are thinking of bringing the law."

Which sent a chill right down Meg's spine since she had only just called the commissioner and there was no possible way for Belle Daube to know that. At the same time, Vidalia's eyes grew wide, and she shrank back to the nearest table of goods.

"Think I'll get one of these for my daughter-in-law. When all that money comes in from my husband, I'll…" She had spoken a bit too loud for casual conversation, and then gasped when she realized she had picked up a dried snake. "Ooo-la!" She threw it back onto the table, again, as if it were still alive. "Better find something else. Don't think she'd…"

"The trouble with tourists is" —Belle Daube went on as if there had been no interruption— "they are not used to the bush. The people of De Ambe do not walk in the bush at night for fear of leopards. And the tourists?" She laughed and shook her head as if it was hard to believe. "They want to take pictures of the leopards. Or find their own way to the mines. Two times the police have come to De Ambe about the tourists, but the answer is always the same. They killed themselves."

"Killed themselves…" Meg murmured.

"Only you do not look as foolish as any of them." Continued Belle Daube. "You want to see the goldmines of De Ambe, missie? I can arrange for my grandson to take you there."

"Right now? By the…short way?"

"As you wish," she replied. "There is supposed to be a big drum party tonight after they find Eddie Campbell's crashed plane. You will enjoy it."

"What? Not the Eddie Campbell who…"

"It has happened many times. Especially when he packs it with too many tourists. That plane is a bucket with too many holes in it, now. But Aram Fada's trackers will find it. They always do. And if he is not dead…there will be a great party. A witch's night for all seasons!"

"But didn't he fly in yesterday, with…"

"He had customers, yesterday. But they stopped first in Kumasi for some music and drink. That's what they said at the post office this morning. They also said if Eddie Campbell dies, there will be no police investigation. Because they already know he is going to kill himself with that plane." Then she laughed. "He is crazy, that Eddie! You will like him."

"Oh, dear Lord!" Now Meg was in a complete state of turmoil. "Professor Anderson was on that plane! Tom will be absolutely beside himself when he hears all this!"

The old woman gave a few rhythmic clicks with her tongue and patted Meg's hand. "Don't worry. If Professor Anderson is in trouble, the whole town will go out looking for him. Aram Fada will insist on it. But I see you will want to get to De Ambe, quickly. It is where the trackers will come in first with whatever they find."

"How do I get there?" Meg asked. "By boat? Can I charter the other plane? "

"That is the Abdu Sadir's plane." Belle Daube spat again, to clear the distasteful words from her mouth. "He has a fine new plane he uses to help with the tours and take his band to places where he sings. But he never hires it out."

"Maybe there's another boat at that little dock near the end of the road," Meg murmured more to herself than Belle Daube.

"No. All the pay boats go home after the tour boat leaves. No more paying customers. My grandson...he has the only boat that goes to De Ambe after three o'clock."

Outside of intercepting Tom, Meg didn't know exactly what she was going to do after she got to De Ambe. Just how did a person go about looking for a goldmine in a tangle of African forest? She only knew she had to get there. Because while it might not be easy to get rid of such a "great name," as Belle Daube had called the professor, a plane crash would leave little for anyone to question.

Even if he was put there after the fact.

Under normal circumstances, Meg would never set out on some river, alone, with someone she didn't know. But children (no matter what culture they came from) she was sure she could handle. Besides, no amount of coaxing could persuade Vidalia to accompany her farther than halfway down the Little River Road where she was supposed to meet the boy.

But she did agree to put in a call to the police and the American consulate in Accra if she didn't hear back from Meg within twenty-four hours. Mostly because she figured it would speak well of her in the event of an inquiry. Especially since she had done nothing at all when Mrs. Cunningham disappeared.

Meg set her duffel down in the middle of the path they were following to reach the little river Belle Daube had directed them to, and looked long and hard at Vidalia Harbin. There were half-moon circles under her arms from the exertion of walking in the heat, and little beads of sweat collecting on her shiny dark forehead. "Just who, exactly, is Mrs. Cunningham? And what do you mean she disappeared?"

"You know. Loud screechy voice, wore every piece of jewelry she owned all at the same time, complained about everything. So happens she's one of my clients from back home. The one talked Ethyl and me into going in on the goldmine in the first place. Said she'd had shares over a year now and was already seeing dividends. Ain't seen her since they hauled her off with the others. That is, not alive, I haven't."

"Not alive...you mean she's..."

"Been dead for a least a day, now."

"Good heavens! You mean, they...they killed her?"

"Don't know."

"Maybe she got away, somehow. Like you did."

"Ain't sure about that, either."

Meg gave a frustrated sigh and reached into her pocket for Tom's handkerchief to dab at the dampness on her own forehead. The heat was becoming unbearable, again, and she felt the tell-tale drumming of another headache coming on. She bent down and unzipped the duffle to search for her umbrella. "Then what on earth would make you say she's dead? Maybe she didn't take to all this voodoo stuff, either, and just decided to do something else."

"I told you I been seeing ghosts, and she's one of them. Been seeing her every time I turn around in this town. Besides that, she screamed like a jaybird when I run off down at the wharf. Heard her hollering halfway outta town. Nope, she's dead, all right."

Vidalia plunked her large tote down beside Meg's duffel and pulled out another brochure to fan herself. "Seeing her plain as day. Always wearing that floppy red hat...same white dress with red polka dots she had on at the market in Ouagadougou. Mad at me, I s'pose, on account of I didn't tell anybody where they took everybody."

"Oh, Vidalia, for heaven's sake, is that the way you saw the professor, too? In some...some ghost vision, or something?"

"No, that was real enough, all right. So, maybe you should call for backup before you go poking around De Ambe all by yourself."

"Call for backup. Just who in the world would I call?"

"Your commissioner friend. I know you private investigators got friends in police departments. Learned it watching television."

"And that's another thing," —Meg closed her duffel, stood up, and pressed the release button on her umbrella— "whatever got into you to tell people I was a private investigator?"

Vidalia half-stifled a giggle before it bubbled all the way out. "You look like Mary Poppins with that thing. 'Specially all dressed up in that long skirt and…"

"Don't change the subject. I am not a private investigator. The idea!"

There was a long, contemplative pause, during which Vidalia stopped fanning her brochure and put her hand to her hip as if she had just caught someone red-handed. "You mean, you're not?"

"Of course, not. I'm a schoolteacher."

"Probably just your cover."

"Vidalia Harbin, I am not a private investigator!"

"I say you are. Because back on the plane, just before that stewardess interrupted to say you got first class, it come over me so strong , the words, private investigator, shot out of my mouth like a belch in public. Wasn't a thing I could do about it. I told you I was psychic. Course, my gift's been going haywire ever since I got to this place."

"Well. It just so happens that stewardess is a private investigator. She's the one I left a message for because I thought maybe she could help us out, somehow. "

Vidalia gasped and slowly began fanning her brochure, again. "Ooo...la! Maybe my gift ain't busted after all! Are you sure?"

"Positive. And her father is the commissioner of police in Akosombo."

"You do have friends in the police department!"

"I would hardly call them friends, but never mind!" Meg snatched up her duffel and began walking, again. "All I know is I've got to find the professor before anything worse happens to him. If it hasn't happened, already."

"I'll think some positive thoughts for you." Vidalia called without following. "Meanwhile, you watch out for pirates! I feel a sense of cheating all around you, girl!"

"Thanks a heap."

20

River of No Return

"I learn that these good people, to make topographical confusion worse confounded, call a river by one name when you are going up it, and by another when you are coming down…"

Mary Kingsley

The only boat down on the little river was a pirogue. The canoe-like wooden dugout had two young men standing next to it who weren't boys, at all. They didn't look a day under sixteen. Being something of an expert on teenagers, Meg knew. The one nearest walked up the path to meet her.

"You are from the shop, missie? My grandmother called me." He waved a cell phone at her with a bright smile. He was a handsome youth with shoulder-length hair braided all over in dozens of thin-stranded plaits.

"Yes, Belle Daube sent me," Meg replied. "So. You're the grandson."

"I am Franklin Hawkins. One of my grandfathers was an Englishman."

"How interesting." She turned a scrutinizing eye on the other one. He looked as if he had no hair at all, for his head was completely shaved. He said nothing, only looked her over as suspiciously as she was eyeing him.

"This is my cousin, who has no English ancestors. He will help with the rowing so we can get there before the rain."

"It's going to rain?"

"Don't worry. It can be some time before the rain." He took her duffel, placed it securely in the middle, and then helped her into the unstable craft, motioning for her to sit on top of it. "So you will stay dry," he said. After that, without any further preliminaries, the two of them pushed the boat out into the lazy current.

The two young men, one ahead and one behind her, paddled in a perfect rhythmic unison. While Meg sat and watched the shoreline recede, it occurred to her that she couldn't get much closer to Mary Kingsley's footsteps than to venture onto some small unknown river with only a couple of native paddlers. Even if they did carry cell phones. She actually might get some marvelous footage out here.

She removed the camera from the bag, which she had strategically placed over her neck and one shoulder to hang more comfortably beneath her new scarf-shawl. As she had trudged along that last long distance to the river, she had also taken a moment to send Miriam a text message. Remembering it took Tom less than an hour to get out of range, she was not about to set out with Vidalia and Belle Daube being the only people who knew where she was going. She had every intention of texting Tom, too, except that the appropriate words had still not occurred to her, and she was leaning more in the direction of simply showing up before he could talk her out of it.

The boy behind her made a quiet sort of hissing sound when she began filming, and the one ahead glanced back, took note of the camera, and then faced forward, again. The heat was almost suffocating beneath the green canopy of trees. The umbrella was no longer a help, so, she put it away. But now her boots were growing unbearably hot, and she was contemplating taking them off for a while, when there was a tremendous splash along the passing shoreline. She lowered her camera for a moment and looked over to where the thick forest crept down to the water and the mangrove trees reached their branches into it to take root in the muddy depths and spring up, again.

"That was a big fish," she said.

"Not a fish." the talkative grandson informed her. "Crocodile."

Which immediately caused Meg to feel unsafe in the little boat that was only three feet across at its widest point and less than six inches off the water. "How long will it take to get to De Ambe?" she asked.

"Not long. One hour maybe. It is a nice trip. No bad currents. And sometimes if it is late enough, you can see hippos feeding."

"Hippos?" Yesterday, she'd been thrilled to see hippos. But the idea of seeing any number of them from this vantage-point was rather horrifying. "Aren't they dangerous?"

"Only if you bump them," he said lightly. "They don't like that."

"Do you ever lose any boats out here?"

"We know where we are going."

"Tip over, I mean. Do many boats like this tip over?"

"Some yamheads who drink too much tip over, sometimes." Then he looked back at her and laughed at the expression he saw on her face, and the young man behind her laughed, too. "But don't worry, missie." He teased. "We have been drinking no beer."

Meg knew they were playing with her and didn't respond. Instead, she fixed the eye of her camera on the chocolate-colored water of the river and looked for hippos. A bit farther along, where the river narrowed, the thick humid heat seemed to engulf them like a steaming vat. Not long after that, those wraithlike wisps of fog, called "smokes," began to filter out through the surrounding forest and lay on top of the water. Recognizing the same oppressive signs of rain as yesterday, she quickly returned the camera to the bag beneath her shawl and set her umbrella in a handy place. Yes, they were going to get caught in the deluge before they even reached De Ambe.

"What is your name?" Franklin suddenly asked over his shoulder.

"Meg Jennings," she replied.

"Is your father very rich, Meg Jennings?"

"It depends on what you call rich." She answered. "He's the captain of his own tugboat, and has a nice little cabin tucked away on a sheltered island to spend the winters in. He and my mother are very happy. I'd say that was rich."

"Do you have brothers?"

"One. He's older. How about you?"

"I think I would like to travel some time to your country. Would you write down the address of your father so that I may know someone there?"

An odd request, Meg thought. Why didn't he ask for hers? Then thinking it must simply be a difference in cultural etiquette, she replied, "If you like, Franklin. I'll write it down for you when we get to De Ambe."

"And your husband's father? Will you write his

address down, too?"

"Did I say I had a husband?" Meg asked warily. "And just who do you think my father-in-law might be? Someone named Professor Anderson, perhaps?"

"Myself, I don't know him. But he is a great name. They say he pays for some of us to go to university, if we have the brains and can keep out of trouble. I would like to write him a letter. You are a teacher, so you should help me."

"I might be willing to talk to him about you," Meg offered. "If you take me where he is. Let's be honest, shall we? I'm sure your grandmother already told you I'm looking for him. And the only way you could know I'm a teacher is if you were spying on Vidalia and me on our way to the river. You could have at least introduced yourselves and helped carry our…"

A flash of light and a near deafening roar of thunder made her flinch and reach for her umbrella. Like the day before, it was followed by several others in rapid succession. Meg had hardly enough time to even get the umbrella open before the rain began to pour down in torrents. The young man behind her picked up a rusty coffee can and began to bail steadily as water rose around their feet and along the bottom of Meg's bag.

A half mile farther upriver, she saw a great streak of forked lightning reach down like a deathly hand and explode the trunk of a giant tree. It was like nothing Meg had ever seen before. Storms here seemed to happen all around instead of up in the sky. She wondered how anyone could ever get used to such wild, unnerving displays of violent nature.

Now, even the talkative grandson became silent as he lent all his efforts to paddling. Meg spent the next half-hour watching the warm rain run in rivulets down his clinging, blue T-shirt and over his jeans as she sat beneath her makeshift shelter. Which was actually doing quite the nice job of keeping herself and her things fairly dry. She made sure her string bag was pulled close under her shawl and protected, and (once again) wondered what on earth she had gotten herself into.

All at once, the two young men, as if by signal, began paddling swiftly toward a passing shore, and to Meg's surprise, banked the pirogue on a muddy finger of land that had nothing resembling a town in sight.

"Where is De Ambe from here?" she asked after they had pulled the boat up onto higher ground, helped her to climb out, and set her duffel down beside her. It seemed to be growing darker by the minute, was it that late, already? Her mind suddenly began to whirl with thoughts of leopards and the hour when not even the locals were out-and-about.

"You will write the names and addresses, now," Franklin Hawkins spoke harshly through the pouring rain. "And give us your camera, too. Otherwise we will leave you here."

"You'll do no such thing," Meg snapped back. "You'll take me to De Ambe like you're supposed to, or I'll write your name and address to that witchdoctor of yours and let him deal with you."

There was a moment of silence, and Meg thought she detected a flicker of concern in the dark eyes.

"You do not know him."

"I most certainly do. He sings in Kumasi twice a month and runs the tour company. It just so happens I'm on my way to see him. Here, hold this." She handed him the umbrella and hurriedly retrieved the long-sleeved khaki jacket that matched her skirt, along with the safari hat out of the duffel at her feet. "I wouldn't be surprised if he was looking for me right now."

There was another long silence as he dutifully held the umbrella over her while she put on her things, and then took it back again. After which her two companions stepped a few feet away from her and conferred together. Meg could have made a run for it, but two summers' experience with a camp canoe didn't give her much confidence in crocodile-infested rivers. And she would much rather take her chances with these two cocky teenagers than be alone in "the bush" at night.

"All right, boys." She walked up to them. "Why don't you just tell me what you're trying to do here?"

The sound of an engine interrupted her, and she looked up in time to see two headlights of a vehicle pinpoint them from a little knoll a short distance above.

"Man, how did he find out?" Franklin Hawkins whispered.

"Miriam must have called him." The boy who hadn't spoken until now, gave a disgusted sigh and turned back toward the boat. "Let's go."

"Stay!" A commanding voice boomed from the direction of the lights, but Meg could see only a tall silhouette descending before the brightness.

There was a heated exchange of words between them that Meg did not understand, and within a few moments, the boys were shoving the pirogue back into the river with much less enthusiasm than they had hauled it ashore. The stranger turned in full view within the lights then, and she could not help the sudden quick intake of her breath when he looked down at her.

"It is safer if you come with me, Megan Jennings." He smiled reassuringly as he picked up her duffel. He, too, had shoulder-length hair in many braids, dark arresting eyes, and a handsomeness that was almost radiant. When he walked ahead of Meg up the embankment, it was with a rhythmic stride that held the grace of an athlete, or maybe even a dancer. There was something stately and regal about him, yet his clothes were simple jeans and a dark T-shirt that clung wet and dripping against his muscular body in the pouring rain.

"Are you...Miriam's brother?" she asked as they neared the jeep. For she had heard the boys say she might have called him, and this man was as strikingly handsome as Miriam was beautiful.

"No." He laughed at the thought. "Miriam is my wife. But she is a wild thing who only comes home when she gets tired. Right now, she is off somewhere trying to catch a thief. Miriam is a good huntress. She called me to come and fetch you."

"How did she know I would be here instead of De Ambe?"

"This is the path to De Ambe. And Belle Daube cannot keep her mouth closed very long for any reason." He opened the door for Meg and motioned her in, then put her duffel in the back before moving around to the driver's side. "She is the third wife of a man who collects foolish tourists. You should be more careful, Megan Jennings. After dark, on this river, all the pay-boats are run by thieves. A woman alone is always tempting." He put the red, late-model Jeep into gear and started off on the muddy road.

"But I had to get here. Especially after I heard about the professor, and the plane crash everyone is..."

"Who told you there was a plane crash? Belle Daube? That old woman should have been a teller of tales instead of a thief. Then she could have lied with honor."

The rain rattled against the metal roof as they slogged along. It was growing too dark to see anything but an outline of towering trees around them, now. Even so, Meg could detect nothing that looked like a town or village up ahead of them.

"How far is it to De Ambe?" she asked.

"You don't want to go to De Ambe," he replied. "It would be too dangerous for you there. They are in the middle of what you might call..." He paused for a moment, as if trying to decide how to phrase it. "... a small uprising."

"But Professor Anderson is somewhere in De Ambe! At the bottom of a goldmine, maybe, and who knows if he's still even..."

They came to a sliding stop in the middle of the road. He switched on the interior light, lifted the brim of her hat for a better look at her, and then let it fall into place, again. "How do you know this?"

"A friend of mine, Vidalia Harbin, only barely escaped the same fate by hiding under a wharf last night. And I'm afraid the professor's body guard, Gilbert Minelli..."

"Have you seen Minelli?"

"Not since the airport in Paris. But Vidalia saw him at the van last night, and Belle Daube..."

He reached toward her, again, and this time ran a finger around the neck of her blouse.

"I beg your pardon!" Meg clutched the open collar

of her jacket tight against her throat. "There's no gold chain, if that's what you're looking for!"

"That is exactly what I was looking for. All who wear them are under the influence of the Abdu Sadir. Now, I, at least, know I can trust you."

"Which is more than I can say for you at the moment! I am well aware of the kind of person Sol Horn is, and I have no interest in his illegal gold investments, or even smuggling it out by way of alligator chains. I only came to find the professor. I have to find him before Tom gets here!"

"Tom isn't coming here. He is headed farther upriver to the Little De Ambe, because he thinks his father is already there. And now..." He switched off the interior light and they were in the dark, again. "I must decide what to do with you."

21

Thief Town

"Tell the chief," I said, "that I hear this town of his is thief town."

Mary Kingsley

Meg had a sudden feeling of dismay. "What to do with me? I told you I have to go to De Ambe!"

"And I told you it was dangerous."

"You can at least take me to the goldmine. I have to find the professor before it's too late!"

"There are more than twenty goldmines between here and Little De Ambe. It could take days to find the right one. We will have to find someone who is part of the plot, instead. It is the only way."

"Then we will have to go to De Ambe!"

"You have the words of a bossy mama." He put the jeep in gear and turned it around as he spoke. "You want De Ambe? I will take you to De Ambe, mama."

"I'm sorry, but it's just that…"

"It's just that you will have what you will have." Then he laughed, as if he would enjoy the adventure, and accelerated until the jeep was fairly flying over the rough, wet road.

Meg held onto the dash and tried not to let the wild ride get the better of her. They barreled along through the dark tropical forest, and it wasn't until he rolled the windows down from a central control that she realized that it was no longer raining. The breeze generated by their movement was refreshing after the airless humidity of the closed cab, and she instinctively reached a hand outside.

Then, as they slowed down for a bend in the road, a figure suddenly darted out and ran along beside them, shouting a loud, long, beautiful cadence of words that Meg couldn't understand. A few moments later there was a glow of open fires ahead, and the headlights picked up a row of brick and mud plaster buildings as people began to emerge and converge on their approaching vehicle.

An arresting volley of drums and chanting started up all around them. Manly voices were punctuated with the higher-pitched shouts of feminine laughter and delight. Excitement mounted like something alive and physical, to course through the jubilant crowd and invade even Meg, with the primitive rhythms.

"Come," said her companion as he pulled the jeep to a stop beside the nearest fire. Then he laid a warning hand on her arm as she opened the door. "But do not become separated from me, mama. If something happens to you, I will never hear the end of it."

It was as if they had been waiting for him. The crowd surged around them with the adoration of a celebrity. "Ashanti, Asantehene! Ashanti, Asantehene!" They chanted as he moved through, smiling, shaking hands, and touching the heads of children whose mothers pressed them close.

Near the fire he and Meg were offered deck chairs to sit in (that mysteriously resembled the ones she had seen on the *Volta Queen*). After that, plates, cups, and calabashes were passed to them. "You don't have to eat all, but take something from each one. It is the polite thing," he whispered.

"Why are they doing this?" Meg whispered back. She took a small taste of a spicy concoction of meat and vegetables, and then smiled in appreciation at the young woman who had offered it.

"It is their right to celebrate me." He exchanged her plate for a calabash that had just been passed along to him. "Little sips of this, or you will be on your ear."

It was some kind of strong homemade beer. Meg merely touched her lips to it, and then quickly passed it along to eager, outstretched hands that were reaching to her. The next offering was sweet potatoes. Delicious. "You should have told me you were a chief or something. I'd have tried to be more respectful. If you're a chief, why don't you dress like one?"

"It is better if a man shows who he is from within, than without. But I am no chief."

"Not a witchdoctor, I hope."

"No. I am the son of Aram Fada. The warrior king of a once great nation these people wish to see restored. I don't necessarily agree, but the responsibility has been thrust upon me by my ancestors. Personally..." He smiled his radiant smile and reached out to touch the face of a shy young girl who offered him her bowl. "I think the answers to our problems lie in education and world peace."

"But you still go along with them?"

"It has been thrust upon me."

"And if there have been murders, do you go along with them, too?"

"I told you before. There is an uprising in De Ambe that has become dangerous. But, as you can see, not all the people here are involved in it. We cannot insult the entire town for the few that have gone bad."

"But we're wasting precious time. When will you ask them about the mines?"

"First, we must eat and be polite."

What followed next reminded her of a neighborhood block party. There was music and dancing, much of which she recognized as the sort of popular western culture depicted through movies and radio. But over all there was the distinct African hum of ancient rhythms that held it all together like some primitive heartbeat. All this was mingled with an immense common happiness in the simplest of pleasures, which Meg could not help but admire.

The son of a warrior king, though, always kept a watchful eye on her. He laughed and danced with every pretty girl who was brave enough to come up to him, and never once refused anything offered to him.

In the meanwhile, Meg let her gaze wander up and down the row of seemingly vacant buildings. Everyone in the place must be out here. She wondered if Sol Horn was among them somewhere. If this was where he lived, as Vidalia had insisted, he was mysteriously absent, at present. Then again, he might have hurried back to the Mole National Park to finish out the tour, and thereby set himself up an alibi.

Miriam could be tailing him at this very moment. Hadn't she mentioned something about a stake-out tonight? But even if there was, Meg found it difficult to take comfort in the fact. Because he only seemed to be leading all of them down a false trail while the real criminal activity was going on right here. In spite of the many confidences that had been expressed in the girl, she was no match for someone as dark-hearted and sinister as Sol Horn seemed to be. And what kind of a husband would let his young wife do something so dangerous? Then again, her father was a commissioner of police for something called the Volta River Authority, so maybe she wasn't working alone in it all.

Because even though there had been no answering message from her on Meg's phone, Miriam had certainly called her husband, quick enough. Maybe even her father, too. Thank heaven! The thought of being by herself for very long in this strange place gave Meg the shudders. But at least she wasn't still sitting out on that muddy finger of riverbank with two belligerent teenagers. Her thoughts were interrupted, then, as someone handed her another calabash of beer, and she dutifully touched her lips to it, smiled graciously, and handed it back, again.

"It is not so bad for you if you cheer up, missie," said the friendly voice beside her. "Keep up your heart."

"The only thing that would lift my heart is to find my friends," she replied.

The man was older, with hair that was peppered with gray. He wore black slacks, a white cotton shirt, and leather sandals. "Are you looking for the men who came yesterday?" he asked helpfully.

"Why..." Meg felt a prickly sensation run through her. "Yes, I am. Do you know where they are?"

"Ask Eddie Campbell. He would know."

"The pilot? Where could I find him?"

"You should know, missie!" He laughed.

"I don't understand."

"Edabe Fada. You came with him." He leaned toward her, slapped his knee, and laughed uproariously. "He knows everything that happens around here, Eddie Campbell. His ancestors tell him everything."

"But he told me he was Miriam's husband, the son of a warrior king!"

"One and the same. He is all those things."

"Well, my goodness, does he have a different name for each one?"

"The people from our village who go to foreign university often choose other names while they are there. Sometimes they bring them home, again. Edabe Fada chose Campbell for his foreign name. Would you like to know how he thought of it? American tinned soup!"

"I guess that explains it," said Meg. But inwardly she was calculating that Sol Horn and the Abdu Sadir might be equally interchangeable. It would certainly explain some things.

"American tinned soup!" He laughed, again, and withdrew a pipe from his shirt pocket that looked like the same one the professor had on the plane.

"Good heavens, where did you get that!" Meg demanded.

"From a monkey thief," he replied. Then he leaned so close to her that the strong smell of beer on his breath almost made her push him away. Courtesy or no courtesy, she decided she had endured quite enough of this wild party. Except at that very moment, a gold chain fell forward from the open neck of his shirt, with a dangling red-eyed crocodile in the center.

"I suppose you wouldn't know where the goldmine is." She could at least give it a try (who knew how long Eddie Campbell would spend being polite?) "The one they took those people to, last night."

"Do I know? Everyone here knows. We all have to

work there when the Abdu Sadir has need of us. It is our..."

Suddenly, there was an earsplitting shriek a few feet away, and Meg looked up in time to see the crowd gathering around a fallen Eddie Campbell. Meg jumped to her feet out of sheer reflex, and, at that very moment, the man she had been talking with grabbed her hand from behind and began to pull her towards the nearest mud and plaster building. Meg tried to resist, but a veritable panic ensued and someone else caught her other hand. She couldn't help but be hustled inside. What was happening?

An oil lamp burned on a shelf in the wall, and she realized the room was a small living area within the larger structure, rather like an apartment, or row house. There was a table and chairs, and a door that led off to other rooms that were probably sleeping areas. The walls were covered almost entirely with colorful cloth hangings, but the thing that caught Meg's eye immediately was a picture of the Virgin Mary hanging on the wall. It might have been comforting if it hadn't had an oversized glowing red heart exposed within her robes.

She had only the briefest glimpse of all these things before feeling a rope slipped over her wrists and pulled tight. "Lord, help me!" The phrase that sprang from her lips was more reflex than prayer, for at that point she was quite beyond thinking. "What are you doing? Let go of me, this instant, or I'll have you both arrested for..."

"Shhh, shhh! It is the best we can do, missie!" The gentleman held his hand out to a young woman beside them, who quickly handed him another piece of rope. It was the same smiling face that had first offered Meg something to eat. "The Abdu Sadir has come! If he looks at you, it will be a bad thing, but don't worry. My daughter and I will help you. We know machinery."

"What kind of machinery? Is there a car or a boat to help us get away from here?"

"No, mission people. We are Christians, and we will help you."

"Oh, you mean missionary!"

"Yes, yes. But you must behave as if you have fainted. Too much beer, you know? Then we can get you away safe before he sees you."

Meg didn't have much choice at the moment, but to trust them. "What about Eddie? Will you help him, too?"

"Do not worry for him. He is the nephew of the Abdu Sadir. The son of Aram Fada. If anything happens to him? Big trouble for all of us. Shhh, be quiet now, so we can get you away."

The rest of their communications were all physical. Once her feet and hands were secured, they pushed her toward the floor, then put a hand over her eyes indicating that she should close them. Meg lay back and tried to go limp all over, but it was difficult considering she was practically frozen with fear. Oh, why hadn't she listened to Tom?

In a moment she felt herself being lifted between the two of them, taken out the doorway, and then, to her horror, they simply handed her off into the frenzied crowd where she was passed along over the top from one person to another. It occurred to her then, that if she really was being secreted away in all the confusion, there were certainly a lot of people in on the secret.

Had she been tricked? The sound of a running engine told her the place she was set down was in the back of a van. Then a heavy press of weight shoved in beside her made her realize Eddie Campbell was being put in there, too. Since he was the one who cautioned her about only taking small sips of the beer, she could only assume it must have been drugged.

Not having actually swallowed any of that strong mysterious brew was the only thing that had saved her from being in the same condition. Meg opened her eyes after an outside door slammed near their feet and tried to look around as the van lurched off into the darkness. Were they being saved? Or were they being taken to the mine to be disposed of like the others?

There were three men crowded into the front seat. She knew because every so often, the thick forest parted to let moonlight flood in through the front windshield to reveal their silhouettes. But they must have assumed the poisonous concoction had done its work. They chatted away quite freely, making no efforts to conceal their intentions by talking in that strange native language she had been hearing since she came here. It occurred to Meg then, that they may not all be from the same town. Africa had hundreds of different languages all pressed together in small places, and English or French seemed to be the common link when necessary.

"But we have done so much work! Last week alone, the taking in was better than…"

"It doesn't matter. The Abdu Sadir said we are found out and must cover our tracks."

"How long until the law comes?"

"They are here, already! How they got here so fast no one knows. Someone must have told them something in Yeji. But do not worry. They are running through all the mines like ostriches!" The van shifted down into a lower gear and began to climb a steep hill. "We are to fire the explosives to destroy the work sites, and then" —the voice broke out into laughter at the sheer genius of the plan— "Then we will help them look!"

22

Left to Die

*"What little time you have over, you will employ in
wondering why you came to West Africa..."*
Mary Kingsley

Halfway up a steep, rocky incline, well hidden
within a thick circle of trees, a large flat area had been
leveled to load railway cars. On it was a length of track
that ran for several hundred feet and then dropped off
abruptly into the river. Meg saw all this through the
front windshield in the bright moonlight after the dark
of the forest. But she hurriedly sank down flat, again,
when the engine stopped.

She felt it was the better part of wisdom to pretend
to be in the same state as Eddie Campbell than try to
oppose three men who could each outmatch her in size
and strength. In a few moments, the back doors
opened with a rusty screech, but instead of being
hauled out like so many sacks of grain, a quarrel
ensued.

"You are the one to carry him," said a voice. "He is
not your headman."

"I will not bring his angry ghost into my house.
Carry him, yourselves!"

"As long as we do not spill his blood," a third

voice reasoned. "He will die by and by and be angry at no one but himself. It is the only way."

"I tell you he will know it was us! We cannot touch him," the first voice said.

"Why don't we let him fall into one of the railcars?" replied the voice of reason. "And then push it into the loading shack. The lady with him."

"I say, we better throw him into the eastern shaft with the others," complained the outsider. "We are running out of time!"

"No – no! If he hits his head on a rock, then we will have spilt his blood! He will come after all of us!"

"Back the van up to the railcar, then. But hurry, or there will be no time to get far enough away after the explosions."

Meg felt one wave of panic after another at each suggestion, but a great calm enveloped her, and she had the most comforting assurance that everything would be all right. Whether this meant that she would soon be seeing either Tom, or the Lord, Himself, she didn't know. The miracle was that she was suddenly no longer afraid, and her mind became perfectly clear.

The engine roared to life again, and if the distance had been any more than twenty yards, they would have flown out on impact when the back of the van plowed into the nearest railcar.

"Stop! Stop, you devil!" The passenger door was flung open, and the voice of reason raised an octave higher as he jumped out. "You are an ostrich and an orphan child in one!" He came around to the back and hollered over the top of the two silent forms toward the driver in the front seat. "This van belong to my mother-in-law! She will have my head in a pot if it gets bust!"

"Tell me where to back…"

"You are backed, you monkey-beard!"

"Stop shouting and move them!" It was the outsider's voice. "Before you raise every ghost in these holes! I am going to set the explosions."

Meg suddenly felt herself lifted and fairly tossed into the bottom of the little steel car. It was everything she could do to keep from yelping when her shoulder came down hard on an unyielding bottom, and then again, when the entire weight of Eddie Campbell landed on top of her, having been shoved out the back by means of some object, rather than lifted. After that, it took both men to push the car along the rusty track and then veer off on the short spur that led to the shack. There was a pause while the corrugated doors were flung open, and then they proceeded a few more feet into the dark of a building that smelled deserted, damp, and rotten.

The doors quickly slammed shut, again. Meg heard another car being pushed up against them from the other side, and then footsteps hurrying away. She could hardly breathe, and her left ribs felt about to cave in where the two cameras in her string bag were wedged under her side.

"Sorry, mama." Eddie Campbell carefully raised himself off of her. "But if I had said one word to those fools, they would have run off before we knew where the professor was."

"I thought you were drugged!" Meg felt herself quickly lifted out of the car and saw the flash of a sharp knife before he began to cut the rope from her wrists and ankles.

"It was the only way to get here so quick with so little time. As soon as they leave, we will find the eastern shaft."

"But how will we get out of here, when…"

A loud thunderous explosion rumbled under their feet and fairly made her ears ring. Before it even died away there was another one.

"Come!" Eddie pulled her toward the back of the building where there was a regular-sized door that opened onto the loading area. It was locked, but only from the inside, and in a moment, they were standing in bright moonlight, again.

"What if they see us?" Meg worried. She didn't think one man with a knife could hold out against three, no matter how afraid of him they were.

"They are all cowards. You see? The van is leaving, already."

"Oh, I pray we're not too late!"

"The professor is a tough old man. It would take more than a week to starve him. Gilbert Minelli? I might leave in for another week. He is a worse fool than the rest of them." He started toward the hillside with Meg following close behind. "Unless they are dead already from the explosions."

Meg stopped in her tracks. "Oh, dear Lord!" There was a great billow of dust pouring out of the nearby entrance.

"Don't worry, that is not the eastern shaft. Because of cave-ins, there are always other tunnels to get in and out of the mines. We only have to find the right one."

The van was gone. But instead of silence, she suddenly became aware of the veritable racket of night birds and insect noises. Even more so than she had heard during the day. Meg smacked at a biting mosquito against her neck and then another. She was about to pull the netting down from the inside brim of her hat when she suddenly realized her hat was gone. And so were her glasses. Lost in the tumult between the town and the van somewhere. She heard a slithering sound in the underbrush they were tramping through, and breathed a silent prayer of thanks that she had not taken off her high leather boots when she wanted to.

Ten minutes later, they came to a small entrance, no larger than three feet square, which was slanted into the hillside.

"Here is an opening," said Eddie, "and we are east." He knelt down and stuck his head inside. "Professor!" he shouted, but even his strong voice seemed to disappear into the blackness. "You killed? Where are you man? Hey, hey, this is Eddie!"

"Pretty…much…" Came a very faint, but familiar reply that made Meg's heart leap (he was alive!). "Tied tight down here…part of the roof…it's caving in!"

"I'll come get you."

"Careful, big drop off, now, from the explosions. At least fifteen feet. You'll need a…a rope, or something."

Meg fished around in her bag and came up with a small flashlight. She handed it to Eddie, and he peered into the dark cavern.

"More like twenty-five," he muttered.

"Maybe we could put the ends of the ropes we were tied with together," Meg suggested. "Then you could lower me down, and…"

"Lower you down, what are you thinking? I can't drop you into that black place!"

"It's the logical thing." She reasoned. "You're the only one strong enough to haul us all up, again."

"You are a bossy mama! Now, let me think."

"Meanwhile you're wasting time. Suppose the whole place caves in down there?"

"I will get a bush rope." He handed her flashlight back and started off, only to turn abruptly around again, and point at her. "You stay there. Do nothing until I get back."

"What on earth could I possibly…"

"Do nothing."

When he disappeared, Meg sat down on a large rock close to the entrance and put her flashlight away. She thought of yelling some encouraging words down to the professor, but considering that he probably believed she had been involved in all this from the beginning, she decided to wait until they were face to face to explain things.

Then she thought how she was quite alone in a bit of West African forest where not a soul in the world, other than Eddie Campbell, knew where she was or how to find her. But the professor was alive! And there had been no plane crash. Tom wouldn't appreciate her coming all this way without him, but she felt sure he would understand after he got over it. With nearly twenty goldmines in the vicinity, and the roof caving in, his father could have been dead before help finally arrived.

The very thought of the professor trapped in such a place and Tom thinking he was safe and waiting for him somewhere else! What if she hadn't run into Vidalia? What if she hadn't come here at all? Who knew how long it would take Tom to find out and get help from somewhere? Then a comforting thought occurred to her. It was a Scripture she had read from one of her favorite Psalms that said, *"The steps of a good man are ordered by the Lord."*

Which suddenly took on a whole new meaning even though she had seen it countless times. It also meant that no matter how lost or tangled up a person became, the Lord was quite capable of bringing order to their chaos. Even when they were outnumbered. And even here on the Dark Continent, where evil seemed to be a way of life for so many. Meg couldn't imagine people "collecting foolish tourists" by way of a business. Collecting them for what? And how did they get away with it?

Maybe they were holding people for ransom. Those two boys had been overly eager for her to write down the names of her family members, but it seemed to her that such a scheme couldn't go on long without someone official coming to investigate. Of course, if it always turned out as if the "foolish tourists had killed themselves" through some unfortunate accident or other...

All at once, everything grew deathly silent.

Which seemed odd since only moments before there had been so much animal racket going on. Then, Meg felt the ground quiver like jelly beneath her.

"What on earth?" She scarcely had time to mutter, before the rock she was sitting on gave a violent jolt and began to plummet on a long sliding decline into the eastern shaft.

Like a wave frozen in mid-advance, the rock and debris beneath her that she had ridden down came to an abrupt halt somewhere in the dark interior of the shaft. What had happened? Was it a cave-in? She got gingerly to her feet, heard the edge of her skirt tear loose from two rocks it was caught between, and felt a warm trickle coming from one knee. Of all things! But nothing was broken. She groped for the flashlight in her bag, again, and clicked it on. The better part of the ceiling was still intact, but she was now at the bottom of the entrance instead of the top. Not twenty-five feet down anymore, but still too far to climb out.

"Professor Anderson?" She swung the beam all around her until it illuminated two figures several yards farther down. They were slumped against a wooden brace that had partially toppled and was now precariously holding up the last portion of ceiling. A fine stream of dirt poured over the top of them from above, like an hourglass with the time running out. But even covered in dirt, she recognized the same man she had seen sitting with the professor at the airport.

"We're dead," said Gilbert. "I can see some dame floating about ten feet up."

The professor lifted a dust-covered head and blinked into the beam of Meg's flashlight. "Why it's…Meg, is that you? Why, blast it all, Gilbert!" He thumped the man with an angry foot. "You said she robbed me, and now here she is, just in the nick of time!"

There was a howl of pain and Gilbert swore profoundly and moaned. "Right in my busted leg, you old…"

"Would I be here if I robbed you?" Meg interrupted the heated exchange as she picked her way gingerly down over the rubble toward them. "I've been worried sick over all this!"

"Figured it out from the deed, did you? I knew you were the kind I could count on! Not like some nincompoops who can't even do what they're paid for!"

"So, I dipped into the coffers and didn't want to get canned," Gilbert complained. "I told you it was supposed to be a staged kidnapping. Rescue the old man and come out the hero. Only they tricked me. Sent me off on some wild goose chase looking for her, so they could do the real thing to you. Had to do a pretty piece of professional work to find you, again, too!"

"You're a nincompoop and you're fired!"

"You can argue about it later," said Meg. "I've got to figure out how to get these ropes undone before the whole roof comes down on us."

"Where's Eddie?" asked the professor.

"He went for a bush rope. He's got a knife with him, but he might not get back in time to use it." She poked tentatively at the giant knot at his wrists beneath the beam of light. "Tight as a piano wire. What have you been doing, pulling it tighter?"

"Prisoner's got a right to escape." He gave a cough as another puff of dust filtered down on top of him. "Worst timing in the world for an earthquake."

"Is that what that was? I thought it was a cave-in."

"If it was a cave-in, we'd be dead. Does anyone else know we're here?"

"The police are looking through all the mines, right now, trying to find you. But Tom thought you were at Little De Ambe, so he went there."

"Blast! Don't you have anything in that bag you can cut with?"

"I've got a knife in my left boot," said Gilbert, "only it's buried under about two feet of rock."

Meg turned the light onto him. He was covered in enough dust to resemble a gray ghost with thick curly hair, but there was no mistaking the gleaming gold chain at his open collar. She gasped.

"Yeah, yeah," he replied to her accusing glare. "There's a sucker born every minute. But would I be here if I followed through with it?"

"I don't know. Here, hold this." Meg stuck the end of her flashlight in his mouth and began clearing away the rocks on top of his leg.

"Owww!" The light clattered onto the ground and rolled several yards away. "It's busted! Did you hear me say it was busted? You got no sympathy?"

"Not much for nincompoops." Meg moved off to pick the light up, again.

"She's the daughter I've always wanted…" boasted the professor. "A chip off the old block!"

"She's as loony as you are," said Gilbert. "…and if she wrenches my leg, again, I'm gonna sue!"

"Which any judge would declare irrelevant when you are on trial for kidnapping." Meg suddenly stepped on something soft and yielding and turned the flashlight onto her foot to see what it was. Red and white material of some kind, but in this light, and without her glasses, she couldn't quite make it out. She bent closer. Polka dots. Huge red and white polka dots. And sticking out from beneath that…

A woman's legs.

23

The Last Stand

"I dare say I ought to have rushed at him and cut his bonds, and killed people in a general way with a revolver, and then flown with my band to the bush; only my band evidently had no flying in them..."

Mary Kingsley

"It's Mrs. Cunningham," the professor replied to Meg's sudden outcry.

"What? Oh, dear Lord, did I do that when..."

"No. The poor woman was dead before all that came down on her. Some kind of stroke, heart attack, or something, just after they brought us here. Couldn't take the strain."

"The old biddy died of apoplexy," said Gilbert. "And if she hadn't done it on her own, someone else would have gladly."

"Mr. Minelli!" Meg interrupted. "I suggest you keep your disrespectful opinions to yourself! Before somebody drops a landslide on you! Or refuses to dig you out of one!"

"OK. But you better keep to your right, on account of Henry Stratlemyer is laying somewhere next to her."

Meg moved her flashlight over the area and then gasped, again. There, indeed, was Ethel's husband. She recognized the rather heavyset man's form even from several yards away. He still had his camera dangling from a neck that was... "What? Oh...don't tell me...he..."

"Leopard," said the Professor. "He was like that before we got here. Must have happened on the photography excursion, trailing too close for the perfect shot."

"I don't believe it!" Meg said. "That's too many unfortunate accidents for one budget tour! As soon as I get out of here, I'm going straight to the commissioner, and..."

"Shhh! Is that a plane? Eddie's back! That boy's like another son to me!"

Meg listened for a moment. "It can't be Eddie's plane. We came in a van."

"Uh-oh..." Gilbert moaned. "If it ain't Eddie, we're dead."

"Gilbert, if there's anything else you're not telling us." The professor warned. "I'm going to break your other leg as soon as Meg unties me!"

Meg startled as if suddenly waking from a trance and hurried back over to finish clearing the rocks away. Where was Eddie? It wasn't that far to the trees, and he should have been back by now. She set the flashlight along a crack in the wall this time. Another drift of dirt poured down on them from the ceiling, and she coughed in the choking dust.

"Watch it! You want to bring the whole place down on us? I can't take any more of this!" Gilbert's complaints grew louder with each rock she threw off him. "Somebody put me out of my misery! They're just gonna blow us all up in that old plane, anyway, so it'll look like a..."

Another beam of light suddenly flooded over them from above, and a long resilient vine unwound itself from the entrance. In a moment, a knife clattered down after. "Come, come!" Came a loud whisper. "You must hurry!"

Meg scrambled for the blade and went back with it to cut loose the professor. It only took a minute, but he had been in the same position for so long, she had to help him to his feet. She tied the vine for him, too, because his hands were numb from lack of circulation.

"Are you sure that knot will hold?"

"Professor, I was raised on a boat. I could tie knots before I could read."

"You next, Meg." He urged then, as he began to be lifted from above. "We can lower Eddie down for Gilbert, afterward."

"Don't bother," mumbled the errant bodyguard. "He said he was going to kill me if anything happened to you."

Meg had an odd sense of urgency now that help had arrived, and it seemed like forever before the bush rope reappeared. The plane must have landed by now, because she could no longer hear the engine. "It could be Miriam bringing the police," she said more to herself than Gilbert. "They said the law was already here, looking in some of the other mines. It could be Miriam!"

"Don't kid yourself, girlie. It's the Abdu Sadir to stage a plane crash. Another change in plans."

Meg shuddered at the thought. "Ready!" She whispered as she wound the vine twice around her waist and then several times around itself before she decided she did not like Gilbert Minelli. Not even a bit. Even if he did have a change of heart at the last minute.

He knew too much about what was going on not to have been involved in the plot from the beginning. Such an obnoxious attitude! Why, as far as she was concerned, he could still be part of this.

Eddie was not as careful as he had been when he lifted her out of the rail car. Maybe he was angry at her having ended up in the bottom of the shaft instead of staying where he told her. But there was certainly nothing she could have done about that. Hadn't he felt the earthquake? "Whatever you're thinking, Eddie," she began when one of her boots suddenly sank into a soft spot of earth and she nearly lost her balance, "I am not responsible for the…"

The grip on her tightened, and suddenly, to her horror, she found herself face-to-face with Sol Horn, instead. Even in the dark she could feel his hatred (yes, hatred!) as she looked into the same chilling stare that he had pegged her with, yesterday, in the crowded restaurant.

"You have caused me a great deal of trouble, Megan Jennings, and escaped me many times." He tightened his grip even more, as if he were angry enough to crush her right where she was standing. "Somebody always helps you! But now…there will be blood."

"Well, it won't be mine because I am not alone! Do you hear?" She gave him a sudden shove. "My friends are coming any minute!"

It caught him off-guard almost enough for her to slip from his grasp, except that she was still wound up in the bush rope and he yanked her back with it, again. Then he reached around from behind and pulled her toward him, his forearm pressing so hard against her throat she could barely breathe.

"Those friends?" He spoke into her ear and pointed with his free hand toward the two still forms of Eddie and the professor, lying in the brush a few feet away.

Meg's heart sank.

Then he put a thumb against her neck under her ear and began to press, causing an excruciating pain. She felt herself going numb all over, and just as everything around her faded into blackness, she heard the far-off sound of other voices. For a moment, the pressure on her neck eased.

Sol Horn hollered, "Get these down to the plane and be quick! The law will swarm like bees when they see the fire! All of them must be inside the plane before they get here!"

Meg didn't miss her chance.

She let go of that iron forearm she had been trying to pull away from her throat and sent her elbow into his stomach, instead. The unexpected offense caught him off-guard again and made him lose his grip. But this time she turned toward him rather than running off, and without hesitation, slammed her fist into his mid-section with every ounce of strength she possessed.

There was a loud "Ooof!" as he clutched his stomach and staggered, and then, to her utter shock, he fell backwards into the hole.

"Oh, dear Lord!" She dropped to her knees and strained to see into the black depths. "Oh, I've killed him!"

"What a hit!" squealed a familiar voice that was suddenly beside her. "I was wrong about you, Meg. Maybe you are law enforcement material!" Miriam, who had materialized from somewhere out of the darkness, was dressed all in black and even had her long tresses tied up in a black scarf. She threw the beam of her own flashlight into the hole. "Oh, it's hardly ten feet to the bottom." And with the spring-like grace of a cat, she leapt in.

Meg felt as if she were going to be ill. What had she done? What if Sol Horn was dead? First kidnapping and now murder! How was she ever going to explain this? She wasn't this kind of person. She had never been this kind of person! She heard a groan behind her and turned around to see Eddie struggling to his feet. "Eddie...oh, Eddie...thank God! But...oh, I...I think I just killed Sol Horn!"

"That snake..." Eddie moved slowly towards her, rubbing a hand at the side of his throat. "He got me in the neck with his thumb before I even knew he was behind me! Where's Miriam? She was here a minute ago."

"She just...just jumped right into that hole like...like it was her own backyard!" Meg peered into the depths, again, and the feeble ring of light at the bottom was enough to illuminate the small dark-clad figure as she flipped over the dazed, still-gasping form of Sol Horn and cuffed him behind his back with a practiced agility. Still alive! Meg breathed a heartfelt thanks to the Lord.

"It is her backyard," Eddie knelt down beside her and gazed into the cavern, himself.

"Edabe!" Miriam's voice could hardly contain her excitement, and for the first time, Meg could hear a trace of the local accent in it. "Edabe, do you see? I have got Solomon!"

"Yes, I see, Nkatia. Come up, now, and leave him for the men to haul out."

"What...what..." The professor's muffled voice came from the brush behind them. Meg turned in time to see him rise up slowly on his hands and knees and then leap suddenly to his feet, circling with an unsteady shuffling and both fists raised to fighting position. "Blast it all! The next person knocks me out, or slips me a mickey, is going to catch it! Are you all right, Meg?"

"Oh, Professor!" It was the best Meg could manage because the wave of relief that flooded over her was almost physical.

"Where is that no-good coward? I'll...why, Miriam..." His gaze suddenly fell on Eddie as he pulled his wife out of the hole. "Have you been down there this whole time? Why the devil didn't you help us?"

"I just got here, Pop," she replied. "It was the best I could do since that trail you were supposed to mark for me petered out somewhere back in St. Louis. I waited an hour for you to show up."

"My own bodyguard submarined me!"

"You want me to arrest him? Where is he?"

"He's still down there with two dead people from the tour," said Meg. "But it's going to take some digging to get them out."

"I say we leave him," said Eddie.

"Edabe...what are you saying?" Miriam pulled the dark scarf from her head to wipe the heat and dust from her face, and her many-braided ponytail fell the full length of her back. "How can we embrace the modern ways when you keep turning back to the old? I must arrest him, first. Then you can do what you want with him."

There was a sound of voices as several more

people came into view over the rise. Miriam stashed her scarf in a back pocket and hollered, "Father, I got him! I got Solomon Horn!"

"You got him," came the deep familiar voice of the commissioner. "It doesn't mean you can hold him."

"I'll hold him. Did you get the others?" she asked.

"Three. But the Abdu Sadir's plane is burning, and he is nowhere to be found. They are putting the fire out, now."

"He's at the bottom of the shaft," said Meg. "Miriam just..."

The large man's eyes suddenly riveted on Meg. "Uh-oh. The little lady with heatstroke, again. What are you doing out here in the bush without your husband?"

"Well, I'm...I'm looking for him," Meg stammered.

"And still obviously affected because that is not true. You knew he was not here. As for the Abdu Sadir, he would never bother with dumping people in holes, or get himself stuck in one."

"He would to cover up murder," insisted Meg. "Sol Horn is as deceitful as the devil himself!"

"But Sol Horn is not the Abdu Sadir, mama," said Eddie. "He is only his son."

"What?"

"I distinctly remember you telling me you weren't married," interrupted the professor.

"I'm not married," said Meg.

"And not in the least ashamed," observed the commissioner. "Edabe, we had to commandeer your plane."

"What for, now? I must get these people home," said Eddie.

"Then take them. We're already finished, so you can have it back."

"Finished…who flew it for you?"

"Tom Anderson," the commissioner replied.

"You mean, he's here?" cried Meg.

"He brought all of us here. We had to land some way down the river, and now he's motoring the plane to the loading dock to pick everyone up. Go on, all of you. My men have arrived with the boats and we'll take care of these others. Hey…"

But Meg had already taken off down the hill, so he called after her. "Slow down! I have enough paperwork without someone else breaking their neck!"

Within minutes, she was down the hill and onto the rickety wooden dock that stretched like a crooked finger out into the river. She looked across to where two motorboats had high-powered lights turned on to illuminate the smoldering fire at the edge of the farthest bank, and saw a thin wisp of smoke that was beginning to rise and dissipate into the heavy night air. Beneath it, the black skeleton of a small plane stuck out from the billows. There were several people watching from the dock, their figures in silhouette against the brightness of the spotlights shining from the boats. They were waiting with ropes to tie onto a large, red and white, twin-engine Cessna that was just coming up alongside.

Meg was nearly there when she saw a familiar figure break away and head toward her. She stepped up her pace and cried, "Tom…oh, Tom!" and fairly leapt into his arms. He caught her, but it was more out of surprise than recognition. Still, it wasn't until Meg planted a heartfelt kiss on a rugged but smooth-shaven face that she realized her mistake.

She gasped and let go of him. "You're...you're not Tom! Why, you're Bertram Hunter!"

"Bobby to family and friends." He gave her the same disarming smile that had made him famous and set her down. "I take it you're Meg."

"Oh, what a way to meet somebody! You probably think..."

"I think that was the nicest way I've ever met anyone," he reassured with a fine good nature as the plane turned off its engines and the rest of the little group approached them from behind.

The professor stopped in his tracks when he came up behind them, blinked twice to make sure, and then demanded, "Why, Robert, is that you? Why the devil are you fooling around down here when you could have been up there helping us?"

"How much more help do you want, Pop? We just about brought the whole Volta River Authority out here. You all right? You look like you fell into a bag of cement."

"That nincompoop Tom hired almost killed me."

The side door on the plane slid open and Meg looked up expectantly, only to realize the man standing there was not Tom, either, but a younger more dashing version of the brother she had so literally thrown herself at. "Sort of went out of your way to get us all to do something together, didn't you Pop?" he called down to his father.

"If your mother doesn't divorce me this time, I'm going to make amends. I've just been through a near death experience. Where's Thomas?"

"Shutting the plane down before he comes after Meg." He jumped down across the narrow space of water between the plane and the dock and landed in front of her. "Hello, Meg." He flashed her another of the winning Anderson smiles. "Want a boost?"

"I sure do!" At which point he took her by the waist and fairly tossed her up into the opening behind him. Meg stumbled through the dark cabin more by feel than by sight, past several rows of empty seats, to where Tom was just turning off the last of the switches and unbuckling his seatbelt.

"Oh, Tom!" She leaned forward to put her arms around him from behind the seat, and he reached one hand up to press the side of her face against his.

"One hour, Meg," he said with a voice full of emotion. "You couldn't stay put for one hour? All I had to go on when I got there was a message from Miriam that Pop didn't show up with Gilbert and you were headed for the mine all by yourself! Why didn't you call me?"

"I tried but you were out of range, already. They told me Eddie's plane crashed, and I thought...oh, Tom...they bamboozled me, and I went to the wrong place!"

"Didn't I tell you it was dangerous out here?"

"But I thought you meant crocodiles and leopards."

"Crocodiles and leopards! I swear, Meg, you'll give me a heart attack before I'm fifty at this rate!" He got up out of the seat but had to keep his head bent to turn and walk down the aisle.

Meg moved backwards in front of him. "But the professor was...well, I didn't think you could get here before something terrible happened to him."

"You could have been killed. Do you realize that?"

"Not when I started I didn't."

"Got me taking off in planes that don't belong to

me and rounding up every pair of eyes I could get hold of just to…" He suddenly noticed her dust-covered hair and disheveled clothes. "Oh, come here, priss." He reached out for her then, as if she might get too far away from him, again. "I can see right now there's only going to be one way to keep up with you. I'll just have to…"

"Thomas!" the professor shouted from beneath the open doorway where they were standing. "Give me a hand up into this blasted…"

At which point Tom and Meg both leaned over to take him by the arms just as someone else gave him a leg up from below.

"Pop, what are you trying to prove, giving us a scare like this?" But the words were accompanied by a spontaneous hug that melted the last bit of remaining gruffness right out of the professor.

He sighed heavily and responded with a reassuring pat against his son's broad shoulder. "Well, I was… blast it all, I was helping Miriam with a gold smuggling case but it backfired on me. I had to sack Gilbert, too. But don't worry, my boy, I'm thinking seriously about hiring Meg to take his place."

Meg was hoping he wouldn't expound on what had given him such an idea, when Miriam landed in the doorway as if she had just been twirled on a dance floor instead of tossed through the opening like cargo. "Don't blame it all on me. It was you two who hired me."

"I thought it was me who hired you," said Tom.

"You hired me to check up on the professor, and he hired me to check up on you."

"You could have at least mentioned that back in…"

"Oh, let's save the explanations for later," the professor grumbled. "You have any cheese and crackers left in that backpack of yours, Tom? "I haven't eaten for two days."

"Replenished my supply in Yeji. It's just under that first row of seats there." Then he raised a hand to clasp Eddie's as he came in after Miriam. "Hello, Edabe."

"Thomas…" Eddie laughed and threw him a playful jab as he passed by. "She would drive me crazy in a week, but she has strength."

"Little too much for her own good," he replied.

Meg felt herself bristling. "Tom Anderson, I beg your…"

"But admirable," he corrected himself, and pulled her close up against him. Which dissipated the small irritation considerably.

The professor settled into one of the seats and began to rummage through the backpack. Meg realized then that this plane was far from being a "bucket with holes." Leather seats, shiny instruments, why, it practically looked brand new.

"Not a blasted thing to drink in here but water!" complained the professor.

"I'll take care of that." Eddie reached into a compartment between the cockpit seats and handed him a leather-covered flask. "Enough to get you to the Little De Ambe."

"My boy…" The professor paused to open it and take a long appreciative swallow. "You have always had a remarkable intuition for what's important! How soon before we leave?"

The younger Anderson leaned his head in from the bottom of the doorway for a moment. "They're bringing Gilbert down the hill on a stretcher, Tommy. I can hear him howling all the way from here."

"Have a seat for a minute, Meg," Tom squeezed her hand before moving past her. "I've got a few things to settle with him whether he's howling, or not."

24

Just Deserts

"I can confidently say I am not afraid of any wild animal—
until I see it—"

Mary Kingsley

Meg felt a delightfully cool breeze against her face and opened her eyes. The gossamer net she had let loose around her bed the night before wafted gently before a scene of breathtaking beauty. Two white French doors stood open onto a balcony that overlooked a garden of fruit trees and colorful, sweet-scented flowers before giving way to the rainforest that surrounded it. Beyond that, one could just make out the ridge of hills they had flown over last night to reach what was fondly referred to as the Little De Ambe, the luxurious residence of Aram Fada, descendant of warrior kings.

She sighed and stretched deliciously in the wide, comfortable bed with smooth sheets, and then caught her breath when she moved against the solid form of someone sleeping beside her. What on earth? She turned over and came face-to-face with a disgruntled, full-grown leopard lying there.

Whether it was an awakening yawn or a snarl that sent a ripple of hot breath into her face, she had no idea. Instinctively, she slid back toward the edge of the bed, trying not to give way to panic...only to be stopped by the rubbing of a massive, but affectionate head against her shoulder.

She realized then that the throaty sounds were not snarls, but only the beginnings of an increasingly steady purr. When the large cat leaned an insistent head into her again, Meg noticed a thick leather collar with the word *Sheba* burnt into it, and realized she was only having an encounter with a house-pet.

"Nice, Sheba..." She scratched between the large ears (it was like running fingers through carpet!) and got up slowly, picked up her string bag under a nearby nightstand, and found a piece of gum. "Mmmm...want this?" Meg unwrapped it before waving it under the animal's nose and then gave the collar a tentative pull. The huge cat obediently jumped down from the bed and followed her. "Go get it and it's yours."

She tossed the gum out into the hallway and then quickly closed the door after the cat went out after it. A mansion on a hill was the last place she would have expected to encounter a leopard! But as it was, nothing about this trip had gone as she thought it would. It occurred to her then that if she had known even half what she would run into in Africa, she never would have had the nerve to leave home.

But she had.

Now, the most sparkling possibilities lay ahead of her, and just thinking about them caused a thrill to pass through her. Not only was she going to return with the film footage she came for, but also with the most wonderful man in the world to help her put it together. Truly, he was her perfect match. The one whose existence she had stopped believing in because of her own quirky ambitions. Of all things, to have met him here on this road to her destiny that she had waited so long to step onto.

It was only the beginning of that road, but he had been waiting for her there. Meg didn't know when, or if, they would ever see the perfection they were heading for. Then, again, maybe perfection was something that came one step at a time, like so many other things in life. The important part was that, for herself, she was finally sure she was on the right road. The one Tom had called the "glory road." She knew, now, that if everything could feel so perfect at this moment, then she would be perfectly content to travel along that path with him *"from glory to glory"* for as long as it took, to wherever it might take them.

Starting with today.

This morning, she was invited to join the family for breakfast on the terrace overlooking the river. There they would finally be able to sort things out and make decisions amongst themselves before the authorities arrived for a more formal inquiry. An impromptu "family conference" Tom had called it, which had been the governing tradition for the Andersons ever since he could remember, he said. It would begin casually at breakfast, but not in earnest until all were present.

Meg quickly traded the colorful nightgown she'd borrowed from Miriam last night, for her own crinkle-cloth dress and sandals. The one in various shades of beige and cream that she had brought along (for the gala dinners) because it was not only cool, but could be crammed into a duffel or purse and still look wonderful weeks later. Her duffel had arrived, to her great relief, sometime early this morning, when Eddie's jeep had been returned.

But just as she was twisting her hair up into the clip, she heard a thump, sounds of a scuffle, and a sudden, rather desperate yell from across the hall. Meg hurried to open her door in time to see Gilbert Minelli pinned to the floor by Sheba. Only a friendly pin, she realized, because the animal was merely licking his freshly-shaven face. However, he sent up a loud howl when the huge white cast that now surrounded his left foot was accidently stepped on.

Meg quickly reached for the leather collar and tried to pull and coax Sheba away just as a young house steward hurried up to them and took over. He made a clicking noise with his tongue to which the large cat immediately responded, and Gilbert wasted no time in trying to crawl away.

"Help me outta here, girlie," he replied to Meg's helping hand, "and you gotta friend for life!"

"Please to excuse, sah!" the steward apologized as he hustled the animal down the hallway. "She is missing breakfast because we are late in the kitchen with so many companies!"

Meg helped Gilbert back into the room, but no amount of coaxing after that, could persuade him to come out again. He was going to lock the door, sleep the day away, and have meals sent in from the kitchen. Meg reminded him there were a few things he would have to answer to, sooner or later, but she agreed to make his amends to the group. Which she didn't mind one bit. Because even though Tom had not been so disgusted with the bodyguard that he would leave him stranded in a foreign jail, Meg wasn't so sure a few days behind bars wouldn't have done wonders for such an obnoxious attitude.

But perhaps she should reserve judgment until she

heard the whole story.

So, she continued alone down the long marble hallway with guest rooms on either side, all the way to the end, where another set of French doors opened up onto a wide, stone terrace that overlooked a portion of winding, milk-chocolate river. The air was cool and refreshing at this hour and elevation. A short distance away waited an elegantly laid table with a white cloth and fine china, where the Anderson men had already gathered.

Tom rose from his chair as soon as he saw her and met her before she even finished coming down the steps. He was wearing his khaki vest over a blue shirt. His hair looked as if he had just run a hand through it, and his hat hung on the back of a chair...all tell-tale signs that he had already been out and about somewhere.

"Sleep well, priss?" He smiled and brushed the side of her face with a kiss. "You look beautiful this morning. Come have some breakfast. Aram Fada's hospitality is legendary around here. But he's in De Ambe dealing with the last of these tribal difficulties, at the moment."

"I hope we'll get to see him, and not just enjoy the hospitality. Good morning, Professor. And..." She sat down in a chair Tom pulled out for her, and looked up in time to catch a winning smile from Bobby, along with a mischievous grin from John. "Gentlemen."

"Best morning I've had in a week, my dear," replied the professor as he added a heaping spoon of sugar to his coffee. "Let me tell you."

"That's good," said Meg. She blew softly on the coffee Tom had just poured for her and took a sip. Delicious. "Because you have a lot of explaining to do to clear my slate with Tom."

"I'm pleased the two of you met. Saw right off you were alike as two people could be. It's why I had your ticket changed to first class. Didn't mean to get you mixed up in all this, though, my dear. I was just trying to figure out a way I could introduce you to Tom. That is, before I realized what a pickle I'd got myself into and had to enlist a bit of your help."

"Well, it was some introduction, Professor. He's been literally dragging me from one end of this country to the other for days, now."

"That's my boy!" The professor chuckled at the vivid picture. "Something needs to be done, he does it."

Meg brought him back to the subject. "I believe it was not showing up when you should have, and then saying you'd been robbed that set him off."

"Oh, Gilbert was the one who implied that," he replied impatiently. "But considering I was out everything you took, I believed him. Strange thing about that, though. Without a passport they couldn't take me out of the country, so they had to smuggle me in with the tour group from the east border, just behind the reserve. Even though I was half knocked out most of the time, it delayed their plans just long enough for you to find us. Gilbert almost got a message through once on the cell phone, yesterday, but it cut off." He twisted around in his seat and looked back toward the French doors. "Where is that nincompoop, anyway? We have a lot to straighten out before the commissioner gets back."

"I'm supposed to make his apologies because he won't be joining us," answered Meg.

There was a spark of irritation in Tom's eyes.

"He'll join us if I have to…"

"Go easy on him, Tom," said Bobby. "If it hadn't been for him spilling the whole plot to Eddie when he did, we wouldn't have got everybody here in time."

"He did it out of self-preservation. He admitted it."

"The point is, he did it," said the professor. "What's more, if he hadn't knocked Sol Horn on his ear, that psychic wouldn't have escaped to tell Meg where we were. As it was, the whole thing went off like it was"—he continued to stir thoughtfully as he chose the right word— "orchestrated."

"Definitely a series of divine footprints," muttered Meg.

"Pop doesn't believe in any of that stuff." John reached across the table for a bowl of cream cheese and spread it thickly over a fresh croissant.

"I do now, my boy. I've personally seen too blasted many of them over the last few days to deny it. Awfully glad you stuck with it, Meg. Not many people would go so far for a stranger."

"You never felt like a stranger, Professor. A bit overwhelming, maybe, but…"

"You mean you're finally going to agree with us, Pop?" John set the croissant back on his plate without taking a bite and looked over at his father with the wide-eyed wonder of a youth that had only just passed.

"Well…" The professor slid his chair back from the table and reached into a pocket for his pipe. It wasn't there. "Blast…" He reached for a glass of tomato juice, instead. (Or, was it a Bloody Mary?) "Let's just say I agree to look into the matter further."

"That's a start, anyway," said Tom.

"Which is exactly what I said to Vidalia, yesterday." Meg pointed out. "And here it is less than twenty-four hours since then, and she's already headed out on a divine trail of her own."

"That crazy psychic nearly got me walloped, again, on the way to Ouagadougou." The professor complained. He finished off his drink and set the empty glass down with a disgusted thump. "Kept talking to me when I was pretending to be passed out. No, you can't convince me she would take the slightest interest in any footprints other than her own."

"The Lord meets us where we are, Professor," Meg said. "Even psychics." She took a small plate of bright orange fruit Tom passed to her. "And you're quite right. She is following her own. Rather a good strategy on the Lord's part, if you ask me, considering almost anyone is interested in themselves, wouldn't you say?"

"I say it's impossible to follow your own footsteps," he replied.

"Unless you're a psychic," said Bobby, and then winked at Meg from across the table.

She cast another glance at the tanned, well-chiseled features of the familiar face she was already predisposed to trust because of the many *Adventure Company* shows she had watched (that would definitely take some getting used to!). But it helped that a few strands of his dark hair fluttered slightly against his forehead in the morning breeze as he looked back at her with that same intensity that all the Andersons seemed to share.

"Not if you're backtracking," she clarified. "I talked to her less than an hour ago, and she is taking a train to Accra this afternoon, where she will then be high-tailing her way home to her husband as fast as she can. Seems he wired her the money instead of abandoning her to her deeds. But I don't think we've heard the last of her, so I'll keep you posted." She stared for a moment at the piece of sliced fruit on her fork, trying to figure out if it was a peach or a...

"Mango," whispered Tom. Then he reached into his shirt-pocket and handed over her glasses.

"Where on earth!" Meg marveled happily as she put them on.

"Man who drove the jeep back was wearing them on top of his head, this morning. Said he was your good Christian brother, so he sold them to me at a discount."

"My good Christian brother! His idea of helping was to turn me over to the very people I was trying to get away from. Honestly, this is the most deceitful place I've ever been to! Nobody thinks twice about lying, cheating, or even stealing as...as an everyday way of life around here."

"Sounds like modern day America, doesn't it?" Bobby commented. "At least most of these people have avoided our habit of being so secretive about it all. They're a happy-go-lucky lot by nature. Makes things more tolerable."

"I suppose," Meg replied. "It does make for difficulties in judgment, though. Look at Eddie. One hardly knows which side he's on, much less how to figure out what he's up to from one moment to the next."

"Eddie is on his own side, mama," came the voice of Eddie Campbell from behind them as he stepped down onto the terrace. He had bare feet and an open white shirt that had obviously been tucked into his jeans in a hurry. Then he smiled the gracious smile of a host and said, "Good morning, my friends, and welcome to Little De Ambe!"

He sat down with them and continued. "It is one of the benefits of being the son of warrior kings. One gets to do with people whatever and whenever he chooses. Ah, but it pleasures me to be a man of justice...which I will remember when you are all put on trial, today!"

25

All That Glitters

*"If I am to be shot for a crime, for goodness sake let me
commit the crime first."*

Mary Kingsley

"Put on trial!" Meg could hardly believe what she
heard. "The only people who should be put on trial
here are Sol Horn and his bumbling…"

"Megan." Tom reached under the table and put a
warning hand on her knee.

"Well, of all the…"

"The Fada council must hear all sides of the story,"
Eddie explained casually, as if they had been talking
about the weather instead of going to court. "It is our
custom. There are some strong accusations being
leveled against you all from Solomon's side."

Meg looked around the table at each of them, but
it suddenly seemed no one wanted to catch her eye,
anymore. "Do you mean to tell me we're all under
some kind of…of house arrest, here?"

"It is the most luxurious residence in all of Fada,"
Eddie boasted. "And because of your tribulations, I
insisted to my father that none of you should be
dragged before the council in the middle of the night
along with the others, which is also our custom. If a

culprit is going to be punished, he is punished immediately."

"A gesture we are all grateful for, I'm sure," said the professor.

"Then I suppose Sol Horn is sitting in his own lap of luxury, right now," Meg accused, "figuring out how he's going to slip his cable and take off for who knows where, while we're all tacking around at a family conference!" She pushed her plate of exotic fruit and finely-baked delicacies aside as if it had suddenly turned to poison. "Tom, this whole thing is a nightmare!"

"Don't worry, priss, we've got plenty of options open to us. I won't let them arrest you, I promise."

Which, to Meg's surprise, made her feel better. That and the memory of the way he had handled things when they came through customs. "Well, what do you want to bet he won't even show up today? Kidnapping and murder, and they just let him…"

"He'll show up, Meg." Miriam, who had quietly appeared at the top of the stairs in a long, white, sleeveless nightgown, meandered over to Eddie, and sat down on his lap. "I forced three sleeping pills down his throat after I cuffed him, last night." She reached for a slice of pineapple and ate it with her fingers. "I wasn't about to let that slippery eel get away from me a second time."

"All right, let's get on with it then," said Bobby. "What, exactly, are we being charged with?"

"I believe the exact phrase…" said Eddie, "…was, the undermining of his character, the…"

"His character!" Meg blurted out, only to feel an uncomfortable increase in the pressure Tom was exerting under the table.

"The injury to his reputation," the son of warrior kings continued in all sincerity, "and the great hardship on his people from the loss of income they will have to endure while he is in jail."

"Loss of income..." Meg put a hand over Tom's and squeezed back just as hard. "He runs a shady tour company...certainly it won't be permitted to keep on."

"Solomon Horn does not run *Bremen Tours*," said Eddie. "I run it myself. It is my gift to the people so that we all may have work in these difficult economic times. It is also a way for us to learn to tolerate our differences. Such as the Abdu Sadir, who is like a lion without teeth since I gave him our old plane to take him and his musicians to various places. However, I'm glad it was insured. Now" —he returned his attentions to Tom—"about the grievances."

"We'll take them one at a time," replied Tom. "Which of us undermined his character?"

"The professor." Eddie paused for a moment to receive a small offering of pineapple from the fingers of his wife and swallow it down. "For not investing the same amount of capital in his new company, known as *USM, Inc.*"

"*United Solomon Mines, Incorporated*," Miriam translated.

"As he did with *Bremen Tours*. Thereby showing a favoritism that has forced Solomon to press his people into working without pay in order to meet expenses."

"I will always show favoritism toward legitimate business practices, as opposed to deceit and usury," pronounced the professor. He picked an orange out of a bowl and began to peel it with obvious irritation. "Take me to jail. I won't back down on it."

"But we will pay for the necessary government

permits to bring the mines back into legitimate operating status, again." Tom offered. "Along with the expense of an outside committee to oversee that all regulations are adhered to."

"Done," said Eddie. "Now, as for the injury to his reputation and loss of income? It seems that mama has managed to publicly strike the son of a respected spiritual leader in the presence of his people, and she must certainly pay for that."

"Oh, for heaven's sake!" Meg fastened the same look on the handsome couple across from her that she reserved for students who fooled around in class. "You called him a snake, last night, yourself! And just supposing I hadn't…"

"Meg will make an apology to the people, and we'll set up a temporary relief account for the families that are affected by Sol's absence," said Tom.

"I'll do no such thing." Meg objected, "I'd rather go to jail with the professor!"

"We'll discuss it, later," he said quietly.

"You can't make me!" she whispered back. He did not follow with the usual reply, but the look he gave her was enough for a compromise. "All right, we'll discuss it, later."

"Done," pronounced Eddie. "And now we come to the matter of Gilbert Minelli, who is the true culprit in this entire incident. If he had not convinced Sol that he could talk both of you"–he motioned toward Tom and the professor respectively—"into investing in the scam in the first place, none of this would have become so serious."

"That nincompoop couldn't talk his way out of a paper bag!" growled the professor. "The only reason I hired Miriam to look into the thing was because he said Tom had already bought in. Showed me the deed to prove it! Which I might add, young lady—" He cast Miriam an accusing glare. "You could have settled right then and there if you had told me you were already working for Tom."

"Client privilege," replied Miriam as she reached for the jam.

"That is not client privilege. That is conflict of interest!" insisted the professor. "For a while I even suspected you. Couldn't figure how that blasted deed with my signature on it got into my pocket on the plane in the first place. I didn't recognize anyone else from De Ambe back in coach. Which is why I had to pass it off on Meg. Figured she'd get it into the right hands somehow."

"One of our new tour guides is from Kumasi." Miriam clarified the matter for him. "He slipped it into your pocket when you were wandering around back there looking for suspects. He also exchanged your bottle of antacids for one with a knock-out pill in it."

"I knew it!" the professor said, then looked to Meg. "Didn't I tell you someone had been tampering with my pills?" But he didn't wait for her to reply. "Why didn't you warn me about the scoundrel, Miriam? That's your job, isn't it? Didn't you learn anything at that university I sent you to?"

"Enough to be able to pick and choose my clients," she replied sweetly. "And I didn't figure out the tour guide was involved until later, when you went missing. He was the only logical suspect, since I was sure I hadn't done it. I'd have bet money it was Gilbert, though, only he didn't even make it on the plane."

"Because I ditched him in Paris!" The professor laughed at his own ingenuity.

"Maybe he let you ditch him, Pop," John spoke for the first time since the true haggling had begun. "If you ask me, it was pretty clever of ol' Gil to get us all working against each other, like he did."

"Misguided admiration, Johnny," said his famous brother as he sprinkled a liberal rain of pepper onto an egg. "Just because the guy lets you stay at his place and play cards all night whenever that spoiled little wife of yours gets mad and kicks you out for something."

"She's a brat, but I love her. At least she doesn't hold a grudge as long as yours does. But you've got to admit, him telling Mother and Tom that Pop was losing his marbles is what really blew everything out of proportion."

"That" —the professor tossed the orange onto his plate so hard it bounced off— "traitor! No wonder she's been threatening to divorce me! He said Tom was helping her set things up for herself in Paris so she'd never have to come home, again! Turning all her company shares into cash just so..."

"Better tell him, Tom," said Bobby. "We're way past surprises, here."

"Since when did you start believing whatever Gilbert told you, Pop?"

"Since you refused to come home yourself, Thomas, because you were too busy systematically converting our assets into French real estate, without even..."

"Would I do something like that? Never on your life, Pop! The only thing that's going on under wraps in this family is that Mother's remodeling *Belle Terrace.* Hoping you'll retire there this year. Been pushing like crazy for me to have it finished in time for your birthday, next week."

"What? What?" He looked at each of them in turn, to make sure it was true. "Well, I thought she was turning it into that health and fitness thing."

"Only for a couple of weeks once or twice a year, to offset expenses. Your health and fitness is what she's interested in most."

"That woman never ceases to amaze me!" The professor looked once more around the table at the faces of his family, and Meg could see a familiar softness come into his gaze. "You know, I...sat there last night at the bottom of that mine with the roof falling in... thinking... thinking it was all over for me. I was going to die like a dog in that hole...right along with the nincompoops!"

"Pop!" John's heartfelt protest tugged at Meg's heart.

"Couldn't see any way out of it, boy." His father reached out and gave him a reassuring pat on the arm. "Actually said a prayer, of my own sort, of course, and next thing I know, Meg shows up. Now, everything working out this way...well... it's so much more than I asked for! Imagine. The Man Upstairs listening to an old nincompoop like me!"

"You are a good man, Professor," insisted Eddie. "A great name. God does not give people like you up, easily. Believe me. And where would we Fada people be all these years after the collapse without your generous investments into our village?"

"Thank you, my boy, but you've always seen me as something better than I really am."

"You have inspired me to be generous, myself."

"Well, that's something, anyway. What exactly are you feeling generous about?"

"I will cancel the rental fees for the new plane you

gave us, and you may use it free of charge! I will even waive the court fees this afternoon!"

"In exchange for what?" countered Tom.

"Gilbert Minelli. I have a great desire to throw him back into the mine and let the ghosts of my ancestors deal with him."

Meg gasped at the idea. "Why, you can't do that…it isn't right! He has to be turned over to proper authorities. And then only if the Andersons decide to press charges."

"I am the proper authority, mama." Eddie pointed out to her. "And I am dealing with the Andersons right now. These are our customs."

"That have been thrust upon you, I'm sure," she argued. "But may I remind you that he is an American, whatever he's done."

"Our judgments are swift and sure. If there is any good in him, he will survive it. The man caused all this trouble just to cover gambling debts he incurred with embezzled money."

"Gilbert never had access to company funds," objected Bobby.

"He developed a skillful knack for reproducing our signatures," said the professor. "Confessed everything to me down in the mine. I forgave him because he saved my life, but then had to fire him for his lack of principles. But I certainly couldn't allow him to be…"

"All right, Edabe"—Tom pushed his chair back from the table and reached into a vest pocket. "What's it going to take to settle it, because we're not giving up Gilbert. We've got plenty of our own ways for raking him over the coals."

"Nkatia would like a small flat in Paris to visit our

children at the University."

"She looks far too young to have children at the university," Meg muttered more to herself than anyone else.

"It's why he calls her Nkatia," Tom answered quietly aside to her. "It means peanut." Then he leaned closer and whispered with a teasing grin. "He married her when she was fourteen. It was thrust upon him by his ancestors!"

Meg's only reply was to toss a bit of orange peel at him, and say, "Shhh!"

"Well, that's a bit more than I brought along." Tom returned his attention to the matter at hand and put the wallet back in his pocket. "Stop by my office next time you're there, Miriam, and I'll take care of it."

"Thank you, Tommy," Miriam happily stood to her feet.

"Don't mention it. And, that ought to conclude all the acts of benevolence we're obligated for, this trip. We haven't even started shooting, yet."

"Done!" Eddie smiled his most radiant smile, took his lovely wife by the hand, and got up to go back inside. "Now, you must all feel free to enjoy yourselves until court this afternoon. Should you desire anything at all, just ask." Then he paused long enough to shout, "Juba! More coffee and tea for our guests!"

Meg watched the two of them disappear through the open French doors, which seemed to be the signal for everyone to relax and drift off into their own various conversations. She leaned back with a sigh of relief that the strange negotiations were over. Nothing, absolutely nothing, was what it seemed in this country. One needed the constant help of angels to even survive, because it was a land of wild and illogical contradictions that even the cleverest and most careful people could not escape unscathed. Why, it hardly even seemed real! She wondered if…

But just at that moment, Tom broke into her thoughts and winked at her. "Now that wasn't so bad, was it? The actual court will be more like a picnic this afternoon."

"But they're nothing but a bunch of trumped up charges!"

"It helps them keep a little self-respect to do things this way. No real harm in it."

"It's degrading. Not to mention the money it cost."

"It's all stuff we would have been glad to do, anyway. De Ambe is our own private attempt at righting some of the wrongs in the world. This kind of thing has been going on for so long, they're really more like family to us."

"I can see that. An unending line of children for the professor to spoil. But what Sol Horn did to him was nothing short of criminal, and should not go unpunished."

"Don't worry, it won't. This is only a family court, trying him for stirring people up to get rid of Eddie, which would have left him in line to be the next Asante king."

"And the professor? Ten minutes later and he could have been dead. Not to mention hauling him across the country for days in a continual stupor."

"Sol's always blamed Pop for passing him by and helping people of less standing, instead. Probably thought getting rid of him would return him to his rightful place with his followers. Then they'd have to depend on all his crooked enterprises, again, which would have been a lot more lucrative for him."

"You mean he's been involved in schemes like this before?"

"Since he first stole money out of Pop's wallet as a teenager. But nobody could ever prove it. Not to mention they were all scared stiff of his father. Now, thanks to Miriam getting almost everything on tape last night, the evidence will finally land him in the hands of the government authorities. He'll be looking at some pretty serious retribution, though. I wouldn't be surprised if it broke him."

"Well, something ought to. He murdered Mrs. Cunningham and Henry Stratlemyer. I should hope he would get something more than a reprimand, no matter who his father is."

"He didn't actually murder them. She died of natural causes, and he got too close to a leopard. So, the verdict on that one will probably be that the foolish tourists killed themselves."

"Well, of all the…"

"No laws against foolishness. Nature does a pretty good job of dealing with that all by itself. Now"—he reached for his hat and stuffed it back into the pocket of his vest. "Let's excuse ourselves, shall we?" Then he flashed a delighted smile, his eyes fairly dancing with some new secret he wanted to share. "Come out to the gardens with me, priss. There's something I want to ask you."

But before she could answer, the harried steward came hurrying down the steps with fresh coffee and the loud announcement, "All these companies want too much! More coffee! More tea! And that missie's husband" —he cast Meg an accusing glare. "Him still hollering for ham and eggs in bed!"

Meg gasped at the inference. "Why…Gilbert's not

my husband," she declared. "Tom is!"

Which caused such a startled silence to come over everyone at the table that she suddenly felt the heat of color coming to her face when all their eyes turned toward her. Well, that wasn't what she meant...what would they think? Oh, of all things! How could she even begin to...

"Is that a proposal, Meg?" Tom pulled her close and gave her a reassuring kiss. "I accept."

****

"For I know the thoughts that I think toward you, saith the Lord, thoughts of peace, and not of evil, to give you an expected end." Jeremiah 29:11

Author's Note

Mary Kingsley
(1862-1900)

Born into an unusual situation, during a time when single women had few choices open to them, Mary Kingsley spent all but the last few years of her life taking care of domestic duties for her invalid mother. She never went to school as a child. But her father, a physician who traveled for months (and sometimes years) with wealthy aristocrats, kept an extensive personal library of science and adventure. These many volumes were Mary's only connection with the world beyond her London home. And it was enough.

Because, at the age of thirty-two, after her parents died suddenly and within six weeks of each other, she finally set off on an adventure of her own. It wasn't easy. Besides the fact that she didn't have enough money to accomplish such a thing, everyone kept telling her she was foolish to travel to West Africa. It was almost certain death, nicknamed the "White man's Grave." So few travelers ever came back from there that the shipping lines refused to sell anything but one-way tickets to that destination. But Mary was more than determined. She came up with a unique plan to partially finance herself by collecting specimens of unusual fish and insects for a certain Dr. Gunther of the world famous British Museum, who would supply all the needed equipment, as well as a small fee for her services. Later on, she also supplemented her travels by becoming a local trader. Mostly because traders had greater freedom to travel and were looked upon with a bit more enthusiasm than other foreigners. But only a bit.

In spite of the many ominous drawbacks, Mary loved Africa and sometimes explained it like this: *"The charm of West Africa...calling you...nearer to you than the voices of the people round, nearer than the roar of the city traffic...[is] the cry of parrots passing over the mangrove swamps in the evening time; or the sweet, long, mellow whistle of the plantain warblers calling up the dawn. Everything that is round you grows poor and thin in the face of the vision, and you want to go back, saying, as the African says to the departing soul of his dying friend, "Come back, come back, this is your home."*

Her scientific studies added a great deal to European knowledge of African culture and wildlife. She brought back one previously unknown species of fish, six unnamed subspecies, an unknown snake, and eight new insects. She walked or canoed through many uncharted swamps and dense rain forests, and was the first European explorer to climb Mount Cameroon. Mary was well-known by her black Victorian traveling clothes, and greatly respected by her African friends, who even extended to various cannibal tribes. Her courage, wit, and wisdom became legendary. Her book, *Travels in West Africa*, became a bestseller, and she was widely popular on the lecture circuit.

Some controversy arose when she criticized certain missionaries for treating the natives disrespectfully, and most books written about her today tend to paint her as a liberal born out of time who went to Africa to escape such constraints. The truth about that comes out best in her own words, where readers will find that she is more than capable of speaking for herself. And if it is true that anyone who does anything new or different from current trends of society invariably risks criticisms, it is also true that actions speak louder than words.

After a lifetime of devotion to family and the ultimate fulfillment of a desire to contribute something of lasting importance to the scientific world, Mary finally volunteered to nurse soldiers and prisoners who were dying, by the thousands, of enteric fever during the Second Boer War in South Africa. Once again, she defied all warnings of almost certain death and went to offer her assistance in spite of it. She died a few months later after contracting the fever, herself.

She was only thirty-seven years old.

Yet, the debate and speculation over her brief life continues even today, stirring up the old arguments, "Was she a Christian, or wasn't she?" Mary says she was. As a writer, I thoroughly enjoyed my research into her life and times, and feel the entire controversy can be settled best by looking at God's perspective on that topic. Jesus says:

"Greater love hath no man than this, that a man lay down his life for his friends." John 15:13

Travels in West Africa is now in the public domain and available for free on www.gutenberg.org. I greatly encourage everyone to get to know this wonderful and inspiring lady for themselves.

Thank you for purchasing this Harbourlight title. For other inspirational stories of Christian Fiction, please visit our on-line bookstore at
www.harbourlightbooks.com.

For questions or more information, contact us at titleadmin@harbourlightbooks.com.

Harbourlight Books
The Beacon in Christian Fiction™
www.HarbourlightBooks.com
www.pelicanbookgroup.com

May God's glory shine through
this inspirational work of fiction.

AMDG

CPSIA information can be obtained at www.ICGtesting.com
Printed in the USA
BVOW021943060313

314885BV00001B/1/P